The Work of Betrayal

Mario Brelich

The Work of Betrayal

Translated from Italian by Raymond Rosenthal

The Marlboro Press
Marlboro, Vermont

The publication of the present volume has been made possible by a grant
from the National Endowment for the Arts.

Manufactured in the United States of America

Library of Congress Catalog Card Number 88-64144

Cloth: ISBN 0-910395-44-6
Paper: ISBN 0-910395-45-4

THE MARLBORO PRESS

MARLBORO, VERMONT

Contents

The Work of Betrayal

Dupin's story (first part)

A GLOOMY CLOUD HUNG OVER THE COMPANY. EACH OF THOSE SITTING AROUND *the table had by now not just a presentiment but the conviction that they would never again gather in their full number and that this supper—with all those now present—would be the last. For quite some time they had seen one after another the premonitory signs of grave events and great changes, but it was the Master's grim forecasts that made for the dreadful certainty in their hearts. Indeed, for some time he had been seizing every opportunity to predict his capture, his Passion, and his death. True, he had made all this look like the necessary prelude to the Resurrection before his Second Coming; yet none of them could rid himself of the nagging suspicion that he might be repeating all this to comfort them or, frankly, to bolster his own courage. In point of fact, it was rather odd that he should be downcast, especially when you considered the glorious transcendental prospects. All would have liked to believe that after the terrible interlude the Master would return among them; but it was precisely this disheartenment of his—unprecedented in him—which opposed such hopes.*

No one felt like talking, for Jesus himself was keeping silent and it was clear to everybody that he was silent because he was distressed; and how else can simple souls show their sympathy for the woe of the great otherwise than by a respectful silence? And yet John, the favorite, who was sitting next to him, found another way to express the deep sorrow gripping the souls of them all: he bent his head against the Master's breast, as though guessing that affection and anguish were not sufficiently eloquent unseconded by actual contact. Not for an instant did he imagine that this gesture of his would provide strength and comfort, as in other difficult situations. At this point his mute despair could only deepen the Lord's inward sufferings.

From time to time that silent affliction was interrupted by a long sigh which, like a tide that fetches up sediments from the sea's bottom, brought to the Master's lips words that revealed how much in his deepest spirit he was obsessed by the idea of death. As soon as he spoke he would allude to this torment. And therewith the lump in everyone's throat would worsen.

Then came the moment that, from the start, they had all dreaded. From the Master's lips there again came that sentence, several times repeated during recent weeks, which had humiliated them and at the same time brought about a feeling of guilt in them. Plainly, the Lord was more bothered by that thought than by anything else, so that, when bitterness choked him, from his lips would spring the impetuous accusation which dishonored them all:

"Verily I say unto you, that one of you shall betray me."

Until that moment they had somehow pretended not to hear, until that moment the accusation had perhaps never been pronounced in so peremptory a tone. Until then, in fact, Jesus had seemed to be alluding to the Psalms and whoever did not wish to understand could even abstain from understanding the allusion. But this time that "one of you" left no way out, the message was addressed to one particular auditor, and the person was sitting there, in their midst—he was one of them, one of the Twelve—and, until it was made clear whom the Master was addressing, the feeling of guilt and remorse would persist in all their souls. Yes, for when they looked frankly into their inmost selves, they had to confess, horrified, that the possibility of betrayal lurked in each of them, without exception. It was painful to admit this, but several times the thought had crossed their minds that, if events took an ugly turn, and the Master found himself in trouble, the best thing would be to beat a retreat, return to one's own village, to one's old trade, and forget the adventure. Naturally, no sooner did this thought appear than they'd banish it as a temptation of Satan's. But the facts were the facts—not one of them could affirm that he had not been tempted by Satan, and not just once but many times.

The accusation had now taken a form so flagrantly provocative that there was no more accepting it without looking like cowards. Respectful silence was no longer warranted; better to protest, a little hurt and vexed, but no less convinced that the accusation was not aimed at them:

"Lord, is it I?"

To ask this question a certain amount of courage was needed, obviously, but each of them had good grounds for hope. Yes, for it was just as true that alongside the cowardly and shameful thought of running away, another had often occurred to them all: that of being ready to undergo any torture for the Master and—if need be—even the ultimate ordeal. So, if Jesus had declared—and this time without any violence or agitation at all, but with pity and profound feeling—if he had declared: "So then, I say unto you, one of you will undergo the ordeal for my sake!"—it is sure that all of them, with a certain fear but also with defiant pride, would have also risked the question: "Lord, is it I?" In that case too they would have awaited the reply in trepidation, as they did now, but perhaps in that case too the reply would have been no different from the one they now heard—a reply that did not dispel their uncertainty:

"It is one of you twelve, that dippeth with me in this dish."

All things considered, this response meant nothing more than "one of you," for at that instant neither the Master nor any one of them was dipping into the dish, whereas a few moments before all of them had dipped, and even several times, albeit without much appetite.

Once again the Lord gave way to his premonitions. As always, he was unable, even now, to hold his feelings in check, and once more he repeated, with the same exaltation, that the prophecies of Scripture were being fulfilled and that all that would happen had to happen. Nevertheless he could not repress his indignation before him who was to be the objective cause of his fate's fulfillment.

"The Son of man," he said, in the pathetic tone he used whenever he spoke of himself (which, what's more, seemed perfectly appropriate to everyone) "goeth, as it is written of him. But woe to that man by whom the Son of man is betrayed! Good were it for that man if he had never been born!"

This malediction, pronounced in accordance with the age-old formula, in its ritual solemnity resounded with such menace that for some moments everyone felt a lump in his throat, and John's boyish head trembled too, and then pressed even more frantically against the Master's breast, as if in sign of horrified protest.

But Jesus was again immersed in his meditations, altogether absent from the world around him, while his inner silence, after that burst of anger, became still deeper and more impenetrable: and from this the twelve realized that, withdrawn into his solitude, he was likely to become inaccessible to their emotions. Little by little, however, as the bitter, oppressive lump dissolved, the grim charge, aggravated by the malediction, led them to react more openly. The moment had come to set respectful compassion aside, and in this way they began to speak among themselves, in moderated voices but with emphatic gestures. While their lips were saying "Who can the one be?" their gestures were signifying "Really, this is a bit too much!" Each by now was nearly certain that it could not be he.

Peter, more aroused than the others, motioned to John. One couldn't leave it at that. He needed assurance that he, Peter, was not the one. Strange apprehensions beset him. He knew for example that if the Master were to depart, the entire burden would fall upon his shoulders of rock. And he felt so weak! That talk about "rock" was, after all, nothing but an ingenious play on words which—though designed to invest him with authority and importance—would, once he was compelled to confront the test of reality, reveal its merely metaphorical nature. The rock, in sum, did not even to him seem sufficiently solid, and his one consolation was that the Lord had expressly chosen him. But what a relief it would have been for him to hear this confirmed, be it indirectly!

Peter was keeping sharp watch. He saw that John was hesitant to break in upon the Master's rapt silence. But then John suddenly raised his curly-haired head and put his lips to Jesus' ear. Only with difficulty did Jesus emerge from his thoughts. He whispered a few imperceptible words to his favorite. Though Peter strained to hear he was not sure whether an actual name had come from the Master's lips. Rather, they seemed to say that there are no hidden things that do not come to light. John indeed drew back, straightened up, and flung an enigmatic glance at Peter, who thereupon decided not to ask the question he desired. But he became attentive again when the Lord, after another deep sigh, seemed to consider the dish anew, in fact broke off a morsel of unleavened bread and dipped it in the sauce of the Paschal lamb. But instead of bringing the bread to his own mouth, he held it out to Judas Iscariot who, quivering, almost flung himself upon it with strange, convulsed avidity. Then Jesus stared straight into his eyes and said:

"That thou doest, do quickly!"

Judas took the mouthful and, casting a desperate glance at the Master, rose and left at once.

Judas' departure and the swift scene that had preceded made no particular impression on anyone. The feeling they all had was that Jesus had sent him out to make some purchases again (since Judas was in charge of the community's purse) or, it could be, to give alms to the poor. Moreover, many of them later declared they had heard the Lord give instructions to that effect.

In any event, no one gave any heed to this apparently insignificant episode, or connected it with the fact that as of that very instant the Lord had come to life and begun to speak. On the other hand, more completely etched in their memories was the difficult moment they spent because of his agitation. The Lord, no doubt because he was unable to keep from doing so, stubbornly returned to his dark forebodings of his coming end and declared that that night would be for him and for them a terrible night, which would put their mettle severely to the test. All of them, but Peter especially, were displeased that Jesus could place so little store by their fidelity and perseverance. It was humiliating beyond measure when, without beating around the bush, he announced that that night they would *all abandon him. "I strike the shepherd and the lambs scatter," said he, quoting the Prophet, and these words sank like so many thorns into Peter's heart, considering that he himself, in moments of discouragement, had used the same image to define the imminent situation. Since however he was the helper chosen to occupy the shepherd's place, there could be no show of weakness from him at that juncture, he was even duty-bound to protest against the Master's accusation, and to try to convince him that his premonitions were unfounded, and were only the notions of a mind that had wandered. So Simon Peter, this time, protested energetically. And as the leader he spoke on behalf of the others too; but above all he was anxious to dispel any shadow of doubt that might attach to his person.*

"Though you were an occasion for everyone's downfall," he said, rising and stepping forward, "you would not be for me," and bowing slightly, aware of having been too daring, he struck his breast proudly.

Jesus quivered in an odd way, like someone awakening with a start. That an interlocutor break in upon that soliloquy of his, addressed to all and to no one in particular, was something he had not expected, and he stared with some bewilderment at his "rock." When, shortly before, he had withdrawn into himself, a profound abyss had suddenly opened between present and future, so that for him, who was already living in the world beyond, it seemed out of place, even comical, to see this little man arrive on stage with a theatrical air, and, inordinately exaggerating his indignation and his faithfulness, worry about things that had long since been accomplished. Just then Jesus had the impression that the whole episode had already occurred in a distant past and that it was taking on a painfully ridiculous quality, precisely because it was nothing but a pale and futile repetition. He had already progressed quite some distance down the road of the future, and in the future's open book it was easy for him to read, not without a touch of indulgent malice, what this figure from his memory would shortly do. A fleeting smile appeared on his face, for the very sentence through which the memory of the future had formed on his lips was in perfect harmony with the comedy of the present moment: the cock would not have the time to crow twice ere this ninny, this rock on which he had founded the entire edifice of his work, would take the opportunity to deny him three times over! It could not be otherwise, of course; it is rightly, necessarily thus. But why does someone protest in the past, when in the future everything is already accomplished?

This response, absent-mindedly uttered by the Master without any intention at all of provoking emotional reactions, as if it were a mathematical axiom, fairly staggered poor Peter. Never, honestly, would he have expected that! Never would he have expected that from him! Even if it was a prophecy, a prediction of indubitable future events, even so his words seemed to him an insult. Gone pale, his eyes full of tears and distress upon his face, he cried to the Lord, on the brink of despair:

"When at your side I must undergo prison and death, I shall not deny you, O Lord!"

And the others, heartened, confirmed that so it would be, both for Peter and for themselves.

The Master stared with weary, almost unseeing eyes at the excited group of his disciples. A kind of pity stirred in his heart. Indeed, they were not altogether wrong . . . They will undergo prison for his sake, and even death. But they will also deny him.

Without uttering a word, he turned away from them, pensive. And in Peter's heart, and in the hearts of the others, remained the searing uncertainty of doubt: to whom among them would it befall to betray the Lord?

No one thought of Judas . . .

Having reached this point in his manuscript, I raised my astonished eyes toward my friend, who sat perfectly still in the old armchair, almost dozing, his pipe drooping from his mouth. Was it possible that the famous discoverer of the Rue Morgue murderer and the man who had solved the mystery of Marie Roget's death had, upon nearing the age most mortals do not live beyond, decided to write stories on biblical themes? To tell the truth, never during our long friendship had I noticed him to lean in the least toward religious practices or to interest himself in religious questions at all. Then the thought flashed through my mind that he might have converted, and that the story was a product of his lately found faith. I remembered that as a young man he had "committed a few peccadillos in rhyme," and so it would not be completely absurd for him to have rediscovered a mood for writing in his old age.

"Right you are, *cher ami*," he said, catching the barely perceptible movement of my eyes, "you have stopped reading at the right spot."

I was much pleased to see that the venerable Dupin was on a par with the Dupin of former times: for, without having once interrupted my reading with a remark or a gesture, he *knew* exactly what point in the story I had got to!

Actually, my fears about how I would find him had vanished the moment I set eyes on him. We had not seen one another since I had left for America. At the time of my departure I had no idea that I was to remain away for so long from the Old Continent, from Paris, and from my favorite friend. Alas, life's unforeseen events, the feverish pace of my work, and various, often vexatious circumstances had kept me from crossing the ocean again. But I had never given up my dream of returning to the blessed places of my youthful happiness, and I decided that, before dying, I would satisfy my decades-long desire. And in actual fact, overcoming not a few difficulties, I had seized the first opportunity to undertake the sentimental pilgrimage, whose principal destination was— needless to say—at 33, Rue Dunot near the Faubourg Saint-Germain, that old third-floor apartment I had purchased and where I had spent long and decisive years living with Dupin, and which had later on become his property and been occupied by him ever since.

To my great surprise I found *everything* just as I had left it. Despite the enormous amount of time that had passed, the furnishings of the old house were not changed, had not been added to by so much as a single piece of furniture, apart from a huge new case for books, whose numbers had gone on growing throughout Chevalier Dupin's lifetime. And not only did I not notice anything new in the furniture, but even its arrangement in each room was unchanged: the ancestral writing desk still stood in the corner, between the window and the closed shutters and the old bookcases I'd known from before, and the two large armchairs in front of the fireplace, still the same and still in the exact same position as in the past, were dimly lit by the same chandelier the two of us had bought during that mythical period. And the old pipes, they too were lined up in the same immutable order on the gueridon—small, low and round—alongside the well-remembered and capacious ceramic ash-tray and the spectacles with green-tinted lenses, which my friend had always worn since his early youth.

It seemed to me that time had stopped. And, in that stagnant atmosphere worthy of an Egyptian pyramid, I accepted almost naturally the presence of that regal mummy called Dupin. Victim as I was of deceptive first impressions, my friend did not appear to me to have changed any more than his surroundings. Perhaps also because of the scant illumination (from oil lamps, as though in the meantime electric light had not been invented!) Dupin, comfortably settled in his armchair and with his inseparable pipe, seemed to me even physically identical to the man I had left in the full vigor of his years. His always well-groomed person was slim, straight, spare, and as he rose to greet me I noticed not without envy the firmness in his step, the crispness and energy in his gestures. Within a few minutes I had found that over all these years he had not changed one iota with regard to his habits either. He was still a faithful adept of the sacred nocturnal hours and, with senile—or puerile?—boastfulness, he right away informed me that it was about five years and seven months since he had last seen the sun. At the first glimmer of dawn he had the habit of closing the shutters, not opening them again until after sundown. He would leave the house at a very late hour, as he used to do as a young man, though now he no longer went out every night nor in search of instructive experiences, but simply for a breath of fresh air.

"I'm at the stage where I walk just for my health," he said with a feigned air of resignation, which was not looking for pity.

"So you have altogether stopped working with the police?" I

asked. "You're not called out anymore even for on the spot investigations?"

"It pains me to observe," he replied, with an amicably ironic smile, "that with the passing of the years you've grown lazy enough to draw hasty conclusions. Things are not quite the way you put them. As a matter of fact, the police still do make use of my services; but, no, I no longer visit the scene of the crime. Age and my congenital fondness for comfort would militate against my involving myself in any investigation that required me to take one step outside the house. On the other hand, my analytical method has reached such perfection that there is no crime or mystery I cannot solve seated blissfully here in this armchair."

He reminded me that the mystery of Marie Roget had been the first instance of such investigations performed while seated in his study. Then, opening the old cabinet, he showed me other "cases" he had solved, cases that had caused a sensation throughout the world and of which I too had heard, though I'd not been in a position to follow all the details from the other side of the Atlantic. It was with almost youthful exuberance that we reviewed all the fantastic crimes whose solutions were linked to Dupin's genius. Indeed, on the desk, as well as on the floor around our armchairs, towered piles of worn, dusty dossiers, monuments to a richly successful life. Deeply moved, I gazed at my old friend.

"Doesn't that leave you at least satisfied?" I asked him, affectionately.

"Not at all," he snapped back. "I did all this to fight off the endless boredom which underlies my life. For my own personal part I have always held life at arm's length. From the time I was very young I amused myself by observing the life of others, while mine, imperceptibly, slipped through my fingers. Oh, how often did I envy the criminals who, thanks to me, finished their existence under the guillotine! Not because of their miserable end, obviously, but because of the life they lived which had brought them to that conclusion! Because of the passions, the emotions, the obsessions which drove them to crime, but were nevertheless complex and experienced realities, particles of a plenitude of life normal people have and *sense* in every drop of their blood. I, who in some inexplicable way was always a stranger to my own personal life, I at least sought to understand what I was deprived of. By dint of understanding, I managed to discover a logic in the criminal, the stupid, the absurd and, perhaps, even the irrational. I enjoyed taking apart and putting back together the intricate workings of that contraption whose reality always eluded me: life. At a certain point I became aware of my incapacity to live it, and then, extremist that I am, I gave up all attempts to take possession of it. Fortunately, I retained the habit of wanting to understand things: not their essence, certainly, which is beyond my scope and because of that odious to me or, at any rate, vexing; but rather their hidden mechanism. You will understand that from such a point of view 'things' can truly be *any* sort of thing provided it is duly complicated and entangled: it's absolutely the same to me, solving a serious crime or figuring out systems for winning at roulette, racking my brains over mathematical problems or thinking up insoluble cryptograms. For someone occupied with such games, life, the only inaccessible 'thing,' passes neutrally by, without causing him much bother . . ."

After a moment's silence, while trying by means of a smile to attenuate the profoundly tragic aspect of his confession, he added:

"To take an interest in things in themselves is the only solution for one who is a stranger to life. And the most appealing things for me, probably owing to my prudence or my cowardice, are those very ones which have nothing to do with life . . ."

Unaccustomed, in our relationship, to talk about intimately personal subjects, I tried to get past my discomfort with a commonplace remark or two on life and the difficulties of living it in such a way as to be able to come to positive conclusions about it, but, seeing that he was listening to me with an impassive and absent air, I struggled up from my armchair and on legs that had gone to sleep limped over to the cabinet again, in this way suggesting that I wished to lead our conversation back to the passion we shared in common.

"Is there nothing further that might interest us in a disinterested way?" I asked in a mischievous tone, while I tried to stifle a yawn. It was already four in the morning. I felt worn out by the exertions of my journey, by my emotions and our intellectual gymnastics; I wanted to go to sleep. I remembered perfectly well that the cabinet contained nothing at all, and so pretended to rummage in it in the hope of finding nothing there. But, by dint of peering about in that dark emptiness, I discovered, in the right-hand corner of the third shelf, a very slender folder which, being of a brownish color and covered with dust, was barely descernible. The melancholy solitude of that folder suddenly roused my curiosity; scenting some mystery, my weariness left me, my spirits plucked up.

"May I have a glance at this folder?" I asked, taking it from the shelf and blowing the dust from it.

"Which one's that?"

"It has EVADENDA written on the outside," I said, not without curiosity.

"*Evadenda?*" Dupin exclaimed, plainly surprised. "*Parbleu!* I don't think I have any more tasks that deserve such an important classification. It's surely an empty folder, a left-over from bygone days."

"Not at all! It contains several pages of dense handwriting."

"I'm intrigued! Go ahead, have a look at them!"

And, astonished, I read to him the opening sentences of the story that appears at the very beginning of these reminiscences of mine. In the margin, written in pencil, by way of a provisional title were the words: *The Last Supper.* A moment or so later and I was interrupted by Dupin's mocking laughter:

"Ah ha, yes, I recall. Go on, but read it to yourself, if you don't mind."

And I started in and had got almost halfway through when Dupin deemed the moment come for me to suspend my reading.

"What do you think of it?" he asked, with a foxy air.

"It's very skilfully handled," I mumbled, more bemused than convinced. "You are a remarkable story-teller. But . . ."

My friend sniggered, amused:

"But? Go on."

"But . . . I must tell you in all frankness . . ." I said, feeling very awakward, "I just would never have imagined that among your other pastimes you also wrote stories with religious themes. A wholly new facet of your so very complex personality is being revealed to me . . ."

From Dupin came a gale of loud laughter.

"Set your mind at ease!" he said, catching his breath. "It's the same old one and only side of me, lover of riddles and amateur detective. But reading those pages, didn't you get a foretaste of one of the most exciting cases in world history? In fact, several years ago I set about disentangling the to this day still unsolved 'Judas Case' . . ."

"The what?" I cried, refusing to believe my ears.

"The 'Judas Case,' *s'il vous plaît*," he repeated in the most natural tone in the world. Then he added, as if by way of apology: "One case is as good as another, even if this one is not of the commonest order. I remember becoming so keenly interested in it that I studied all the relevant literature. Then other cases of a more urgent and financially more promising nature came my way, and I ended up forgetting about it completely. You see how strange chance is . . . When I think of all the delightful hours I devoted to its study and to reading about it and pondering over it! My impatience to get a handle on it led me to write those pages so as to summarize, perhaps tentatively, my first impressions and intuitions. By the way, perhaps you have your own theory or at least some idea as to why Judas betrayed Jesus Christ and as to how the whole thing actually transpired?"

"To tell the truth, no, I don't," I was obliged to admit. "I don't know anything more than what the Bible says about it."

"My, then you know rather a lot!" he chuckled in a slightly ironic tone. "I take it then that you are straight on what the Gospels say on the subject?"

"I don't have a precise recollection," I confessed. And unable to hold back a yawn, I added: "And right now I feel incapable of the least effort to remember."

At that Dupin rose from his armchair, went to the window and pulled the shutters to.

"You have every right to think about sleep," he said. "The sun is coming up, it is time to go to bed. But find a moment to reread the pertinent passages in the Gospels. We'll talk about them this evening. The case lends itself perfectly to armchair examination. It will make a charming diversion for two little old chaps of the sort we are. And, for my part, it will provide me with the greatest satisfaction—for I can guarantee you that the subject at hand is wonderfully devoid of current relevance."

On the traces of the Gospels

THE NEXT DAY, DINNER OVER WITH, WE ESTABLISHED OURSELVES COMFORTABLY in the the old armchairs, as we had been in the custom of doing as young men, and we each lit an old pipe. With youthful ardor, my friend Dupin proceeded immediately to the order of the day:

"So then, have you had a look at the Gospels? What's your impression?" Then, without waiting for an answer, he continued: "I'm confident, *cher ami*, that after having consulted the Bible, the 'Judas Case' appears to you even more mysterious than you thought at the beginning. To make you feel better I may point out that the Sacred Writ does not contain the elements needed to clarify either the 'why' or the 'how' of the wretched apostle's treachery. But I may add, also for your consolation, that you would not have got much farther from the scrupulous study of everything in the two thousand years of literature on the subject, from the

Church Fathers to the efforts of modern specialists and writers: to this day, Judas' behavior remains shrouded in obscurity. Concerning the betrayer's personal motives more or less ingenious hypotheses can be put together, but the actual role he played in the arrest and in the criminal proceedings brought against Jesus (another thorny and still unsettled problem!) has never been given a convincing explanation.

"In my opinion, the unsuccess of the scientific and literary reconstructions is owing precisely to the absence of the basic elements upon which they ought to rest. Although I am familiar with a good part of the literature on the subject, I do not remember ever having encountered an author who in all honesty declared his surprise at the incomprehensible silence of the four evangelists upon a subject that for two thousand years has fired theologians, scholars and artists. But I am the sort who is surprised when there is something to be surprised about, and I am unable to disregard this or that astounding phenomenon. You, with a still fresh memory of the lines in the Gospels, should have no trouble verifying what I am saying. As regards our 'case,' the one monolithic truth upon which all the sacred texts agree is that Judas betrayed Jesus. But that the betrayer had a valid motive for committing his crime is adduced nowhere, nor is it shown in what this crime consisted *in concreto*, nor in what plausible manner it was committed.

"Why this strange way of behaving on the part of those who were the witnesses as well as the victims and heroes of these fatal events? After cudgelling my brains over this for some time, a luminous hypothesis gradually dawned upon me: if the evangelists did not go deeply into the question of the betrayal it was because they themselves were unable to make head or tail of it! But did it ever occur to you, or for that matter to anyone, that the apostles, who all unawares and unsuspecting had witnessed the work of betrayal, were so taken aback by what happened that not even afterwards did they attempt to understand it? Or that, though having tried, they failed to find a valid motive for Judas' deed, or a plausible explanation for the manner in which he performed it? Finally I reached the conclusion that these 'valid motives' and 'plausible explanations' perhaps never existed, or else lay far beyond their comprehension. Right now I am tempted to think that if the evangelists have not handed down to us a complete and realistic picture of the betrayer and the betrayal, this is not so much through lack of shrewdness and inability to observe and to reason; it is very simply because instead of falling into the error committed by their descendants—who looked to testimonies, documents, historical, archaeological and juridical research for an understanding of a mystery whose reality, *raison d'être*, and logical justification are hidden in wholly different spheres of thought and existence—they wisely did not try.

"So don't expect me to venture into the labyrinth, the blind alleys explored time after time by far more competent and gifted pesons, for I have come to be thoroughly convinced that, by proceeding along the already well-trodden paths and persisting in the use of the methods and means adopted up until now, one will never arrive at a solution of these problems, already, by their very nature, defiant of solution.

"But of course there is no danger of our stopping at the point where for various reasons the evangelists and the specialists were unable and the writers and dramatists unwilling to pursue the matter farther. If we now review one by one and analyze the salient features of our riddle it will be for the sake of refreshing our memory, but also in the express hope of running up against some new and troublesome questions which will lead us little by little to an unexpected formulation of the 'Judas Case.'

"So, to work! According to theology's cardinal thesis—which I deliberately accept as the basis of my analytical work—the four Gospels not only do not contradict each other but are squarely in agreement or, in the worst of cases, complement each other; and rarely is this thesis more eloquently borne out than by their closemouthed treatment of Judas' betrayal. The four sources of the Good Tidings vie with one another for the record for inexactitude in everything concerning the details relative to the so-called 'Trial of Jesus' and where the betrayal is merely a secondary circumstance. We readily agree that not one of the apostles or disciples was in a position to follow events step by step: what little they were able to find out and pass on was truly a hodgepodge of not very credible information."

"Actually, the story presented by the four Gospels does not give a complete picture of Jesus' trial, which is today the cause of serious headaches for Christian historiographers. The evangelists' meager accounts do not seem to tally with each other and it does indeed require the tricky acrobatics of doctoral reasoning to bring them into line. Some scholars are tempted to deny even historical reality to this extravagant trial, so lacking in the characteristics of logical structure belonging to events that have actually occurred.

"Many scholars contend that the imprecision the evangelists show in reporting the circumstances of the betrayal is simply the consequence of the method and the aims they consciously chose when presenting their recollections. Their exposition is a tendentious chronicle which most often does not even respect chronology, but is always mindful of the audience it is addressed to. Out of their exposition must come the teaching, with all its luminous and seductive aspects, out of it must shine forth the Master's divinity. Biography is not asked for here, and documented historiography even less. If in the four Gospels facts of an informative character or various descriptive elements do appear, it is never out of a seeking for historical exactness, but always out of the necessity for making plastically evident a reality which must penetrate a very particular group of readers.

"According to these scholars it is therefore very likely that the evangelists would not have reported their Master's trial with greater precision even if they had been in a position to reconstruct it point by point, and they would not have spoken in much greater detail about the betrayal even if this had been something more accessible to ordinary human understanding. For them it was necessary and sufficient to give prominence to the fact that the Son of God had been vilely betrayed and put to death, but in the end had succeeded in triumphing over the powers of darkness by coming gloriously back to life.

"Despite all this it is equally true that on the trial, where they had not been present, the evangelists do supply some information, though second-hand, while one fails to find the least shadow of an allusion, be it casual or gratuitous, to the personality of the betrayer—whose intimates they had been—or to the real motives that might have driven him to the betrayal. It seems that the figure of the betrayer went unnoticed during the long years of living together, and that his ignominious act so caught the little community by surprise and left it so perplexed that no one ever succeeded in explaining it. No hint anywhere that anyone glimpsed in Judas the future betrayer. And no attempt to understand his deed! A chance remark in one of the Gospels: 'And then Judas Iscariot, propelled by hatred *or* wounded vanity *or* disappointment *or* desire for money . . .'—that would suffice to dissipate all the doubts that have remained unanswered for twenty centuries. But nothing of the sort. Historiography affords no other example of reticence to match this in the Gospels regarding the reasons for an event of such decisive importance. It seems that the apostles, until then without suspicion in regard to Judas, only really understood when on the Mount of Olives they with their own eyes saw him coming up with a posse. Only at that instant did the realization strike them, coming like a bolt out of the blue, that they had warmed a serpent in their bosom and that it was to him the words of Scripture referred: 'It was he the man who had broken bread with the Master and lifted his heel against him.' But it was a bit late to find out any more about him: for that was the last time they saw him! No, nobody had ever suspected Judas, and John himself, who in his Gospel devotes more attention to him and seems more fully informed about him than his fellows, implicitly confesses that he too had had no suspicions either: according to the favorite apostle, the idea of the betrayal was suggested to Judas by Satan, who had installed himself in his heart shortly before the Last

Supper. John, a mystic above all, who prefers to call upon supernatural reasons to explain events and situations that are hard to unravel, lays the blame on the Devil's intervention and, despite the presumed bad faith toward Judas Iscariot with which some scholars tax him, does not bring up that business of the thirty pieces of silver.

"Those thirty pieces of silver seem to be the only concrete thing in the Judas affair, but the idea of identifying them as the motive for the infamous deed did not even occur to the evangelists, who, not being witnesses to the events, could only report whatever had come to their ears, and without even that minimum of zeal that even the most blasé police reporter would bring to it today. Matthew, true enough, says that the betrayer's first thought is to pocket the 'blood money,' but this in itself does not prove that it would also have been his major concern. In Mark's and Luke's versions the question of the money has only secondary importance. Judas declares himself above all ready to betray the Master, and thinks only about arranging with the representatives of the religious authority how Jesus is to be delivered into their hands: only later on do the high priests, delighted, promise—on their own initiative and not at Judas' urging—to give him money. Matthew alone specifies that the reward is to be thirty silver coins; the other two synoptics are not aware of or do not tell us what the retribution amounts to. If Judas was driven by the thirst for money, he certainly made a poor bargain: not only was that a small sum for the service which, in his view, must be valuable to the high priests, but it was also small in itself. With it the traitor would have been able to buy himself approximately one ounce of nard ointment, that is, one tenth of what Mary, Lazarus' sister, had used to anoint the Lord's head and feet. Even if that precious perfume went for an arm and a leg, it certainly wasn't worth it, for ten times less than its price, to sell one's Master and bring down upon onself the malediction of the ages and eternal damnation. If Judas had some notion of how much he could get in payment for his betrayal, there is no doubt that his deed was motivated otherwise than by thirst for gain. If, however, the amount of blood money had no part in the negotiation, that signifies that for him the question of money was truly secondary, or perhaps of no importance at all. The fact, reported by Matthew, that he gave back the thirty pieces of silver, indeed, flung them into the faces of the priests, seems to confirm our thesis: accepted or repudiated, for Judas the money had at most a merely symbollic value; in my opinion, which is that of someone well acquainted with the world of the police, this paltry sum was the price established, by law or by custom, for delations. The police the world over have always and everywhere paid their informers badly!

"There remains, as an historical reality, one further fact, indisputable but not less mysterious on that account: I refer to Judas' visit to the house of the high priests. According to the consistent testimony of the synoptics, that was when Judas offered to deliver Jesus into the hands of the authorities and began the attempt to carry out his project.

"It does not take much to see that such an interpretation of Judas' visit is only too elementary, and emanates directly from subsequent events, from, in particular, the fact that Judas was at the head of the guards and turned Jesus over to them, revealing his identity by means of the infamous kiss of betrayal. Since Jesus turned the Master over to the authorities, the purpose of his visit must have been to offer them some such service—thus do the evangelists seem to have reasoned. They, in keeping with their practical objectives and their method of writing history, could satisfy themselves with this sort of solution to the problem; but for us problems inevitably multiply.

"One must not forget that according to Matthew and Mark, the Master was still in Bethany when Judas went off to see the high priests; whereas Luke and John, without specifying at what moment Satan purportedly came to inhabit Judas, give us to understand that his visit took place well before the Last Supper, that is, shortly after the triumphal entry into Jerusalem. In either case, at any rate, it appears that Jesus hurried to the house of the high priests and left it with the definite task of delivering the Master into the authorities' hands. Yet what happened in the house of the high priests, between his going in and coming out, remains surrounded by a deep mystery.

"Anyone denying the existence of that mystery in so doing contributes, precisely, to deprive Judas' betrayal of that realistic look which in the end was imposed on the historical version. What is so mysterious, indeed nigh to miraculous, resides in the fact itself that Judas succeeded in getting past the door and getting assigned to the task.

"Our astonishment becomes plausible when one considers the betrayal from the viewpoint of the high priests: what for them was the real value of Judas' intervention? Was it worth the thirty pieces of silver? Or far more? To answer this, we would have to know the intentions of the high priests regarding Jesus, but on this point also we have only what the four Gospels say to refer to. Our four sources jointly affirm that during Jesus' public ministry attemps to capture him were frequent. But one thing does not seem very clear: whether these attempts were a consequence of public indignation or of orders issued by the high priests. If you care to go by what the Gospels say, both cases would become possible, and we would have to suppose that it was sometimes the one, sometimes the other. But, at this point, our uncertainty is reinforced by the position taken nowadays by ecclesiastic historiography. The latter maintains that Jesus, when by fleeing he avoided the threat of capture and withdrew to safer places, should not be mistaken for an ordinary delinquent being sought by the law; he was not pro-scribed, nor was any warrant issued for his arrest, so that his flights and his disappearances must be regarded as legitimate self-defense, almost as a precautionary measure to gain time, in order to hold out until what he judged to be the opportune hour to surrender himself into the hands of the authorities. Put in other terms, this means that, down to the last moment, he was a free citizen, free to exercize his trade as prophet, constrained only now and then to flee to avoid the consequences of the ire and indignation of other free citizens, to whom his Word was a nuisance. The authorities did not have it in for him.

"Only John records a meeting of the Sanhedrin during which the priests called Jesus a public menace to domestic peace in the State. Caiaphas therefore proposes that they kill him, and from then on—as John says—there were attempts to kill him. Personally I do not feel competent enough in these matters to judge the credibility of this testimony in the fourth Gospel, but my layman's brain perceives an obvious discrepancy with the other Gospels or with the position of the Church's modern historians. There is, in fact, a pretty big difference between having someone bumped off and having him arrested with a regular warrant. Even if to your mind John attributes to the high priest a somewhat exaggerated concern over Jesus' subversive activity, from the cited passage the most that results is that the priests leaned toward having Jesus assassinated, perhaps in the course of a brawl provoked by popular indignation. This is the way you renconcile the apparent contradictions in the Gospels."

The clearer the historical circumstances become, the denser grows the mystery surrounding Judas' betrayal! Being neither a writer of history nor a theologian, I advance cautiously and do not rule out the eventuality that in the midst of our investigation things take a surprising turn, and show that, contrary to the thesis put forward up until the present, Jesus was actually persecuted by the authorities. In this case I would ask only one question: for what purpose did Judas betake himself to the high priests? To tell them to lay hands on a man whom, even without his invitation, they were ready to lay hands on—there was no need for it. To tell them to lay hands on him during a quiet hour and as quietly as possible—advice for which Judas' perspicacity was not required. To present himself in person and offer to indicate the best time for making the capture and the way to the Master's place of refuge— likewise superfluous: spies shadowed every suspect person, and henchmen took care of the rest. But, in this case, what does the most horrible betrayal in history come down to? It comes down, to tell the truth, to a deed whose vileness almost vanishes in the face of its insignificance, and above all in the face of its foolishness. Thus, the most infamous traitor, the traitor *par excellence*, Judas Iscariot, would have done no more than lend a hand in a simple, easily dealt with affair that would have followed its course even without his involvement—thus furnishing the most sensational example of superfluity in the world's history. It is after all amazing that the high priests would have accepted his completely super-fluous collaboration. But if for some reason we do not know—for the sake of convenience, perhaps—they accepted it, such services were surely not even worth thirty pieces of silver.

"Nevertheless, it seems to me that one can rule out the hypothesis that Jesus Christ had been legally outlawed and that the authorities intended to lay hands on him: the absurdity of Judas' collaboration would be enough to exclude this. But then the problem of his mysterious visit to the house of the high priests presents itself with even greater insistence. If the authorities had no intention of arresting Jesus, it is because they had no reason for doing so. And even if it would not have displeased the Sanhedrin to see the Prophet murdered, this does not mean that it had sufficient grounds for arresting him. Judas, therefore, with his offer did not represent a new and precious element capable of resolving the difficulties the Jesus affair could have caused for the priests: the problem, in fact, was not whether or not to put him bodily in jail, but to find a justification enabling them to do so.

"When Judas decided to go to to the high priests, he must surely have realized that serious though his personal motives might have been—hatred, jealousy, hurt pride, avidness for money, or any other purely hypothetical motive—they would not be enough to induce them to arrest the Master. Even were he of limited intelligence or blinded by emotion, he must surely have been aware that if he wanted his wish granted he must offer something reasonable and useful, in conformance with the eternal laws of supply and demand. And despite the fact that the evangelists skipped right over this moment in the betrayal, I am fully convinced for my part that precisely on the occasion of that mysterious visit Judas Iscariot *had to have said something of extreme importance to the priests*, something essential, which they did not know and which indeed provided them with a sufficient motive for Jesus' arrest. But what could this insignificant person say that was of such importance that it could cause the high priests 'to rejoice'?

"The historical investigation must ponder this hypothesis. Never shall we know what Judas told the priests that they did not know already. It would be going too far to suppose that the betrayer made up out of whole cloth some dreadful accusation which prompted the Sanhedrin to act at once. The truth is that the priests did not act at once, but let four or five days go by and left to Judas' discretion the choice of the hour for the arrest. Everything gives us to suppose that what Judas said represented, in the eyes of the high priests, neither something important nor something new; and that at the most it was said at a propitious moment. It truly required a lucky combining of heterogeneous elements, of unforeseeable, almost miraculous circumstances for the betrayer's insistences to be taken seriously. Whatever the motive at work in him, there is one thing the betrayer could not have foreseen: his action's success.

"Looking to our four not very precise sources, we indeed find two points of use to us in our desperate effort to reconstruct the historical truth in some credible manner. One of these points is the accusation formulated against Jesus: 'Are you the Christ, Son of God? Are you the King of the Jews?' At the same time, the evangelists more than once cite the Master's severe prohibition against propagating the great revelation: to no one are they to reveal that he is the Christ, Son of God, hence King of the Jews! How then were the high priests and Pilate able to formulate their accusation in those terms? A little more and we might be tempted to answer that the charge was suggested to them by Judas Iscariot . . .

"But this answer seems too obvious not to arouse our suspicion. It could be the right one if the apostles had really kept the secret and Jesus himself had never rendered it a matter of public knowledge. Unfortunately, neither the Gospels nor their exegetes are in agreement on this score. Carried away by his eloquence, Jesus did make incautious statements before strangers and, in the heat of discussion, even before some adversaries and enemies. That he considered himself the Son of God, the Messiah, that is to say, the King of the Jews, was at the most an open secret that could not escape the attention of the authorities concerned. If these authorities nevertheless did not bestir themselves, it means that they had thoughtfully weighed the possible influence of these messianic declarations upon public order, and their possible political consequences. For the high priests, Jesus' declarations were bombast devoid of any real foundation. That Jesus was not the Messiah was to them a fact so obvious there could be no room for discussion. The whole thing was of interest to them only on the practical plane, in the event Jesus succeeded in convincing too large a crowd with his nonsense, and in the event his mystifications were able to provoke a disturbance. Nothing, however, seemed to warrant such a concern.

"Since we have ventured into the realm of hypotheses, I make free to propose one of my own. Judas, unable to tell the priests anything they did not know already, or to invent lies they could not check upon, must nevertheless have told them something that shook them out of their torpor. But what knowledge did Judas possess that could have appeared to them an absolute *novum* worthy of attention? It seems to me there can hardly be any doubt as to the answer. The one thing Judas knew and the priests didn't know was the *truth* about Jesus—namely the fact that he was *truly* the Christ, the Son of God, that he *really* was the Messiah, hence King of the Jews. His vindication of the Master's divinity must have been a desperate speech, a furious pleading filled with terrifying eschatalogical prospects, still more so with menacing images of a future near at hand. He said absolutely nothing that the high priests had not already heard, and yet that nothing pronounced by him had a *different*, an impressive aspect! I don't know whether you've ever met a person with absolute faith, but it is an overwhelming experience, it reduces you to nothing at all, or at the very least it puts a scare into you. I believe that for a few moments the high priests also experienced the paralyzing magic of Judas' volcanic faith. But, once they recovered their wits, they realized that they now had enough elements in hand for a concrete indictment that would take that fanatic out of circulation, in accusing him of outrage against religion but above all of political subversion.

"But for Judas to achieve such a result—and we do not have the right to forget it!—Judas had to pronounce, for the second time in the world's history, the Credo first pronounced by Peter. This plausible hypothesis of mine, which even strikes me as the only one of its kind, has the merit of providing an idea on the 'how' of the betrayal, and at the same time of flatly excluding and of rendering useless a good part of the fanciful conjectures and of the baseless theories as to its motives. The absolute faith in the divinity of Jesus, the as it were mathematical certainty that Judas displayed before the high priests, eliminates baseness and vulgarity from among the motivating factors of his criminal act. And for my part, as you shall see, I have reason to believe in the sincerity of the betrayer's Credo . . ."

At this precise point Dupin thought to relight his pipe, which meanwhile had gone out. He had conducted his argumentation at one go, without any interruption, just as he used to do in the past when he had a thesis or a theory all ready. Even though he had kept his eyes fixed on me all the while he spoke, he seemed to become aware of my presence only now. And, noticing my perplexity, he smiled a little smile of satisfaction.

"Your turn to talk," he said, with a polite gesture. "Go ahead, ask me at least one question."

"Well, my dear friend, I must tell you," I replied, "the whole subject being so foreign to me, my confusion nearly outdoes my curiosity. And, frankly, I find it a bit depressing, this inferior position I am put in by my complete incompetence in the matter."

"Don't be discouraged. If you are willing to follow me attentively, you'll pick up the necessary knowledge in a jiffy and we'll be able to advance together into an area where I myself no longer feel all that safe . . . and so we'll be back on a par. After that you will be able to help me in the most effective way. But right now I am waiting for you to formulate the one possible logical question, frightened though you may be by its childish simplicity . . ."

"As a matter of fact," I said after hesitating for a moment, "such a question has crossed my mind, and I didn't dare ask it, not wanting, indeed, to show my naïveté in this regard . . ."

"And what is it?"

"Very well, it's this: I was thinking of asking you why, given the way things stand, given, that is, the correctness of your hypothesis—why then did Judas Iscariot betray the Lord?"

"Bravo, you're still as sharp as ever," Dupin exclaimed contentedly. "That is exactly the question that required asking. I wish however to repeat that I do not claim the merit of having hit upon the correct hypothesis: I called it the only plausible one, in the original sense of the word, because I find it beautiful, attractive, almost poetic. But it is also of course the only one, and it would be the only one even if it were not so beautiful and so exact. I add, moreover, that we can leave this hypothesis out of the picture without compromising our subsequent investigations—but in that case we must give up arriving at an idea, however vague, of the 'how' of the betrayal. The 'how' along with the 'why' of the proditorious deed would be fated to remain a mystery . . ."

"But then you do not know the 'why' either?" I cried, almost indignant.

"I do not know it, I know it still less than I know the 'how,' " Dupin admitted, though without any loss of his composure. "Even if my hypothesis, the only plausible one, does not shed light on the personal motives of the betrayal, at least it explains its substance and renders comprehensible the high priests' decision on the subject of Jesus' arrest. And one must keep in mind one further advantage my conjecture provides. Following it, it is obvious that if Judas had not been sure of Jesus, if he had not believed and had confidence in him, he would not have even tried to betray him. Why? The answer is simple: because apart from his faith and his Credo, he had nothing to apprise the high priests of. And his faith must have been uncommonly solid for him to believe that it could suffice for the betrayal. Owing precisely to this obsessive faith, the most absurd deed in the world ended up enveloped in all that probability which characterizes every historical event.

"It is a strange thing that while the essence itself of the betrayal aroused no interest over the centuries, scholars and writers let loose their imaginations over the personal motive, nobody being satisfied by the story of the thirty pieces of silver. Some great minds—and lots of mediocre ones—were tempted by the figure of the betrayer and, in every literary genre, poems and novels, stories and plays, they all tried to uncover the mysterious motive for the betrayal. We have seen Judases jealous of the Master's greatness, envious, suffering from an inferiority complex, Judases humiliated by everybody, Judases as national heroes and precursors of Zionism, we've even seen Marxist and confrontational Judases. But whether they be works worthy of attention or of scant value, all of them swim in the selfsame sea of gratuitous hypotheses. And how could it be otherwise? Of the historical figure of Judas we in fact know nothing, absolutely nothing. And for my part, perhaps with your disapproval, I would resign myself to passing over the entire problem. For a clear understanding of this betrayal is it really so important, so indispensable, to know Judas Isacariot's personal motives? Of course, it would be interesting; but not any the more indispensable on that account.

"I believe, my friend, that if I had not thrown him the life-saver of my 'only plausible hypothesis,' Judas would still be standing there in a quandary, wondering under what pretext to approach the high priests and what he should say to them, so unclear in his mind was the 'how' to betray Jesus! Well, I am just as strongly inclined to think that neither did he know 'why' he had to betray him. This hypothesis of mine, so surprising at first sight, shouldn't surprise us anymore once we consider the Judas personage from the point of view of his role, betrayal. What counted, what was important and indispensable was the betrayal in itself, and not its motives and modalities. Next to the absolute necessity of betraying, Judas' personal motives and machinations had only a relative importance, were indeed futile and irrelevant contingencies. The betrayal *per se*, its transcendent purpose and its historical consequences were of such boundless import that Judas' eventual personal motives were of purely apparent value and consistency, serving at the very most to create that atmosphere of historical verisimilitude or credibility I alluded to earlier. That is why to attempt to discover them would seem to me an unnecessary waste of time, or at least a gratuitous chore."

"So then," I broke in, "if I understand this correctly, you think the 'why' of the betrayal may be sought outside of the person of Judas?"

"I think that is where it *must* be sought," Dupin affirmed. "Were we to suppose, even as an eventuality, that the betrayal could be important for events or persons more important than Judas, the personal motives of the execrable apostle immediately lose all interest, or, perhaps, all consistence: they might even not exist at all."

"How is it possible for you to admit of a human act devoid of all motivation, detached from that 'inherent logical necessity' you are the proponent of?"

"We'll come to all that later on," said Dupin, his mind on something else. "Let me remind you parenthetically (and refrain from rushing to construct theories upon it!) that there exist acts committed by human beings without their conscious participation: acts in which they behave as automatons, in a state of hypnosis, for example, or of plagiarism, of blind obedience, of total subordination, when these human beings are no longer anything but simple means and have a merely instrumental function . . ."

"You think perhaps . . ." I began, hardly able to conceal my disappointment.

"I don't think anything," Dupin cut me short. "I am simply calling your attention to the existence of enormous interests that were closely bound up with the 'work of betrayal.' According to theology—but this is obvious to anyone—the betrayal was a necessary prelude to the Passion and the Crucifixion, a *conditio sine qua non* of the Redemption. This is obvious both for the right-thinking and for those who don't think one way or another, because it is also a historical fact and you don't trifle with historical facts: they must be accepted as they are. Only the heretical could raise objections, sceptics and unbelievers who blindly and without distinction reject facts and events, from the truthfulness of the Gospels to the real existence of Jesus Christ, who don't want to hear about the Redemption either and, in the best of cases, behind the story of the Son of God see just one more prophet's career, thus depriving it of its logic and its fatality. They are even capable of alleging that the events could also, when all is said and done, have taken place differently. Hence the betrayal could just as well have not taken place. In fact, say these anti-historical talents, putting forward their clinching argument, the Almighty God and His Only Son could have thought up a thousand other ways to save humanity or, at least, to sacrifice the Redeemer, supposing that this was truly necessary. If our 'only plausible hypothesis' comes to the intelligence of these gentlemen, they will unfailingly exult, for they will see their position reinforced. If the betrayal presents no advantage either for Judas or for the high priests, there could just as well have been none, and God and His Son would have been able to arrive by other paths at the so-called redemption of mankind.

"It is difficult to take the fierceness of the unbelievers seriously, and it would be to display too much indulgence were we to allow for their arguments. At any rate, their final conclusion strikes us as irresponsible, premature anyhow. Can one call it right to resort to divine omnipotence to justify gratuitous hypotheses, and to exclude the very one that comes down to us as a historical fact?

Doesn't it occur to anybody that divine omnipotence could have brought the whole thing off exactly as it happened in fact? Personally, I don't find it so surprising that divine omnipotence should have chosen betrayal, with its elusive 'whys' and 'hows,' as the instrument for Redemption; and, the opposite of our adversaries, I think that it is precisely in the fact that it preferred the difficult and the almost impossible over other, simpler solutions, that the greatness of omnipotence comes through—something which, after all, is not without precedent in the relations between God and mankind. As does a hunting dog seeking where to go next, I stop and point; and as of now I am ready to believe that the divine plan must have attached particular importance to having the redemption of man be preceded by a betrayal.

"And here rationalistic historiography and reason itself come to our assistance. Jesus could not afford to have his program depend on the whims of the high priests. The latter paid little attention to prophets so long as they did not publicly endanger the political and religious order, and their indifference was sometimes such that they did not prevent them from being stoned and killed by the mob. It was the ideal way to be rid of undesirable elements. Jesus who, at least in appearance, was nothing more than just another prophet, could very rightly fear the same fate. But to let oneself be killed by the irate crowd under some run-of-the-mill circumstance would have been tantamount to acknowledging and confirming that he was truly nothing more than a run-of-the-mill prophet.

"According to the Gospels' testimony, Jesus, with the very longstanding desire to die crucified, sought to avoid—and did indeed many times avoid—the commonplace death of prophets, for this purpose not hesitating to put his magical powers to use. By disappearing from sight in the midst of the raging mob, he seems to have wanted to preserve himself for the sole satisfactory death, which was to come about at a specific time and place and under specific circumstances, in keeping with a pre-established plan of his. This being so, Judas' betrayal assumes an extraordinary importance. The choice of the propitious hour for his capture having been entrusted to Judas, the possibility of dying during Passover, and not on some ordinary day, lay in Jesus' grasp. And besides has it never occurred to you that it was during the interrogations of Jesus that utterance was first given, in public and in official surroundings, to the solemn truth destined ever to resound after so many centuries? Who then, but for the intervention of Judas, would have asked Jesus if he was truly the Messiah, Son of God and King of the Jews?

"Compared with these enormous interests that Jesus had, all the possible motives and personal reasons of the man who betrayed him are of only secondary, nay, negligible importance. Just as compared with huge quantities modest decimals do not count, so Judas, as an individual, did not count before the immensity of the plan for Redemption. That is why we can further confirm, with one more reason, that it wasn't even necessary that Judas have personal motives: Jesus had them in abundance.

"If it be admitted that there is no common measure between the divine plan and the obvious modesty of Judas' own personal motivation, we may reach conclusions that the positivo-rationalistic historiographers would not find distasteful, conclusions indeed already deduced by a number of specialists of that school: in clear language, we find ourselves with, on one side, a Machiavellian or 'jesuitical' Jesus for whom the sublime end justifies the knowingly chosen cruel means, and, on the other side, a victimized Judas who, driven perhaps by some trivial, futile personal motive, but much more probably deceived and hoodwinked by the Master's supreme will, and in any event ignorant of the true purpose, all unsuspectingly carried out the task he had been assigned. And why can we not imagine a Jesus extremely conscious of his own objectives, to the point of not balking, in the interests of final success, at the most cunning, the most refined measures? Within the rationalist conception, the impossible does not exist in History, and in the name of truth one may very well reconstruct facts and events in such a way that they are in complete contradiction with their intrinsic evidence. For them it is even possible that Jesus didn't exist at all.

"Actually, from the rationalist point of view the problem is easily resolved. Jesus chose eleven apostles as spokesmen for his message, pillars for his Church, martyrs for his religion; and he chose one by whom to be betrayed. This twelfth apostle was deliberately chosen on the basis of certain clues or certain precedents which made it possible to foresee, if not the probability, at least the possibility of the treacherous deed. Jesus took note, when he chose him, of the weaknesses in Judas' character, with a view to utilizing them at the suitable time for his own practical and divine ends. A sentence of John's seems to confirm this secret calculation. The favorite, in effect, maintains that Judas was a thief and, being responsible for the purse, would filch what was put into it. If we go by the centuries-old belief which grants so much importance to the thirty pieces of silver, it becomes evident that Jesus counted on his disciple's criminal tendencies, and precisely on his greed for money. Entrusting the purse to a thief, he also subjected him to permanent temptation by Satan, and could hope, not without reason, that such a fellow would not hesitate to betray him the minute he was offered the chance to earn thirty pieces of silver. The Machiavellian figure of Jesus thus shines out in all its superhuman perfection. The Jesus dear to our imagination and to secular tradition most certainly would not have exposed a weakling to temptation and sin; yet the 'jesuitical' Jesus who had pulled Peter from the water after he had fallen into it through his own cowardice, let Judas drown in the whirlpools of damnation. Continuing along this line, the image of the betrayer as the unconscious and innocent victim of a higher plan would even so be without the tragic, demonic aspect which has distinguished it over the centuries, the traitor being nothing but a mere thief. Jesus, on the other hand, whether God or superman, would be stripped of all the attributes which symbolize his traditional image and which are indispensable for our affection and filial respect. Great though the work of Redemption may be as an end, the means was unworthy of the Son of God, fountainhead of goodness and justice: for instead of saving a weak man, he sacrificed him.

"The general aversion it arouses would be enough to reject any such reconstruction; nor, fortunately, is there any objective reason that obliges us to accept it. Nothing forces us to believe that desire for money was the motive for Judas' betrayal, and moreover the only source that calls the betrayer a thief does not bother to correlate his kleptomania with his criminal act. And yet, from whom might we expect some light on the role played by the twelfth apostle if not from John, who claims to be the evangelist who knows most about him? That the favorite disciple knows a lot about Judas, and never, of course, anything pleasant, has aroused in many critics the suspicion that John is biassed toward the betrayer. When all is said and done, a deep dislike is altogether understandable in the one who 'loved most and was most loved,' indeed even the deepest hatred would be understandable. All the same, it is not possible to trust unconditionally a historian who does not approach his subject 'sine ira et studio.'

"John in fact is the one the Master told the betrayer's name, he is the only one who knew from the beginning why Judas left after receiving the dipped bread from Jesus' hands, and from his same account it emerges unequivocally that he was to keep this knowledge to himself for a long time to come. Indeed none of the other three evangelists reports the version John transmitted to us. This fact, anyhow, is one of the so numerous mysteries of the New Testament and arouses our curiosity with regard to the favorite apostle. To the ordinary mind it would seem natural that, if not before, then at least after the betrayal, John immediately inform his companions that Jesus, thanks to his divine prescience, had identified the betrayer: so outstanding a manifestation of Jesus' prophetic power would have been worth pointing out, and worth the other evangelists' mention too. Oddly enough, they are silent on the matter, as though they knew nothing about it. Only Matthew mentions the discovery of the betrayer, in a version which at first sight contradicts John's. According to Matthew, all the apostles, terrified and humiliated by Jesus' declaration, ask the question: 'Master, is it I?' Judas like the others dares ask the same question: 'Would I be your betrayer?' And Jesus answers: 'You have said so.'

"If it were absolutely necessary to choose between the two variants, we would have to give preference to John's. But there is actually no real contradiction. Matthew seems to reduce the episode to its essence, in the light of subsequent facts. It would have been a psychological absurdity had the apostles, as one man, not reacted violently against the unmasked betrayer. Nor would it have been in Jesus' interest to endanger the work of betrayal by a thoughtless revelation. But our having set limits to Matthew's credibility does not add to or lessen John's truthfulness. However, difficulties of all sorts crop up, even in his regard. We do not wish to question that Jesus really identified his betrayer to him, but we fail to understand why John, in his turn, did not reveal this secret to his co-disciples immediately after the betrayal. Or if he did reveal it, why the others failed to take note of it. The biggest difficulty is of a psychological order. John, so vain, so proud of his position as favorite, so loquacious when it came to his own glorification, how was he able, over all those decades, to resist publicizing this episode, this subsequent confirmation of his privileged position? Did he perchance fear that his companions would not believe him? Or, what is worse, did he hasten at once to communicate to them this evidence of favor—but did none of his companions believe it? Why? From envy? From dislike? Or because they considered him a braggart?

"No one is able to present a sound argument that places John's truthfulness in doubt. It remains nonetheless that he is privy to certain things which are not confirmed in the other Gospels. By way of example we may cite the episode of the anointing in Bethany. In John, after the sister of Lazarus anointed the Master's head and feet with the costly spikenard, we read 'Then saith one of his disciples, Judas Iscariot, Simon's son, which should betray him, Why was not this ointment sold for three hundred pence, and given to the poor?' John however, lest we imagine Judas impelled by an offended sense of social justice or any howsoever idealistic motive, goes straight on to tell us that the future betrayer was only an ordinary thief, a thief who was sorry to see the pretty sum of three hundred pieces of silver wasted, since the money, once gone into the common purse, would wind up, some of it at least, in his own pocket.

"Without expressing an opinion on John's wounding accusation (betrayers also have a sort of honor, upon which they are touchy)—since to understand the motive and the essence of the betrayal it makes no difference at all whether Judas was or was not a thief—we must point out that here once more is a fact with which only John is acquainted. None of the other evangelists seems to be aware of Judas' kleptomaniac tendencies. But supposing that John, even in this regard, knew more than the others, it is difficult not to notice a generous dose of perfidy in the way he recounts the Bethany episode. The favorite, in this particular instance, is not the sole witness and his version can be compared with that of two synoptics (Luke neglects the episode). The comparison leads us to some painful conclusions. Mark in fact speaks not only of Judas, who protests at the sight of the anointing, but of *several* disciples, and Matthew gives us to understand that it was actually *the whole group* that was scandalized. These at first sight would seem to be three irreconcilable versions and we are almost tempted to seek out the reason for these divergences. Mark speaks of 'some' shocked disciples, thereby leaving open the possibility that Peter, to whom he was faithful, was not necessarily to be included among them. Matthew, instead, who was certainly among those who expressed indignation, declares, out of devotion to the truth, or with some slight exaggeration, that it was a shocking moment for *all* the apostles, using the general indignation to excuse his own. Without wishing to insist upon the fact that reasons of this sort were behind the accounts of the two synoptics, it is important for us to show that upon this occasion Judas' behavior was not exceptional or different from that of the others. From a comparison of the synoptics it simply appears that Judas *too* was, or may have been, among the indignant. But if we hold with Matthew, one must fear, or rather consider as certain, that John also joined in the choir of disapproval! Among all the evangelists, John is surely he who exculpates himself the most ingeniously: by saddling Judas with the entire revolt, he divests himself 'by the processs of elimination' of the role that must have been his during the regrettable episode.

"Nonetheless, it is not difficult to conciliate the information from the various Gospels: it is indeed possible that all the disciples were scandalized, but that only some of them asked why so much expensive oil was being wasted, and that only Judas expressed himself in the manner reported by John. Thus the favorite would have employed the poetic form *pars pro toto*, citing the most characteristic exclamation to render his account more dramatic. But he can still be reproached for having kept silent about the general indignation (in which consequently he too would have participated) and for presenting Judas as being the only one— owing to his native wickedness—who opened his mouth to utter disdainful words.

"Unless we wish to call this attitude of John's irresponsible, we must find where its perfidy lies; and someone about whom one is able to show that to the extent he spoke the truth, he did not speak the whole truth and nothing but the truth, becomes suspect on all the points in his testimony that are not supported by other witnesses. So it is within anyone's right to entertain reservations even in regard to the privileged position that John claims he occupied in the Master's heart. And it is certainly not on the basis of the information provided in the four Gospels that we can change the mind of anyone who is reluctant to accept Judas as a common thief. As for our own selves, we would be inclined not to look upon him as a thief. If the synoptics were to come to our aid on this score, the most that would come out would be that Judas, having nothing of his own, occasionally dipped into the common purse, as I myself would have done in his place, to buy tobacco for my pipe. But that was not a sufficient reason to betray the Lord; and with so venial a peccadillo Judas could have become a saint, just like John, his accuser.

"This swift and partial examination of the fourth Gospel was necessary to demonstrate that, however well informed he was, John offers us no new elements apt to give some solidity to the betrayer's evanescent figure and help us discover the why of the infamous deed. Nor was the favorite interested in such details. All that interested him was to apply grim and unpleasant colors to a figure he neglected to define.

"What with the indescribable poverty of the elements which might shed a little light on the profound mystery of the betrayal, we must however hail the very fact that John deals with the figure of the betrayer in so personal a manner, and consider as an important item of information his hostile and spiteful attitude toward Judas Iscariot. Can we, in our situation, confine ourselves to acknowledging this fact without seeking the reason for it? Why, indeed, does John devote special attention to the figure of the betrayer? And why does this attention focus on the person and not on the importance and motive of his deed? And though he is upon one occasion disagreeable with Judas, why does he resort to circumlocutions, approximations, allusions, unproven accusations instead of flying out at him with overwhelming hatred, which would be proper and understandable and even compatible with his excitable temperament? Nothing of the kind. Risking the appearance of a mere slanderer, the apostle of love deals with him *maliciously*.

"If it is true (and unfortunately we must make this reservation, for elements concerning the curious relationship between the disciple and the Master are to be found only in the fourth Gospel), if it is true that John was the favorite apostle and that the Lord's affection was manifested in the forms reported by the favorite himself, I believe we can discover the reasons behind his deplorable attitude in regard to Judas; and, it should be added, it is of little importance, from this point of view, whether John actually had a privileged place in Jesus' heart, or only boasted that he did. It is

however important to us that he set great store by it, and
undeniably he did. John, undeniably, loved the Master, egotistical
though his love may have been, and he was loved in return,
possibly a bit less than he thought or wanted to give people to
believe, and in a manner more superficial than he would have
wished: at any rate he was loved in a certain way, and this feeling
the Master had for him he had turned into a title of glory or
vainglory. This sentimental tie will help us identify a little more
narrowly the favorite's 'perfidy.'

"We must keep in mind the fact that John's Gospel is a sort of
memoir, published sixty or more years after the events that make
up its contents. These are the recollections of a dignified and
respected old man, whose word inspired an at once original and
fundamental current in the development of Christian doctrine.
When he undertook to set his evangel down in writing he was a
prominent leader, nearing the end of his life. And this majestic old
man, whose declarations about the privileged place he held in the
Master's heart could easily be much more than just boastings—
that is, could be in some way true—, unhesitatingly stoops to
calumniating and showing in an unfavorable light a man who is
dead, and who died miserably. And he does all this without any
reason, without any purpose, does it gratuitously, to give outlet to
sentiments or resentments which since his youth have stewed in the
depths of his heart. His ugly remarks about Judas do not aim at
explaining any facts. He simply takes pleasure in denigrating him.

"But what are the feelings urging to this defamation? John, the
first of the mystics, could surely have exposed in Judas the
principle of Evil. But he doesn't do this, neither does he assail in
him the betrayer of the Son of God. Thus John is no exception to
the general rule: he pays no more attention than anyone else to the
betrayal's essence and motivation (and we are by now certain that
his precious friendship with Nicodemus could not have been of any
great usefulness to him on this score). John does not go after the
betrayer; he has it in for Judas personally. But Judas was not an
enemy of his, or a competitor in the rivalry that developed for a

position in the Messiah's kingdom. Resentments of this sort would have been, at a pinch, more justified toward any other apostle than toward Judas, who after all had done away with himself more than fifty years before, while he, John, had risen to one of the uppermost positions in the hierarchy. But what was it then that he could not forgive him for?

"When a great man, become great as no one ever was before, looks back upon his past, he is able to forgive all those who stood in his way, for each obstacle overcome is a touchstone of his greatness; but never will he be able to vanquish his antipathy for him who took his place in the heart of the woman he loved. The truer the love was, the longer jealousy lasts. The rival, even if he was no more than the object of a passing fancy or a shortlived passion, will forever remain a disturbing mystery for the lover who is the less able to understand the spell the rival exerted over his beloved the more furiously he remembers the obvious defects to which she remained blind for too long. And if the rival, as foreseen, ends by becoming unworthy of the flame kindled in the fought-over heart, it is a masochistically voluptuous relief to call to mind all those signs which, to eyes less charmed, would at the outset have revealed the unworthiness in his character and his behavior.

"John, in his Gospel, behaves exactly like the lover who has had to bear humiliations and torments because of his beloved's incomprehensible attraction to an abject rival. No one, however, is to be misled by this somewhat audacious analogy of mine, and no one is less ready than I to imagine a triangular romantic relationship between Jesus, John and Judas: I am not the sort to fall into the trap of fantasizing, which I reproved in the poetic reconstructions of the story of Judas. Yet there remains the favorite's peculiar attitude toward the person of the betrayer, the special malevolence he brings to bear on him; and the analogy holds up not just in the case of love between men and women, but in every sentimental relationship. And as between Jesus and John there did exist a relationship of this kind, I have every reason to think, with the encouragement of the testimony implicit in the fourth Gospel, that to the favorite Judas looked like a disturbing factor for his sentimental harmony. To arouse his jealousy it may have been enough for Jesus to treat his future betrayer with special attention, an attention slightly different from that reserved for all the other apostles, and a bit similar to the kind reserved for him: an attention of a *personal* character. That someone other than himself could have a personal relationship with the Master seemed inadmissible to the favorite, who saw this threatening the exclusiveness of his rights to Jesus' human affections. His lover's eyes were on the alert and his favorite's heart detected an indefinable, inconceivable menace. It truly took the ultra-sensitive seismograph of John's jealous soul to sense that between the Master and Judas existed mysterious ties, too subtle to be perceived by everyone and too strange to be given a name. John had never succeeded in understanding this relationship between Jesus and Judas, but he intuited its existence, and that was enough to quicken his jealousy, which, sixty years later, would be exuded in the calumnies and perfidies of his Gospel's recollections.

"To you does it perhaps seem too risky to assert that between Jesus and his future betrayer there must have existed altogether unusual relations?" were Dupin's concluding words as he rose to prepare the coffee, without which he would have been unable to go to sleep.

A relationship verging on the absurd

THE FOLLOWING EVENING, AFTER I REPORTED ON MY TRUANCIES IN THE CITY
of Light *à la recherche du temps passé*, my friend Dupin raised his
hand and pointed his finger at me:

"Did you give an occasional thought to Judas Iscariot?"

"Oh, you've infected me, all right," I answered with a laugh.
"Sitting at the Café de l'Opéra, or standing in front of the
photographs of the *stripteaseuses* outside the Moulin Rouge, I
realized that my thoughts were constantly wandering through
Palestine, in the company of Jesus Christ and his betrayer . . ."

Dupin nodded, visibly satisfied.

"So then you agree that the relationship between Jesus and his
twelfth apostle must have been delightfully special?"

"Theirs must have been a relationship bordering on the absurd!"
I rejoined, going him one better. "If Jesus foresaw everything, he
knew from the start which one was to be the betrayer, and yet he

continued to live with him, both loving and fearing him at the same time . . ."

"Stop, for heaven's sake, stop!" Dupin burst out joyfully. "You've said enough for me to realize that you are not insensitive to this problem, beautiful because devoid of all practical interest—but which on that very account deserves more than a flash of intelligence and enthusiasm.

"The sentence you brought out all in one breath is worth dissecting piecemeal and will serve as the guiding thread for our thoughts this evening—if one evening turns out to be enough to exhaust the subject. For example, for you it seems obvious that Jesus identified his future betrayer from the very start, but now I am going to put before you an enormous number of collateral problems. To begin with, I could ask you this question: would you, after first identifying him, would you have chosen your future betrayer as an intimate collaborator?

"The first reaction of a thinking person who foresaw or sensed in someone the cause of his own undoing would be to try to get away from him, not to make him one of his principal collaborators. Jesus, on the contrary, made Judas his apostle, nay, he even did so after a minute preparation. According to Luke's testimony, Jesus already had behind him a long and felicitous period of activity when he chose his collaborators. His disciples form a fairly sizable cohort and people came in large numbers from the whole of Judea and from Jerusalem and from the littoral by Tyre and Sidon to listen to him and be cured of their infirmities. At a certain moment Jesus felt the need to choose some among his disciples to be his closest collaborators, his emissaries, who could act on his behalf and in his name. So one day, and it is again Luke we are quoting, he went up on the mountain to meditate and pray, and there he spent the night. At dawn he summoned his disciples and from them he chose twelve.

"This passage from the evangelist suffices to convince us of the great importance Jesus attributed to the election of his apostles. By the words 'Did I not elect the twelve of you?' he himself underscores that he has acted consciously and freely in this regard. We would have to challenge Jesus' own words were we to want to maintain that he was the victim of a 'misjudgment' in connection with Judas.

"It follows from all this that Jesus not only foresaw his betrayer in Judas, and not only did nothing to keep him at a distance, but that it was with full awareness that he chose to have him as a collaborator. However. this being what Jesus did, normal human understanding finds itself confronted here by something deeply mysterious.

"If we abide by official theology, the answer should present no difficulty. Jesus, the son of God, God Himself, endowed, though in a human body, with a divine nature and with all its prerogatives, by virtue of omniscience knew everything, therefore also foreknew and foresaw his life, Passion, death and Resurrection, all of it in every least detail, betrayer and betrayal included. Thanks to these divine gifts, Jesus recognized his future betrayer at first glance, vividly recalling the moment, the place, the circumstances under which he was to encounter him. He recognized him on sight, perhaps without having ever seen him before, as if he knew him *ab æterno*, and from the beginning he knew what deed Judas would commit against him. And yet, fully conscious of what he was about, he chose him, despite all that. Or precisely because of it . . ."

At this particular point Dupin paused and drew a deep breath, and took advantage of it to relight his pipe which was not tolerant of such lengthy disquisitions.

"Precisely because of it!" I said, something of reproach in my voice. "Just as I supposed . . ."

Dupin nodded his assent.

"If that is just what you supposed, do have the kindness to bear with me a little longer. I would rather defer the attentive examination of this problem until later, so as not to drown in successive waves of new problems before we have succeeded in coping with the flood of old ones. For now let's confine ourselves to drawing, on an altogether human plane, the conclusions of Jesus' foreknowledge regarding his fate. What we have here is nothing less than so-called determinism, the doctrine according to which everything happens in a manner established beforehand and all our individual or collective efforts are vain in the face of the destiny which weighs on History. The future can already, in the present, be considered as past, and it is upon such premises omniscience and prescience find a rationally acceptable basis. We ordinary mortals, ill-provided with sixth senses and revelatory presentiments, can go on discussing determinism, accepting or rejecting it as we like, for no absolute proofs will ever be forthcoming to end the matter. Not at all the same is the situation of those who foresee certain events in their lives or in the world and who, furthermore, have managed occasionally to convince themselves of the exactness of their predictions. We can express all the skeptical reservations we like, asserting that these are matters of pure chance or of people in a state of over-excitement, but these same people think otherwise. Foreseeing for them is the equivalent of knowing, of identifying a future occurrence that cannot be constrained, altered, or avoided. A true prophet never doubts the ineluctability of what he foresees; and the more authentic a prophet is, the less he is able to lull himself with the hope that he can be mistaken.

"Once we allow Jesus the gift of foresight, it indeed seems childish to ask why, having identified his future betrayer, he did not seek to eliminate him. Holding off for the moment on the problem of the intrinsic necessity for a betrayer, Jesus' prescient powers sufficed to convince him that the betrayer was an integral part of his destiny. And if I foresee something the while being above all else convinced that not only must certain events inevitably come to pass but that their realization is even highly to be desired, I will put no obstacle in the way of these events, not only because all my machinations would be in vain but also because they would be immoral. Seen in the light of determinism every individual life is an accomplished whole which can attain to the rank of the perfect work of art. The superior man, especially if endowed with virtues enabling him to embrace with a single glance the indivisible unity of his life up until his death and beyond, will never attempt to resist his fate or modify it even in the slightest details, rather he will accept it in its totality, identifying with it. It is thus construed that we may if we like talk about free will, of which *amor fati* is precisely the supreme expression. Upon me there mainly depends—seemingly at least— only the act of accepting or refusing my destiny; and the great are great precisely because, by accepting it, they provide its value: they breathe life and soul into the raw material of pre-established existence, and rather than inanimate puppets they are the actors of their roles. To do something else than what is expected is the property of children's play. But adults' play consists in fulfilling destiny, by promoting it or retarding it, with the artist's creative instinct. Even if it excites terror or the fear of death, the thunder of the wheels of destiny's chariot is not without a joyous note: for him who foresees his destiny and is one with it, it is always gladdening to ascertain the ineluctability with which events come about, especially if he is conscious of having creatively contributed to their fulfillment. The culminating moment in the tragic existence of a man at the mercy of predestination is the one when he wholly accepts his destiny and, instead of surrendering to it, lends it a hand: at that moment he becomes master of himself and also of his destiny, for instead of struggling against it and running away from it, he goes to meet it and, in making it the instrument of his elevation, in a certain sense dominates it.

"For Jesus, the predestined being *par excellence*, in whom the *amor fati* was always at white heat, the encounter with Judas must have been a decisive experience. Discovering in the multitude of his followers the person of his future betrayer, he may perhaps have known terror and the shudder of the fear of death, but at the same time he also experienced great relief, the relief every prophet and seer feels when he meets with an indisputable sign of the accuracy of his foretellings; such signs, in fact, are the touchstones which unequivocally distinguish the real contents of prescience from fantastications. Recognizing the future betrayer in the person of Judas, Jesus could once more be convinced that his foresight had a real foundation. When he chose Judas to be his follower and his apostle, he simply conformed to his own predictions and to prophecies, dreadful ones, yes, but not the less ineluctable for that.

"Before coming back to the analysis of the 'choice' of the betrayer, we must open a brief parenthesis and say something about the influence that messianic prophecies may have exercized on Jesus' ideas and behavior. Among the various positivist-rationalistic hypotheses there is one which attaches an exaggerated importance to the fact that Jesus was very expert in everything in the Scriptures that concerned the Messiah. According to this theory, which unhesitatingly denies Jesus all his divine and supernatural qualities, and takes him more for a clever fellow than for a man of genius, his great trick consisted in impeccably adapting himself to the words and allusions of the prophecies, or, conversely, skillfully adapating these to the circumstances. There is without any doubt a certain amount of truth in such a thesis; but anyone who accepts it unreservedly forgets that Jesus, in fooling his followers, would first have fooled himself; and it was not illusions he was in need of but rather proofs of his mission. It is for this reason, and not for some other, that Jesus was mindful of the prophecies of the Scriptures (and of so many others that the Holy Writ has not preserved) and that he was very eager—and often very anxious—that they be fulfilled in his person. For him, who called himself the Son of God and foresaw the future, the coincidences between the predictions of the prophets and the events of his life must have seemed neither more nor less than the substitution of a concrete number for the unknowns of an equation, and nothing short of total analogy guaranteed the perfection of the mathematical operation.

"But for us the problem is not of essential importance, since Scripture contains no explicit prophecy, or even any recondite allusion, having to do with the betrayer, let alone with the necessity for the betrayal itself. The quotation with which Jesus, after the washing of the feet, alludes to the betrayer, comes from David's Psalm XL and certainly did not have the same coercive force as a prophecy concerning the Messiah. Coming at this juncture, this quotation does provide authoritative support for a fact considered as an already accomplished one, but it must not have seemed sufficiently solid to serve as the basis for a prediction. With the Gospels as our evidence, we may resolutely assert that when Jesus spoke of his betrayer, he never invoked the support of Scripture, but relied upon his prescience alone. This fact, however, does not rule out the possibility that, adding itself to his clairvoyance or omniscience, some prophecy unknown to us further strengthened Jesus in his deep expectation of a betrayer. In his choice and in his later behavior he might thus have been doubly influenced: by both clairvoyance and Scripture.

"On a generous impulse we make one final concession to the most tenacious bad faith concerning the person and fate of Jesus Christ: we'll posit—by way of hypothesis—a fanatical Jesus, a crank, obsessed by the idea he is the Son of God and of having to prove it, smart enough, clever enough to find followers and capable of using Scripture and every possible illusionistic mystification to get himself believed. We'll say—still as a hypothesis—that this Jesus, sustained only by his lucid madness, was not endowed with any supernatural or out of the ordinary virtues, nor with divine prescience or telepathic intuition, but that by means of cunning stratagems he sought to fit with existing predictions about the Messiah. A Jesus of this sort would surely have more difficulties fulfilling the destiny of the Messiah than the other Jesus, backed up from the start by the Divine Word and by his divine or metaphysical foreknowledge. With nothing to build upon apart from the prophecies and analogies with pagan gods, this fanatical Jesus must coldly calculate how to prepare his path to Golgotha, and do so beset by very understandable misgivings. To get there was not easy, and the final outcome could not be left to chance. If this Jesus had not the ability to foresee that Judas Iscariot would betray him, it follows that he was going to entrust one of the essential elements of his earthly fate to the fortuitous workings of circumstance. But such a supposition being incompatible with the scheming prudence of such a Jesus, it is more logical to accept the hypothesis that the betrayal was part of his plan from the very beginning. However, if this were so, Jesus chose Judas, not in accordance with the prophecies or thanks to the illumination of his divine prescience or to a telepathic intuition, but indeed with the deliberate purpose of turning him into his betrayer! 'Is it not I who chose the twelve of you? And one of you is the devil!'

"Between the fanatic rogue and the pure God of the Monophysites we could imagine innumerable other figures of Jesus and ascribe to them all sorts of ways of thinking and acting, but the result would always be the same: even though the reason for it is mysterious and still to be elucidated, the person of Judas and his function—that is to say, the future betrayer and the future betrayal—were essentially and existentially of extremest importance to him. This point established, we have got rid once and for all of the preliminary problem: namely, why the Master chose for his apostle the man who was going to betray him. Chose him not *in spite of* this, of course; but precisely *because* of this. And with this concluding observation we now turn back, to our great satisfaction, to full-fledged Christian orthodoxy. Obviously, neither official theology nor the four Gospels give much prominence to this awkward fact, but neither the former nor the latter leave any doubts as to the consciousness of the choice, founded on clairvoyance or, flatly, on the Master's divine foreknowledge.

"Since it was so important for Jesus to be betrayed by Judas, we must deduce that whatever the motive the latter had for betraying him, it was negligible compared to the vastness of the Lord's objectives. Even as he was electing Judas, when Judas was without any doubt still in a state of innocence, Jesus was compelled, by his prescience and by his predestination, to foresee, to desire and anxiously to assert that Judas would betray him. Therefore Judas

was from the very beginning condemned to commit the most
ignominious crime in universal history; and the Lord, in choosing
him, ratified the sentence. The certainty that he had his betrayer
and had him near to hand gave him a joyous and cruel but
unshakeable sense of security.

"There, reduced to its essentials, is the situation as it appears
when the first encounter takes place, or after the long meditation
on the mountain, when the future betrayer was named an apostle.
We have used some tough but appropriate language, corresponding
to the tough material out of which the situation took shape at the
moment of the choice of Judas. Tough material, but still raw
material which, like a block of marble under the artist's chisel,
may assume unforeseen forms, from the most horrible to the most
highly poetic, forms throbbing with feeling and others metaphys-
ically abstract, in accordance with the particular image we have of
the figure of Jesus. His personality determines his relationship
with the betrayer, and by now you understand perfectly that this
relationship will assume varying tonalities, indeed divergent and
irreconcilable characteristics, depending on whether one prefers,
let's say, the Machiavellian Jesus of the inveterate positivists to the
pious Jesus overflowing sentimentality of the worthy women in the
parish, or—to both of these—the Jesus who is one with God, as
the ancient heretical current once proposed, et cetera. To do an
honest job," said Dupin, lifting his voice and aiming the stem of
his pipe at me, "every time we come to an important moment in
the relations between Jesus and Judas we would have to review the
entire history of Christology, weigh and discuss all the theories,
take into account all the doubts and all the counter-arguments. No
need to tell you that the sojourn you contemplate in our dazzling
metropolis would not suffice for such an exhausting task.

"So following that path is therefore out of the question," he
concluded, but from the sly twinkle in his eyes I knew he had no
intention of giving up. "Whence my decision: with a Copernican
turnabout, instead of evaluating, discussing, rejecting the theses of

others, I shall present my own figure of Jesus, basing myself on this
image I shall conduct my investigations, and I shall leave to others
the trouble of counter-attacking, should they think it worth the
effort!"

I was disconcerted. Suddenly, however, a light went on for me:

"If I understand correctly, you intend to define a figure of Jesus
as a working hypothesis . . ."

Dupin nodded, visibly pleased:

"This is why I like talking with you, *cher ami*—you grasp things
at once! It is indeed impossible to investigate the relationship
between two persons—if both of them are elusive. In our case,
fortunately, one of the two is more or less accessible: the person of
Jesus. Accessible, I say—which is not the same thing as graspable.
And it's not through any fault of mine, it's not a 'sin' on my part.
Personally, for the objectives I have set myself, I would be content
to adhere to the dogmas and official positions of the Church: I
would be content, in fact, with a simple catechism written for
grade-school children, but I am forced to the horrified recognition
that despite so many 'imprimaturs,' catechisms are very different
from one another, even very divergent. And, what is worse, in our
day there is a veritable flowering of new catechisms, which do their
best to introduce disorder and confusion even into articles of faith
of well-tested stability. Not only is the Tridentine Creed discred-
ited with the approval of our bishops and cardinals, but they are
even depreciating the value of Peter's Credo, the more authentic
one. I am not formulating an opinion of my own on the subject,
I am saying only that at present the Church can be of no help to
a private detective. She has left in shadow or has failed to clarify
over her two-thousand-year-old past certain points which ought to
have some importance for her, and which for us would be essential.
I am thinking, notably, of the general question of Jesus' dual
nature, divine and human, and of the 'system' of his foreknowing,
in particular. Left on my own and encouraged by the Church's
permissiveness, all I can do is formulate my modest hypothesis.

"No telling what you are expecting now, but I do hope that you will be disappointed. You surely don't suppose that I am about to set up as the initiator of a new trend in heresy! There'll be nothing of the sort, my friend. I on principle entirely accept the Apostles' Creed and unreservedly subscribe to that of the Council of Trent, with everything that ensues: descent into hell, resurrection, ascent into heaven. I subtract nothing; all I do is add one thing without which I would not be able to continue.

"Our Jesus is the Son of God, he is the Christ, he is himself God, and up until this point I am in agreement with the Roman Catholic Church. But—and this is the nub of it—in my view this Jesus of ours, once incarnated, found himself bereft of divine prerogatives in their pure state. Human nature, without excluding or impairing his divine essence, somehow limited and blurred, without completely eliminating, the qualities inherent in it. To sum up, Jesus was God, was the Son of God, was convinced of it, but in his human guise he had to face all the uncertainties of this miserable condition, and his own divinity *presented itself to him as a thesis to be demonstrated, not so much to humankind as to himself and to God the Father.*

"Well, there—that will be our working hypothesis, which, as you will be able to verify as our investigation unfolds, is by no means an arbitrary one. Our methodological position here may perhaps elicit a few disapprovals from the rationalists, but it's not apt to bother the minds of theologians who haven't been much bothered by the problem of Christ's dual nature for the past seventeen centuries or so. The Monophysite heresy, condemned at the Council of Chalcedon, maintained that it was Jesus' divine nature that had absorbed his human nature, and so far as we know nobody else has ever put forward the same thesis: they who, instead, insisted upon the supremacy of human nature in Jesus ended by denying the existence of his divine nature. In fact, it was the Roman Church that insisted on the coexistence of both natures, without, however, managing to render it familiar to the imagination of the faithful, and without philosophically convincing disbelievers. The matter does not seem to be of much importance for the Church, or at least it has never been of immediate interest. Official theology, in this connection, makes do with indefensible compromises and to this day goes on considering dual nature as a concomitance that Jesus can maneuver at will, with suspensions or interruptions under the control of his will. When he performed miracles, healed the sick and foresaw his passion and death, Jesus was giving free rein to his divine qualities. But when he was suffering, when he was letting himself be tempted by Satan or wanted to give Judas the opportunity to change his mind about his traitrous intentions—well, at such times he had his divine qualities on hold.

"However, maneuverable divine qualities, which at once strike us as the product of a childish imagination, never, in the course of Christianity's twenty centuries, captured even the popular or artistic imagination. Indeed, just as it cannot conceive of a Jesus reduced to within purely human limits, or the inordinately divinified Jesus of the Monophysite heretics, so the faltering human mind cannot conceive of a Jesus simultaneously pure God and pure man, two perfect natures in a single person, and at every instant equally efficacious, or voluntarily maneuverable. The human imagination has always preferred to see in Jesus a God who, once become man, resigned himself completely to the miseries and restrictions of human nature. While we recognize the meaning and divine plan in the Redeemer's earthly destiny, we also like to see the deeply human tragedy. But what sort of human tragedy if mental restrictions upon the hero's divine nature are hiding in the wings? The religious and artistic imagination of two thousand years of Christianity has always cherished a Son of God subject right until the Resurrection to petty human nature: for to one enjoying the inordinate supremacy of divine nature, to undergo the tragedy of human beings cannot be a serious business.

"The Church is not against this humanized conception of the figure of Christ and tacitly shares the general opinion of the faithful, retreating into vagueness or rhetoric on all those occasions when the two natures seem to be in conflict or disharmony. And this attitude on the part of the Church is possible precisely because, for centuries, the problem has mainly slumbered. But if ever it were to enter a virulent phase, how would the Church confront the problem of Jesus' dual nature? It would suddenly come out that it is not simply a matter of clarifying the two natures' possibilities of simultaneous coexistence but also of plainly defining what divine nature essentially is! How can one talk about a greater or lesser degree of presence of divine qualities in Jesus Christ if one does not provide even so much as an idea of those qualities? You have got to specify exactly what that other nature is, and what manifestations of it we must discover in Jesus, before discussing their dosage and the combinations they form with human nature.

"Actually, they graciously acknowledge the existence in Jesus of divine properties, ill-defined or not at all, without their ever going to the trouble to examine what these qualities are, not only in Jesus but in God Himself. For instance, we accept or reject divine prescience in Jesus without first knowing what it is in itself and how it is manifested in the Almighty. Not long ago I read a book*
which *per tangentem* raises the problem of divine omniscience, whose modest results are worth recalling as an admonition to those who think that theological concepts have a self-evident or unequivocal meaning. Divine qualities, it is said there, are on a scale, like God Himself, inaccessible to our minds and our imagination, are therefore inconceivable and unimaginable, and it would be the grossest error to describe them by analogy with human qualities. Anyone committing such a mistake must very speedily realize, whether it be Revelation he consults or historical and everyday experience, that God is neither all-knowing nor all-powerful, and man, were he endowed with those same divine qualities, would be much more omniscient and omnipotent than God Himself. In fact, both in Biblical stories and in everyday life, it is as plain as day, wherever you look, that God doesn't know anything about certain events, didn't foresee them and is not doing what he ought to do, from which we must deduce that our good, just and mighty God

---

* The author alludes to his own book *The Sacred Embrace*. (Translator's note.)

is ignorant, capricious, nay, wicked. Since, however, such a God is absurd, it is reasonable to suppose that our ideas about Him are mistaken, just as are our ideas about His divine qualities. With the idea we have of divine omniscience, the picture of an ignorant God necessarily leads us to believe that we're the ignorant ones and that in spite of everything God is omniscient, but not in the way we understand omniscience. And the situation will be identical with other divine qualities: thought perfect and complete in themselves, beheld by our puny mental categories they will seem full of gaps. But being unable to change our reasoning and imaginative apparatus, we must once and for all give up trying to understand divine intentions and surrender unconditionally, perhaps by obeying the revealed commandments and prescriptions. Even if we sometimes feel we have guessed the Almighty's intentions and are following His path, we can be very sure that it is an illusion. On the other hand, our faith must not collapse just because our God often appears to us as a being unworthy even of His indeed very deficient creatures.

"Thus, in the curved mirror of the human mind and history, divine qualities are reflected in a very vague and disquieting fashion. God—who whether by definition, whether as is evident from the facts, seems to know everything and to be able to do everything—sometimes, owing to our mental myopia and as is shown by the facts, seems to be ignorant of present and future developments, and to be helpless before them. On the plane of practice and of experience, the divine qualities seem to oscillate between measureless power and childish naïveté.

"So much for the resumé of the book we read a little while ago—and after that it is not surprising if these qualities, so very oscillating and vacillating in the Almighty Father, turn up again in the Son, where they are even more uncertain and still more defective because limited and contaminated by the effects of human nature. Though supremely endowed with divine qualities, why should Jesus have been better able to use them than the Father? Like God the Father, he probably knew everything, foresaw everything and could do everything in his own way, that is, in the divine way, different from all humanly imaginable ways: notwithstanding all that, in human practice, that is, on the historical plane, his omniscience and his omnipotence, like those of God his Father, operated in a way that one may well call defective. In him too boundless power and childish naïveté alternated like the ebb and flow of the tide.

"Conformably to this theory of ebb and flow, which has has been the unconscious concept of believers throughout two thousand years of Christianity and which the Church itself has in practice accepted, we see no difficulty in acceding to the simultaneous coexistence in Jesus Christ of divine and human natures. Surely, his divine virtues did not make his life in human guise any easier, while his human nature certainly did not impair the efficacity of his divine nature. We might put it this way: far from being of much use to him in neutralizing the vexations and perils of human life, his divine qualities served—and it is to that end he employed them—to bind him implacably to human nature and to his earthly destiny.

"A divine nature as volatile as this will not, we think, be able to shock even the most sensitive of the hardcore rationalists. At the very most they might ask what leads us to believe that divine qualities exist in Jesus. We could answer them in several ways. First of all, that it is a working hypothesis, made to our liking. Secondly, that since the essence of these qualities cannot be defined, no one is in a position to deny them. Those who instead deny the historicity of Jesus' life and consider it a mere fable will only the more readily accept our thesis: superhuman qualities are characteristic of the heroes in fables and belong among their customary ingredients.

"Jesus performed miracles and foresaw a number of future events, but to do that it was not of course indispensable that he have divine qualities, let alone that he be God. It is usually on this particular point that for the rationalists the divinity of Jesus either stands or falls. But by what right are these gentlemen more easily satisfied than was Jesus himself, whose divine qualities by themselves would never have sufficiently convinced him of his divinity? That is why he had to follow his path the whole way down to death, to resurrection, to ascension.

"According to the Gospels, Jesus performed prodigious miracles with extraordinary ease, but not always with the same extraordinary self-assurance. How often, and with what clarity, would he say that the miracles were due to the Father! And how much anxious worrying preceded certain of his miracles, and what relief followed them! Where you have a divine prescience, as such a thing is understood by humans, any uncertainty as to a miracle's success would be absurd, but it is by no means excluded in a divine prescience like the one that has emerged after our deeper analysis. Well might Jesus know that he was the Son of God, perfectly convinced of it might he be, yet in the ebb phase of his divine qualities he was nevertheless beset by doubt, by uncertainty, by confusion and other weaknesses inherent in human nature. Very often Jesus found himself miserably prisoner of his human nature, and constrained to *believe* in that which he knew and was convinced of from the beginning of time: his own divinity. If thanks to his omniscience and thanks to his omnipotence he could be 'divinely' (again in the sense the human mind understands the word) sure of success, why then would he have been forced to *rely* upon the Father's infinite goodness in order to accomplish a miracle? The logical answer to this question can only be this: Jesus' alleged self-assurance, his through his divine nature and from time to time proven to him anew by the reflux of divine qualities, was necessarily accompanied by the interferences of human uncertainty, which, somewhat like what occurs in radio reception, caused fade-outs on the divine wave-lengths. Only thus can we explain Jesus' anxieties, his permanent concern to carry out to the letter, or at least to carry out figuratively but down to the last detail, the prophecies of Scripture, and only thus can be explained the most ambiguous episode in his life: his tempting by Satan.

"We can only suppose a Jesus totally subordinated to the

physical and psychic laws of human nature, when not even the most refined theological quibblings fail to dispel the suspicion that this was a manifestation of pure hysteria. It is obvious that temptation by Satan is a phenomenon reserved for human beings only. It is equally incontestable that, having decided to tempt Jesus, Satan saw the possibility of getting him in his clutches. Likewise we may be sure that Satan was well aware he was dealing with the Son of God. On what could Satan base his prospects for success? Certainly not on the absurd idea that even a God can be tempted, or that Jesus, once he turned into a man, would cease being the Son of God. The Scriptures do not contain descriptions of pranks, even of a supernatural kind. Satan's temptation was a serious event in Jesus' life, it was an exceedingly dramatic episode, the moment of the decisive choice. It was *as a man* he resisted temptation, during one of those ebb phases of his divine consciousness. If baptism in the waters of the Jordan confirmed Jesus in his divine nature, the temptation confirmed him in his human estate. Indeed, the sole element upon which Satan could build his hopes was not that Jesus was not the Son of God or did not know that he was, but that at this precise moment he could only *humanly* believe it and that, in order to resist, he could only *humanly* hope for the aid of the Father. With the refluence of his divine nature, or, at any rate, in the full possession of his divinity, Jesus could have satisfied the wishes of Satan or driven him away—but in that case Satan wouldn't even have gone to the trouble of coming to tempt him, or the episode would have ended as a farce. As, however, Satan did make the attempt, he had a chance of succeeding.

"Perhaps, later on, we shall have occasion to analyze the hypothetical consequences of this chance, minimal as it was. But for the time being let us be content with the fact that, theoretically, Jesus might also not have resisted the temptation, either by inopportunely revealing his divine nature or by yielding to human weakness, but in any case compromising his mission once and for all. He remained humanly strong precisely in order not to give proof of his divinity.

"Indeed, so prodigal when it came to miracles, Jesus steadfastly refused to perform them whenever the request was addressed to him in the way of a challenge or 'temptation.' This is a fact too important not to be pointed out, for it always occurs in circumstances where had he shown proof of his divinity—that is, unequivocally and prematurely shown himself to be God—he would have jeopardized his mission. No one, howsoever unsophisticated in matters of theology, can help but wonder whether the work of Redemption would have been achieved, and how, if Jesus had escaped from his guards, or if he had come down from the cross. But it is precisely at the most critical moments of his life that he did not call upon his supernatural powers. For some mysterious reason, Jesus' life and work had to unfold on a rigorously human plane, where his divine nature was a burden that made his existence more painful: the inflow of his supernatural qualities kept alive the consciousness of his ineluctable destiny, while their withdrawal left his soul filled with anguish and uncertainty. The miracles—apart from his predictions the only visible signs of his divine virtues during the years of his ministry—were not performed by him to alleviate his earthly fate: for him they had only an instrumental value in respect to his true mission. The terrain of divine drama having been reached, the miracles came to an end. Rationalists are free not to believe in the miracles and to denounce them as out and out sleight-of-hand: the fact remains that at the decisive stages of his life Jesus was always human, hopelessly and heroically so.

"Forgive me, *cher ami*," Dupin went on after a brief pause, "do forgive me for this long parenthesis filled with theological materials; but, in addition to sketching for you a figure of Jesus we'll use as a working hypothesis, I hope I have given you a feeling for the problem of his dual nature and that you have put all your doubts away as to the possible coexistence of two natures within the same person, without that person necessarily turning into some hybrid monster. Only after this *excursus* do I feel entitled to confirm a statement of yours, pronounced earlier on and with a rather too youthful impulsiveness. Yes indeed, Jesus knew beforehand of the betrayal and identified his future betrayer before electing him as an apostle: which means that he chose him not only 'in spite of this,' but 'precisely because of this.' Having dealt with those preliminary problems, we are at the point where—"

"I now feel even more justified in qualifying the relationship between Jesus and Judas as something bordering on the absurd!" I interrupted, carried away by my visions and perhaps also by the need to hear my own voice. "Why, put yourself in the Master's place! . . . Wouldn't you say that from the very moment he identified the future betrayer, and realized that the wheel of destiny had been set in motion, he found himself, psychologically speaking, in a situation we all have the right to call *absurd*? It is hard to imagine that he would not have felt horror or terror, and often hatred too, in the presence of this innocent caterpillar who, in time, must necessarily turn into the butterfly of death. But the good will, the faith, the fervor, the innocence and absolute confidence shown by the future betrayer were probably awfully unsettling, cruelly distressing, sure to rouse deep feelings in Jesus' heart, confused, ambivalent emotions which sometimes bordered on the torments of remorse. One rather likes to imagine a Jesus in the grip of a mad temptation to go straight up to Judas and tell him the true state of affairs. If Jesus was as the imagination and devotion have wanted to picture him over the centuries, he must frequently have felt the urge to tell Judas flat out that it was useless for him to delude himself, useless for him to hope for redemption, that it was even rather dangerous for him to let himself be carried away by the dream of the new order, from which he would be excluded; and to boot that he would have to commit the supreme sin and that eternal damnation was to be his lot! There must have been times when, his glance falling upon this disciple, Jesus felt irremediably ill at ease, times when the game must have seemed infamous to him: for he was consciously treating as a lamb the wolf that for the time being, and in good faith, did in effect imagine himself to be a lamb, and perhaps would have remained one had it not, instead, been pre-ordained that he become a wolf. His human outlook must sometimes have advised Jesus that the decent thing would be to disclose to Judas the horrors that lay ahead and to provide him with the possibility of taking to heels, of at least attempting an escape—doomed, of course, to fail, because contrary to fate's decree. Furthermore, if my memory serves, the theologians claim that Jesus tried several times to forewarn his unhappy apostle.

"The uniqueness of Jesus' psychological position vis-à-vis the condemned man," I continued, in as much as Dupin was listening attentively to me, "takes on various colors and all sorts of nuances with your theory of the ebb and flow of divine content in his dual nature. Your theory allows us to assume some weak areas in Jesus' divine lucidity, indeed states of depression and of doubt regarding the credibility of his own conscience. I have no trouble imagining that this Judas, model of good will and epitomy of innocence that he was, must have generated a feeling of uncertainty in Jesus, and often a feeling of despair as well, as to the wisdom of his choice. Everything depends, really, on the manner, the degree, and the moment in which the flashes of omniscience illuminated him . . ."

"Indeed, the less frequent or evident these flashes were, the more he must have been tormented by worries," Dupin resumed. "But I'm not thinking so much about his emotional and moral crises in regard to Judas, as about the need he had to keep an eye on the disciple fated to betray him: in as much as Judas was an element he could not do without in the pursuit of his course, Jesus must have had to transcend sentimentalisms and allow the prudence of the serpent to vanquish the meekness of the dove, both of them components of his character.

"This prudence of Jesus appears also in the fact that before chosing his apostles he decided to spend a night on the mountain in prayer and meditation. If thanks to his divine prescience he had the clear vision of the future to go by, he would have had no need to pray or meditate, but only to reproduce exactly the images perceived of things to come. But during his brief life Jesus did only too much praying and meditating before taking an important decision, and this proves that the decisive moments were the ones when his divine qualities tended to ebb. Like other mortals, Jesus was constrained to use his reason, and his many prayers show that instead of appealing to his own divine wisdom, he invoked paternal illumination.

"The choice of apostles, at any rate, was preceded by intense spiritual concentration. During those still hours of the night, Jesus mentally passed his most devoted followers in review, and whilst some of them appeared to be up to their mission, he had to give a great deal of thought to others. But his main concern must not have been so much to analyze all their attitudes as to discover amongst them the one who would assure the work of Redemption. Even if he had already long since recognized the future betrayer in the person of Judas, he had to weigh on the scales of reason the real premises of this pre-established betrayal, and examine, in the twelfth apostle's psyche, the deep-lying factors that later on must guarantee his recourse to actual crime.

"*Just what* he knew about the future, *since when* he had known it: thereby hangs the dramatic intensity of that famous night. To spare ourselves the labor of reviewing all the variations and combinations, it will suffice to mention the two extreme cases. All his apostles may have been thoroughly known to him ahead of time, so that he was altogether clear upon what rock to build his Church and who was to be his betrayer. Nevertheless, owing to the strange law of ebb and flow, Jesus could still have hesitated over the persons to choose as collaborators, and in this case prayers and meditations were indispensable. In this case—that is, the worst of cases—Jesus possessed very few concrete elements on which to base his meditations: there were the great objectives—founding the Church, getting himself betrayed—and there was a group of followers, whom he more or less knew. In this group he must find eleven men who would become the columns of his Church, and one man who would become the condition and guarantee of the achievement of his ultra-terrestrial objectives.

"That night he had to take a decision and choose the eleven and the one. I simply cannot picture a Jesus who first selected twelve from among his faithful and then, after a long and silent examination or else after having resorted to psychological provocations, would have singled out the one who was to serve him as betrayer. Moreover, it seems out of the question that Jesus might have thought, in this regard, of Peter or Andrew, of James or John, or of anyone at all of the eleven. Actually, those simple souls appeared utterly incapable of committing any infamy whatever against him. Their simplicity had been the source of their faith, of their strength and their constancy, simplicity had defined what was great in them and what was weak. It was absolutely improbable that, aside from little, vanity-inspired quarrels, backings-off and backings-down prompted by terror, or some doubts and uncertainties, their human pettiness could ever get near the frontiers of turpitude or dastardliness. If Jesus did not divinely foresee all this, we may be sure that his reason told him so, or at least that it was his intuition, his belief, his expectation, his trust, like the trust he had in certain characteristics belonging to the twelfth.

"The choice of the twelfth was the most delicate problem. The others had but to follow the path he indicated and they would lead him to triumph; whereas the twelfth, the while believing he was aiding him as the others were, was to lead him to death. But could he entrust this difficult role to just anyone? Naïveté also has its limitations, and, above all, simplicity of mind and narrowness of reasoning are more resistant and more stubborn than granite. The betrayal could not be entrusted to Peter, not only because he was destined to another mission, but also because, once he had finally become aware of the double game, he would have rebelled and, very simply, would not have lent himself to it. Never would any of the eleven have accepted the messianic prophecy knowing that the price of its fulfillment had to be betrayal on their part. Peter, Andrew, John and the others, ideal for preparing and continuing Jesus' work, would never have been willing to help him bring it to its conclusion. In this grave and sensitive affair Jesus could not rely on his disciples' fidelty, their fanaticism, their spirit of sacrifice. For the role of betrayer he needed an unusual person, whose reaction would not be mute rebellion, but rather . . ."

Dupin halted there and with an abrupt gesture reached for the famous green spectacles he ordinarily put on when he wanted to conceal his most secret thoughts from others. But he changed his mind, and smiled at me as if in apology.

"Although . . ." he murmured in the midst of a sigh. "Although . . . When you interrupted me a little while back I was thinking of what the next step in the investigation should be. I would have proposed to tackle the problem of why Jesus chose Judas in order to be betrayed by him. More simply, the question would have been this: Why did Jesus need a betrayer? And in yet more exact terms I would have couched my question this way: Why must the work of betrayal be the condition *sine qua non* of the work of Redemption? But your passion for rare and absurd psychological situations has me back again on the right track anyhow. As a matter of fact, it is not possible to move ahead without talking . . . about him. About Judas, yes. You, probably struck by my presentation of him as not being conscious of either the 'why' or the 'how' of the betrayal, a little while ago you went so far as to call him 'an epitome of innocence' and 'a suckling lamb.' And behold, I too have arrived at an 'although' . . ."

"But you wanted to finish your sentence . . ."

"No, I couldn't have. But an image came to me, a metaphor if you prefer . . . On Judas' brow must have shown a mark, the mark of vocation. In one way or another, he must have stood out sharply from the other apostles . . . in such a way that, before asking why Judas was chosen *for precisely this*, I would like to examine the problem of why *precisely Judas* was chosen for this . . ."

At that point I must have cast a glance of entreaty at him, for I saw him relax and saw his wrinkled hand fumble about in search of the box of Swedish kitchen matches (those dating from the prehistoric age of matches, which he had dug up who knows where).

"All right, my friend," said he with a touch of complaisance in his voice, "I am willing to take it into consideration that during daytime you play the tourist, a rather sorry aspect of your personality, running counter to that other which fits you to appear in the role of indefatigable interlocutor in a nocturnal dialogue. I shall be indulgent with you and allow you to go to sleep. As for me, I've still got things to do: twice a week I'm obliged to work out arithmetic problems for the little niece of our dear old concierge—remember her? You in the meantime need have no care but to get a good rest and to be in form for this evening, so as to give me a hand when I try to put together an historically plausible reconstruction of the figure of Christ's betrayer."

Chosen to evil

THE FOLLOWING EVENING (WHICH HE—THANKS TO HIS SINGULAR CONCEPTION of time—had yesterday referred to as "this evening"), Dupin launched right in without much by way of preamble.

"Before picking up the thread of our conversation, I must warn you, if you yourself haven't noticed already, that, for the purposes of our investigation, attempts to trace the outline of the wicked apostle interest us only up to a point. You'll see that in the sublime regions where our investigations will take us, the human characteristics of the protagonists absolutely do not count.

"However I must not forget your congenital psychological curiosity nor yet—strange coincidence—my fragmentary short story 'on a religious subject,' as you too generously qualified it. There I could not avoid sketching the portraits—very approximate ones—of two human figures; but I never thought I'd run into someone who would oblige me to flesh them out.

"Do you realize what you are asking of me? I wouldn't dare claim we did a brilliant job with the reconstruction of the figure of Jesus, but you must remember that we wouldn't have got even that far without the aid of the science called theology. But now, as we turn to the figure of the betrayer, theology too ceases to be of any aid to us, and the task seems to become impossible. Just think a moment! Whereas regarding Jesus we have, what with the Gospels, other sacred writings, ecclesiastical tradition and Christology, a surfeit of data which could enable us to reconstruct his personality down almost to the last detail, to evoke episodes in his life with a certain accuracy and to imagine his behavior and his reactions in any hypothetical situation—, when it comes to his betrayer we find ourselves in the most total ignorance. We have already mentioned how little the New Testament has to say about the betrayal, and anyhow those few facts have absolutely nothing to do with the person of the betrayer. It is impossible, on the basis of historical data alone, to reconstruct the figure of Judas Iscariot, and that is why we must reject all the reconstructions that have been attempted until this day: all of them have the fault of attributing to him a character invented out of whole cloth, a hypothetical personality, without any basis in history and reality. The numerous Judas figures created by world literature serve only to lead us away from the truth—which, I may add, is perhaps destined never to be uncovered—and to fill our imagination with rigid clichés that do not and cannot have anything in common with the betrayer of Jesus.

"Even without knowing anything about the person of Judas Iscariot and the antecedents of his private life, we may willingly accept your 'innocentist' thesis, particularly in what concerns the period of the first contacts between the future betrayer and the Master: obviously, he did not approach the prophet from Nazareth with evil intentions. On the contrary, everything leads us to believe that he approached him with the best intentions and with the greatest hopes, as did the other disciples.

"In general, all those who gathered around a prophet did so to satisfy deep spiritual needs, convinced that the man of God might say or do something to fill the empty spaces in their souls and corroborate their vague and confused hopes. These hopes, as everyone knows, were then oriented toward a religious and moral rebirth, whose direct consequence was to be a political rebirth: the realization of an independent Jewish State, comparable to that of the Egyptians, Assyrians, Babylonians and Romans. These splendid dreams, expressions of the impotent impatience of an oppressed and sorely tried people, had no other foundation in reality than an age-old longing built exclusively on the promises of their God, called Yahweh. In fact, the political situation of the chosen people, now become a part of the Roman Empire, offered then so little hope of reconquering a yearned for and so rarely enjoyed independence, that the Jews, instead of hoping for the impossible, placed their hopes in the coming of the Messiah, which to them seemed less impossible. Of course, the Messiah too, the glorious successor of King David, had been promised only by God, nay, only through the intermediary of His prophets, but, on the other hand, Yahweh's promises were all they had left to put their hopes in . . .

"It is by now a commonplace to say that the history of the Jewish people has a character all its own, distinguishing it from the history of all other nations. It unfolds as a direct result of the relationship between this people and their God. The driving forces, the sources of energy as well as the ideal aims of this strange history, which certainly did not seem destined to affect universal history, were the various covenants concluded at various periods between the leaders of the people and Yahweh, who, in good times, promised demographical and political might and, in periods of decadence, rebirth. Only these particulars enable us to understand in a certain way why this small people—who, apart from the modest beginnings of the era of stability inaugurated by David, and the subsequent age of prosperity and oriental luxury already condemned to collapse, knew in the course of their history only the sufferings and horrors of servitude—never ceased believing with unshakeable faith in a future of splendor and national greatness. Only these particulars enable us to understand in a certain way why this people of slaves considered themselves at every moment in their history, even at the most desperate and humiliating moments, as the holder of a definitive victory.

"They enable us to understand it in a certain way and up to a certain point, but not with absolute clarity. Faith in divine promises could not be enough to cause the chosen people to believe in and hope for a decisive turn in their fortunes. A faith which again and again reveals itself devoid of any real basis will begin to totter and will end by altogether collapsing. In order to persevere in their exasperated attitude of mind, the Jewish people needed to believe in something that had more solid, more palpable and, so to speak, more vitalizing foundations than the divine promises, and which at the same time would also explain their not having come true. And I do not think I am wrong in saying that they found this concrete factor in their feeling of guilt, in their conviction that they did not deserve divine grace.

"The covenants with God, like any other covenant, were bilateral covenants: the two contracting parties mutually committed themselves to observe the assumed commitments. The Jews fully suspected that God did not hand out His promises and His aid for nothing, and that He expected fulfillment of the promises made to Him. The chosen people, by way of return for having been chosen, had promised Yahweh to accept Him as their only God and not only to respect His rights, but to make them respected by all the peoples of the world. To worship their God and make His greatness visible to everyone, that is the most sacred duty and at the same time the most sacred right of the people of Israel: rights and duties that they would never have thought or been able to neglect without exposing themselves to misfortunes, humiliations, or calamities.

"Yahweh was for Israel, Israel was for Yahweh. But a failing in the covenants was their obscurity on an essential and delicate point. Never had it been specified which of the two contracting parties was to fulfill his assumed commitments first. To their great despair, the Jews each time saw the Lord withdraw into His majestic inaccessibility. The covenant once concluded, Yahweh left things up to the chosen people, and not only did things never really go very well, but constantly kept going badly. Yahweh, it cannot be denied, several times intervened spectacularly, with showy generosity, but instead of heading them effectively in the direction of their historical mission, He confined Himself to saving them from certain death with last-minute rescues. The true, radical assistance was never there, and for this the Jews ended by holding themselves exclusively to blame. In order that history begin, thought they, rather than waiting for God's help should we not perhaps become worthy of it? The chosen people ought then to take the first step, by rendering themselves more deserving of divine promises. And the more severe the trials were, the more they must strive to merit celestial favors. As even so divine assistance was slow in coming, the chosen people tried several times to address themselves to foreign gods for the long-desired aid. But the foreign gods were not more merciful, and the Jews, like beaten dogs, returned to their former master in even greater despair than before, for through their attempted escape they had become even more unworthy of the goodness of Yahweh.

"This intense and steadily intensifying feeling of guilt was the chosen people's luck: to it alone they owed their survival and their indestructible dreams of greatness. Indeed, belief in divine promises and in a national rebirth to follow, gainsaid by the evidence of reality, is an attitude that cannot be maintained indefinitely, and Jewish history abounds with recollections of lassitude and disaffection. But it was these symptoms themselves that fed the feeling of guilt, itself a flesh and bone reality which could not be doubted. Not even the most critical spirit would ever have accused God of not keeping His word: divine help would probably come as soon as the Jews carried out their preliminary obligations. The prophets, sent by God, men with long beards and thundering voices, saw to it that faith in the divine promises was not allowed to die out; they even increased the number of those promises, enhanced their effectiveness and allure, but at the same time they stressed that it was up to the Jewish people to take the first step by becoming worthy of the Lord.

"Thanks therefore to their feeling of guilt heightened to the point of exasperation by its prophets, the chosen people had over the course of their history grown accustomed to having before them an immediate duty, apparently easier to achieve than that of being the world's foremost nation: namely, to become worthy of their God, duty number one—prerequisite *sine qua non* of their historical mission, duty number two. Thanks to this chronological stratification of the purposes of their existence, the chosen people managed to preserve intact their boldest and most fanciful dreams. Forced to think only of the necessity of rendering themselves more worthy, the task which in theory and in practice looked to be the more achievable, about that other, despairingly unachievable task, it was enough just to dream. For as regarded the realization of the vision of a splendid national rebirth, that would be the Messiah's job. The Messiah was Yahweh's last and most interesting promise, and also an excellent occasion for the chosen people to free themselves of their worries in connection with the supreme goal. The Jews could from now on concentrate all their forces upon trying to merit divine mercifulness and the coming of the Saviour; the Saviour would handle everything else.

"In this tense atmosphere of expectation and dreams, of hopes and compunctions, the people pressed enthusiastically around those who, with some authority, exhorted them to repentance and to purification of the spirit and announced to them the coming of the Messiah. After a long period of stagnation, prophets were arising again, and dreams reduced to embers blazed up anew. It was now worth making great final efforts in the way of religious concentration, repentance, and expiation!

"Crowds of thousands upon thousands of people gathered also to listen to the Word of Jesus; dozens upon dozens of persons followed him about, so as to be near him at all times. We have no reason to suppose that the forces of a general sort that were driving malcontents, penitents and dreamers toward the prophet in multitudes, were not at work in Judas Iscariot as well. Indeed, we do not know why Peter and Andrew, John and James chose to follow Jesus or were, before that, assiduous disciples of John the Baptist. Within this ensemble or conglomerate—that we could also call confusion—of aspirations to a thorough and overall renewal in every sphere of life, political and social, spiritual and material, it is difficult, first of all, to disentangle the individual components, and, secondly, to confidently attribute preeminence to any one of them to the detriment of the others. But what the disciples were seeking above all from the prophets and rabbis was enlightenment on how to put themselves right with the Lord.

"The greater part of the disciples hoped to find in Jesus the solution to grave religious and moral problems, and the decision to follow him was most often preceded by sensational conversions. Who indeed would have abandoned the most tattered fisherman's net in order to follow a prophet, had he not been convinced he was making the better choice? Should we deny good faith only when we come to Judas?

"We do not know just what brought him from his distant Kerioth, a village in southern Judea, to Galilee, where Jesus began his ministry. We do not have any reason or any right to suppose that Judas followed the prophet solely for want of something better to do, let alone that he expected social and economic advantages from joining the Master's company. At that moment the Messianic revelations had not yet taken place, Jesus did not yet offer any hopes for those who might dream of high honors in the Messiah's later kingdom. And yet he too responded to Jesus' invitation: 'Follow me . . .'

"The Gospels, it is true, do not expressly say that Judas too was summoned by those words. It was thus the Lord spoke to Peter and Andrew, to James and John, thus did he invite the publican Levi, afterwards called Matthew . . . But the words 'Follow me' were never pronounced by Jesus at the end of his long and conscientious discussions with the candidate disciples. Actually, this invitation was issued like an order which, by its very nature, precluded all discussion. One can hardly imagine those that were invited politely declining or postponing their decisions. The exegetes insist upon the fact that these invitations were addressed exactly in the manner the Gospels report. At the words 'Follow me,' Peter, Andrew and the others instantly laid down their nets and let their boats drift off, and Matthew did not even go to collect his month's pay. By means of these magical words Jesus communicated his decision, and from it there was no appeal. The great fisherman of souls was unerring in his work. Caught in the often violently cast toils, hesitant and hostile ended up yielding too. Even the conversion of Saul on the highroad to Damascus is nothing, after all, but the result of the irresistible appeal of this magical 'Follow me.'

"In view of all this is it correct to speak of any initiative at all on the part of the early disciples? At the urging of who is to say what impulse coming from deep within, they consorted with the Master without thinking that it would mean having someday to abandon their nets and their boats. A number of them had certainly seen other prophets and knew from experience that their lives were not at all enviable. The public's reception could even be hostile and then, from raillery and insults to blows and thrown stones, a thousand difficulties and dangers threatened the prophet and his followers, not to mention long treks through the desert and the permanent question of getting enough to eat. Any reasonable and sober person would have thought it over a thousand times before quitting his trade or daily occupation, modest though it might be, in exchange for the uncertain fate of wandering prophets. The truth of the Word must have captivated their souls for them not only to be unable to resist the hare-brained idea, but to actually desire it and thereby carry through to conclusion in their minds and hearts a psychic process that made them reply yes to the Lord's summons. It pleases us to suppose that, in the majority of cases, Jesus addressed his orders to persons spiritually and morally ready to accept them, so that these orders instead resembled invitations, and his decision coincided with the consent and desire of the future disciples. But, as Saul's case illustrates, his decision was unyielding even when faced by the elected one's fiercest resistance and hostility.

"Owing to the complete absence of data and testimony, we know nothing about the circumstances in which Judas was called and in what frame of mind he accepted the offer. It seems probable to us that he accepted it with pleasure, with enthusiasm, and unreservedly. We even have good reasons for crediting Judas with more than ordinary fervor and zeal: we must not forget, after all, that Jesus later on made him his apostle! Between the first summons and the selection of the apostles there passed a certain time, a sort of trial period lasting several months, during which the Master had the opportunity to get to know his men thoroughly. Even if from the very start Jesus had recognized his betrayer in Judas, and had in spite of that picked him to be an apostle, he still had to take into account the opinion of his disciples and, especially, of the other elect. And let it not be forgotten that later on he even entrusted him with the purse. All this proves, for us, that Judas, at least apparently, was well regarded by Jesus and his colleagues, and it seems to us beyond question that he was on good terms with his own conscience as well. Judas, in all likelihood, was perfectly sincere with himself and hoped innocently for his own redemption.

"Judas' sincerity was no doubt also nourished by the fact that the Master had invested him with all the privileges and prerogatives, all the virtues and gifts with which he had invested the eleven others, in order that they be able to spread the doctrine more effectively and gain believers for the new faith. We have no reason to doubt that Judas made good use of the favors lavished on him over the years of Jesus' public ministry and that he announced the Kingdom of Heaven with as much fervor and success as his colleagues. To give added force to his words, he healed the sick, performed miracles, and perhaps even resurrected the dead, like the eleven others, and if he didn't, it was solely because the eleven others didn't either: the Gospels do not tell us whether the apostles actually made use of the privileges of investiture during the Master's lifetime. Nevertheless, it seems certain that the future betrayer was not deprived of any of the gifts Jesus bestowed on the apostles, and indeed that he preserved them down to the very last moment when, if we are to believe one of the evangelists, it cannot be ruled out that he partook in the Eucharist! But if this is not ruled out by Mark, it is by the theologians, and also by us. For it would really be overdoing it to imagine Jesus, in an excess of demonism and bad taste, using the exquisite flavor of his body and blood to incite the twelfth apostle into committing his ignominious crime. We prefer to believe that when Judas rose to leave for the house of the high priests, all he had in his mouth was the less exquisite savor of the morsel of bread soaked in the sauce of the lamb.

"At any rate, Judas had every reason not to consider himself the worst of the apostles, and from the vanity that is so frequent in human beings he probably considered himself one of the best. We have no way of determining which of his dreams had turned into reality, which of his deeper needs found satisfaction, and neither do we mean to assert that he was enthusiastic about having been chosen. But one thing is sure: there was not the faintest doubt or suspicion in his soul. When the young man from Kerioth heard from the Master's lips that he had become his apostle he did not imagine for a single instant that he would also become his betrayer. And to picture him thus, so unaware and so trusting—it staggers us and it gives us the shivers, especially if we remember that when he told the good news to him, Jesus already knew that he would have to perform the betrayal.

"Whatever may have been the real figure of Judas, his fate, seen in this light, takes on an assuredly tragic aspect. It is not necessary to seek comparisons among the models offered by Aeschylus or Sophocles to understand the quality and gravity of the fate which from the beginning hung over the head of Judas Iscariot. The Yahwehist order of the Jewish world offers numerous examples of tragedy preordained by the will of God and of tragic heroes chosen for the working of evil and predestined to failure. At any rate, just when he thought he had found the way to salvation, the young man from Kerioth started on the downward path to damnation. And in this particular case, both the first of its kind and archetypal, it was not a matter of metaphors: the way to salvation was truly the way to Salvation, in the strict sense of the word, and the downward path was truly that of Damnation, with Gehenna and everlasting fire.

"The tragic in the life and figure of Judas Iscariot was wonderfully sensed and expressed in an ancient legend related by Jacobus de Voragine. My wish, in spending a little additional time on this product of popular fantasy, is not to seek in it elements for the reconstruction of the historical figure of Judas. This tale of horror—which cannot be dated and which reveals not the slightest trace of credibility—would not recommend itself as a historical source even to the most fanciful writer. But the ancient story contains a great deal that is instructive and edifying, and above all else it will open our eyes to a new way of looking at the figure of the betrayer.

"In fact, while the legend contains nothing about what Judas was like as a historical personage, it does on the other hand tell us very clearly what he was like for the medieval popular imagination, not yet revised to fit the viewpoint of those learned heads who in their studies and research were intent on making this personage acceptable and credible in the role of Jesus' betrayer. What could, what must the man have been like who committed the supreme crime? This is the problem the legend deals with.

"Such a man must for a certainty have been the wickedest in the world. Before committing the supreme crime, this Judas—as you shall see—had already soiled his hands with the dreadful crime of Cain, for he had slain his own brother. Then he had also committed Adam's sin, and, just as Adam had offended the Father in order to have the forbidden apple, so Judas, worse than all other delinquents, had, on account of an apple, befouled himself by the worst thing one can do to a father, for he had killed him. The prompting to this shameful deed had come from a kind of serpent, from Pilate, his friend. Nor was this an ordinary parricide: for that crime engendered the sin of Oedipus, since Judas afterward married the murdered man's widow, that is, his own mother. So what could be more natural—and this is the implicit and fundamental idea within the legend—that, after so many black crimes, Judas should also commit the most horrible and unforgivable one of all, the betrayal of the Master?

"That is the moral of *The Golden Legend*. But if we who are modern readers undertake to read the story with the naïve eyes of the literal-minded public of those days, we are tempted to recognize there, beyond the foreseeable lesson, a more distressing and impassioned message. In listening to the incredible adventures of this black personage, whom the pious legend seeks to make horrible and loathsome, we have the sharp feeling that before us stands not a delinquent but an unhappy man, among History's figures the unluckiest of all, whom the pitiless hand of fate made ascend the stairs of every *tragic* misdeed, to the supreme crime and to despair.

"This feeling of ours is owing to the fact that the legend of Judas Iscariot is a masterpiece of psychology—though not of course in the sense of the psychological novel of the last century. The psychological understanding of the common people does not extend to the emotions or spiritual states of its heroes, but rather to the psychic reality underlying them; and psychic reality, for the mythic and even fabulistic imagination, is indissociable from higher realities, cosmic or metaphysical, of which psychic reality is simply a reflection. Hence that imagination has no need of realistic descriptions in order to represent reality to us. That is why the Judas legend, so beyond belief in its details, but overall so strongly coherent, manages to impress itself upon the reader's imagination and to gain his credence. For Judas to get to the supreme crime it took more than being a commonplace thief; he had at the very least to be the greatest delinquent of all time. He presents all the characteristics of the classical tragic hero: he is not in himself a bad man, he does not have the ruling passion or fixation which brings the heroes of romantic tragedy to their inevitable downfall. Like the protagonists of ancient tragedies, he is the simple instrument of an inexorable fate, he is someone chosen for the doing of evil.

"Upon this tragic hero in the ancient style destiny lies heavy even at the moment of his conception. On the very night of the impregnating embrace, a divinatory dream reveals to his mother that the child in her womb will become 'A son so evil that he will be the downfall of our race.' After such a dream as this, what serene happiness throughout those months of pregnancy! Whatever they were like, the son is born and the parents wonder what they ought do do. Mortals always greet divine revelations with ambivalent feelings: it is always possible to misunderstand them. Never knowing how much to believe in them, their attitude itself becomes ambivalent. They do not dare oppose destiny openly, but neither do they resign themselves to letting it take its free course. Therefore they devise compromises. Killing the little monster would be a sacrilegious act on the part of Judas' parents, an interfering with the divine plan; while to raise him would be too grave a responsibility vis-à-vis mankind or, at least, the Jewish nation. So the parents put him in a little box which they entrust to the waves of the sea. And there you have an excellent 'semi-solution,' the only proper one. God gave him to us, let God do with him what He wishes.

"So Judas becomes a foundling, as had been Zeus, Telephus, Oedipus, Romulus and Remus, or—to remain on familiar territory—Moses. If, as is most unlikely, instead of dying by the wayside or ending up in an orphanage, the infant connects with the teats of a she-wolf or of a royal princess, we may be sure that he benefits from the special attentions of the powers above. For the latter it would be easy to let the drifting newborn sink, but rather than the simple solution, the powers above—and this is very characteristic—prefer the elaborate one and so they arrange for the little box-boat to wash up on the shores of an island.

"In the legend recur the initial circumstances in the story of Moses. The island's queen spies the floating crib, takes the babe unto herself and, being without offspring of her own, passes him off as her son and raises him in a manner befitting an heir to the throne. If we like we may even suppose that Judas would have become a fine king of the island in the legend.

"But Judas was not chosen for that task. Fate, or else the powers above, remained mindful of that final scene where the betrayer, having fallen from the tree of his suicide, would lie on the ground, amid the bowels spilled from his burst belly. From the comforts, the pleasures and advantages of the princely life to the potter's field at Aceldama, the distance seems enormous. But a mere nothing is enough to reduce the life of human beings to a shambles, and it can even be done quietly: to undo or make a mockery of one of their favorites, the powers above sometimes choose the irreproachable expedient of conferring their bounties upon a third person, who will take it upon himself to strike the great blow. The powers above therefore let their blessings descend upon the queen, who very shortly gives birth to a son, a son born from her womb, so that what usually happens in such circumstances happens now: the favorite, the hope of the future, the presumed heir to the throne, all at once becomes an intruder. The affectionate mother is transformed into an unkind stepmother and in the boy's soul jealousy, bitterness and hatred take root. The legend relates briefly that young Judas began to mistreat his little brother and at last murdered him. Our own belief is that the adolescent's deed had all the extenuating circumstances of an unintentional crime: unconscious intentions, which shun formulation in thought and still more so in utterance, always find their pretexts and expedients. In any case, young Judas has to flee, and so it is that he turns up in Jerusalem.

"There he has no trouble finding his *locus naturalis* in Pilate's court and, we might say, this plainly fabulous episode in the legend is also just where it belongs from the standpoint of probability. Who welcomes a dethroned crown prince if not the upper circles in his land of exile? It is likely enough that the Roman governor have taken some pleasure in the company of the well-mannered and perfectly educated young aristocrat. Who knows but that he was able to converse with him about various problems in Hellenistic philosophy, perhaps even discuss them in Greek, an unexpected treat in that arid province. Judas must have become a familiar in the house, for otherwise it would be inconceivable that he and Pilate between them come up with the scheme of stealing fruit in the adjacent garden.

"Here again we have a patently fabulous episode, but the surprising thing is how simple, almost inevitable, it is to discern the logical connection between events. In fact, if we bear in mind that Judas' life is a pattern of horrible and wonderful sins, which, moreover, are also the great mythic sins, the absurd episode of the stolen apple (that is, of fruit in the original Latin text) does assume a mythic significance, with nothing lacking except an Eve who would have taken it into her head to demand the forbidden fruit. It really seems to us out of the question that Pilate could have asked Judas to hop over the balustrade of the terrace and down into the neighboring garden and steal certain apples, solely because he had an irresistible yen for them. Between men suchlike behavior is just about unthinkable, even in fables. However, everything becomes possible and takes on poetic likelihood if we bring a woman on stage, more precisely Pilate's wife. This neurasthenic woman, whom the Gospels also present as a hypersensitive being, and who following a bad dream sided with Jesus before her husband, may be easily imagined, in an altogether womanly moment of caprice, stubbornly and obsessively insisting on having some fruit, certain fruit in particular, that is, some of the fruit growing right there, a few steps away, on the neighbor's tree, perhaps the only pieces of fruit outside her reach among all the pieces of fruit in the whole of Palestine. Only thus does it become comprehensible how the young friend of the family, in a gallant gesture, ventures down into the neighboring garden and, protected by the evening shadows, plunders the tree. But lo! out of the dusk steps an older man. The two exchange words, then they grapple, finally the young man, striking the older man with a stone, puts him out of action.

"The next day it becomes known that the old man is dead, and in addition it is discovered that he was not some night watchman or other, but the owner himself. As to the consequences, they are shortly disposed of in the legend: according to it, everyone finally subscribes to the version that has the old Ruben (or Simon) suddenly taken ill, while Pilate sees to it that the old man's property passes into the hands of Judas and also that he marries the widow.

"Undoubtedly this 'unfortunate affair' must have meant some bother for Pilate, a brief headache or two, he may have had a scene with his wife and felt sorry for the disconsolate widow. If at first he felt a bit annoyed with the young rascal he soon became seriously worried about him: Judas was completely overcome, on the brink of despair. This unintended homicide would certainly have reminded him of the earlier unpremeditated fratricide, so that for the first time it must have occurred to him that a curse hung over his head.

"In this frame of mind Judas was probably endlessly prey to an unrelenting desire to make reparations for the wrong he had involuntarily done. Together with his powerful friend, he did all he could to soothe the widow in her grief and to help her with the bureaucratic formalities and with the practical matters having to do with administering the inherited property. Acting as a good neighbor he became a regular visitor in the house left without a master. We have to suppose that the widow was not yet old and ugly, on the contrary she must still be fresh and youthful, and not unprovided with feminine charms. They were both in a despairing state, wanting to receive and to give comfort. The woman needed someone she could lean upon and give her tenderness to, as though to a son. And the young man, for his part, amidst an existence he bewailed, sought a woman on whose bosom he could lay his head, as though she were his mother. Neither of them could have thought that marriage, which guaranteed the unrestricted fulfillment of these affections, would prove to be the one solution they ought not to have chosen.

"And so here is the error of Oedipus committed in this context too. And inevitably the day arrived when the couple discovered they were mother and son.

"How many other things became clear to Judas at the same time! And among all those things, probably the least distressing was that he had married his mother. With that discovery came the realization that the man he had slain was none other than his own father. Of course he kept this horrible discovery hidden from his wife-mother who, in the intimacy of their shared life had naïvely told him about her dream, that is, that he would be the very worst of the worst, the incarnation of evil, traitor to his own race. Thereupon it was easy for Judas to convince himself that her dream of long ago had been truly prophetic. Everything became clear, and his life sank into nothingness. The young man, aware now that he belonged to the Jewish nation, understood, stricken, that he was one of Yahweh's chosen, one of those condemned to evil, like Cain, like Ham or Esau, like all the damned remembered by tradition, but smitten in his one person by all the curses that his predecessors, luckier than he, had shared among them.

"Horrified, he fled into the desert. He had already committed every imaginable crime, and even those unimaginable. Only one point of the foreboding dream still remained obscure: that is, that he was someday to bring ruin to his whole people. Well, for doing this he had not had either reasons or means, not up until now. But now, loathing himself and the world, without aim or ambition, in quest of oblivion and expiation, he could honestly hope that, by exiling himself in the desert, that absurd prophecy would not have to be fulfilled.

"But he met Jesus, and the wretch could never have thought that Jesus was the one person he should have carefully avoided . . .

"In telling you the pious legend," Dupin resumed after a brief pause, "it was not among my intentions to give you the illusion that there could be a grain of truth in this story of Judas Iscariot. Instead, my purpose was to bring out the difference between the workings of the naïve popular imagination and the modern attempts to reconstruct an important figure about whom nothing is known. Modern writers, in order to be able to understand it, construct a figure *ex novo* and around it a plot that unfolds in keeping with the rules of romantic tragedy: indeed, not one of them would ever be capable of imagining that Judas' dreadful deed may have been motivated otherwise than by emotions, passions and moral attitudes. The pious legend is far broader in its ideas in as much as it discerns in Judas' deeds the inexorable and irresistible work of destiny. It is not necessary to define the character of the betrayer closely, or at all costs to presuppose a tragic opposition between him and the Master: the supreme crime can be arrived at by even an everyday sort of person in a state of perfect innocence or unawareness, who becomes a tragic hero through the simple fact of being an instrument of destiny.

"The figure of Judas is not described in the legend, but even so there emerges from it an unequivocally clear picture of what the man who betrayed Jesus Christ must have been like. To the popular mind's mythic imagination nothing would have been more absurd than reducing the tragedy of the betrayal to a fortuitous clash of character or opinion between Jesus and Judas, or to some peccadillo on the latter's part. The 'divine matter' of the Redemption deserved characters of a different stripe from small-time thieves, ambitious men, persons suffering from inferiority complexes. The betrayer had to be the sum of the greatest evils, and the supreme crime had to be independent of any contingency: the betrayal had to be fated, the product of the iron logic of an inexorable destiny, and not subject to a fortuitous combining of circumstances, to the wishes or the free will of individuals.

"In the legend, as in the Gospels, Judas is without a distinctly defined face. But in the legend Judas has a *life*. Although this legendary biography has no historical value, it draws our attention to the fact Judas was not, for Jesus, just an empty first name, a mere materialization of his intuition or his prescience, but a concrete person who, before getting to the betrayal, must have had a life behind him, a life that had been really lived. Judas, the historical person, was a man of flesh and blood who, in following the Master, carried with him the burden of a past and probably more memories to be forgotten than fervent messianic feelings. The Judas of the legend ends up in the desert to obtain expiation and forgiveness for his criminal acts, and who knows whether, on this point, the pious tale is not right on target? In that case it would be normal that Judas' personality make a strong impression upon Jesus, and not so much, indeed, because of his aspirings to salvation, as because of the fact that in the past he had already committed every crime—possible and impossible—and thus offered the guarantee of committing still another, the gravest and most absurd.

"If Judas had been like this, Jesus' uncertainties would surely have been allayed. To carry out tasks requiring specific abilities, we generally prefer to turn to specialists; and what question could there be for anyone that the Judas of the legend was far and away ahead of all other specialists in crime? Wherever he put his hand, there had been catastrophe. On Jesus' part it would have been a grave error to give any other of his apostles a try when he had at his disposal the ideal person, who had not only a talent for crime but an out-and-out gift! If the condition *sine qua non* of the work of Redemption had been—according to Scripture, or after the model of a mythological experience—that a woman from among his followers dally with the high priests or with Pilate, Jesus would probably not have looked to Martha, sister of Lazarus, or to Mary, wife of Zebadiah, but, without doubt, to Mary Magdalene, even though she had come to him in search, precisely, of purification.

"At any rate, the legend indirectly confirms what, on the basis of my analyses of evangelical texts, I have maintained from the very beginning of our conversation: to wit, that Judas must not have had any personal motive for committing his crime. The legend illustrates for us how it is possible to commit villainous acts without being a villain and how one can perform the most glaring misdeed at the very moment one is seeking one's salvation. Through their reticence, the Gospels confirm, or at least do not exclude, that the case of Jesus' betrayer could be similar to that of the legendary figure. Only thus is it conceivable that the apostles knew nothing of the impending betrayal prior to the moment the Master was arrested, and that regarding Judas they had harbored no suspicions."

And here Dupin brought the conversation to a close.

"Summing up, how would you describe the stage we have reached in our investigation?" he inquired with his wily look, and hardly able to stifle a great yawn.

My courage returning, I too let my weariness show itself, producing a great yawn of my own.

"Allow me to put off my answer until tomorrow," I said rising from my chair.

"Fine," he agreed, "but I am going to tell you right now where we are: at a standstill. If we go on this way we'll get nowhere. For tomorrow evening I'll have to find another thread for us to follow. And as a matter of fact I already have something in mind. Prepare yourself for something really sensational . . ."

Behind the celestial scenes . . .

THE NEXT EVENING DUPIN WAS UNABLE TO HOLD OUT UNTIL THE END OF
dinner. He was still in the midst of peeling a pear when he turned
to me with a question:

"Now then, are you ready for the *coup de théâtre*? Before us this
evening there shall appear an illustrious, a most illustrious, not to
say an archillustrious personage, who will depose in the capacity of
witness."

I sat there dumbly and tried to recall some renowned scholar,
some theologian, historian or writer or Sorbonne professor whom
Dupin might have invited to sit in at our discussions.

"Who might it be?" I finally asked.

My friend confined himself to making a vague gesture with his
hand, and we immediately transferred to our old armchairs.

"From now on," Dupin began, "our way of posing the problem
will be altogether different. Up until now the 'Judas case' has been

the object of my passion as an amateur detective, eager to reconstruct a crime and identify its motives. But, as occasionally happens in the history of criminology, the investigator suddenly realizes that he is confronted by a very complicated case indeed, where the crime itself and its material executor are the least interesting factors: the secret lies hidden off-stage, one presumes the existence of mysterious instigators, clues point to important State interests, and then the investigator reins in on his policeman's instincts, tries to bow out of the picture, to shelve the dossier, and to let subside into oblivion the crime that he so unwisely uncovered.

"I am experiencing the same discouragement," he added, with an almost contrite air, "as I see that in order to get at the truth I am going to have to involve none other than Almighty God and subject Him, though only this evening and only from love of truth, to a stiff interrogation. My boldness, however, finds an excuse in the fact that even though illustrious personages contribute richly to the discovery of truth, it is always very easily they wriggle out of difficulty and preserve their respectability. But the 'Judas case' has taken on such dimensions in the course of our investigation that, out of our wish to reassure a public opinion thirsting for truth, we must carefully examine the interests and responsibilities of all those directly or indirectly implicated in the affair: the betrayer and the divine betrayed, the Jewish nation and humanity, and, above all, the one about whom we have not spoken until now—the Almighty.

"I propose that we open a grand jury hearing!" he exclaimed at this point, concluding with a resounding laugh. "Were we content to take generalities from this Most Illustrious Personage and to verbalize only what He permits us to know about the 'case,' banal passages from catechism would be all we could transcribe. Redemption was the work of His mercifulness, the fulfillment of one of His long-standing paternal desires, the realization of one point in His divine scheme. Jesus descended to earth mandated by his Father, who had planned *ab æterno* to redeem man from original sin and throw the gates of salvation open to him. It was the task of the Son, divine person and himself God in essence, to save humankind and teach it how it was to save itself in his name and following his example. With his sacrifice a new era opened in humanity's history, an era which, though apparently following the beaten path, is in truth a sharp improvement upon it; indeed, man has become free, damnation does not have to be his fate, in fact, if he likes he can earn himself eternal bliss.

"The deposition of the Most Illustrious Personage ends there, and the presiding judge does not deem it necessary to trouble Him with any more questions. Furthermore, we perfectly understand that it won't be possible to get Him back on the stand later on: He has already deigned to contribute over much to the discovery of the truth. But after His departure we are more convinced than ever that He knows a great deal more on the subject and has some hidden reason for not revealing anything further to us. Therefore, with all due respect, we formally wrap up our inquiry and file away the dossier; but no one can forbid us, intrigued as we are by the reticence of the Most Illustrious Personage, from pursuing *privately* our amateur detective investigations. We shall take the very best care not to give out any interviews to reporters from the yellow press."

"So you're claiming that you've got something on the Lord!" I exclaimed, amazed.

"Yes, I'd say so," replied the unruffled Dupin. "I am sure that, before the arduous undertaking of conducting an investigation of the Lord, many others would beg off, saying that everything one can know about Him has already been stated by theology, a science with two thousand years behind it; and that outside theology, the Lord is and remains inscrutable to our lightweight human intelligence and that all our inquiries are consequently destined *ab ovo* to failure. But we are of a different opinion. For us, God is not only a metaphysical being, whose essence and whose properties can be defined only in philosophical and theological terms. He is also a personage, one of many personages (although a most illustrious one) in our human history, and His actions, reactions, interventions, manifestations, and revelations can be verified and checked, at least within the chronological space that extends from the first line in Genesis to the last line in the Apocalypse of St. John. Actually, Holy Scripture, from a certain viewpoint, is nothing but the minutely detailed chronicle of relations between God and mankind. With Scripture as your reference, it would be overdoing it to expect to arrive at an exact physiognomy of God, or a complete picture of His divine plan; but you have to be pretty blind not to notice certain characteristics in divine nature and in divine behavior toward mankind over the course of a long historical period. God, having entered History, became part of the world of phenomena, just like His creatures: thanks to the testimony—for us authentic and indisputable—of the Bible we have more abundant and more precise information about God than we do about cosmic rays and certain deadly viruses. This fact signifies, first of all, that about God, taken as phenomenon, as object of our experience and observation, we are in a position to express judgments—judgments if not about His essence and His *true* purposes, at least about His way of manifesting Himself in our human world—; secondly—and still more important—this signifies that we are also able to behave properly in His regard. I do not exclude that a Copernican revolution in our knowledge of God *an sich* might stand our phenomenological observations on their heads, or provide a truer interpretation of them. We should not forget however that the geocentric world did not work any worse than the heliocentric world, and the sun shines and warms in the same way whether it turns around the Earth or the Earth turns around it.

"Our fundamental observation is that the Lord, once having entered History, must abide by the laws of the world of phenomena and must take them seriously to be in his turn taken seriously by His creatures. His position vis-à-vis mankind seems a little like that of an adult who condescends to play with the little ones. In this there is no danger that the former's authority and dignity become less, just as there no danger that the children fail to perceive all that is immeasurable and incomprehensible about him. Even if the adult plays ball with the children, or blind man's buff, or hide and seek, he remains superior throughout, even able to interrupt the game at any moment and go off about his own business. However one essential thing is not in his power: he cannot, while the game lasts, exempt himself from accepting and respecting its rules. An adult who does not respect the rules of the world of children, or who violates them, risks becoming odious and ends up banished: the little ones will find as playmates other, more appreciable grown-ups or will withdraw into their private world, safe from strangers.

"Even the simplest relationships between children and adults entail, for the latter, certain commitments, and when the adult is the father these commitments become serious and burdensome. Any adult at all can remain indifferent to what other people's children think about him, but a father cannot be completely without interest in the ideas and feelings of his own offspring. And the relations between God and men are the same as those that obtain between father and son. It would seem that He at one time cherished the dream of not having to bother too much about His creatures, after having created them. By forming man in His image and likeness, He perhaps thought everything had been attended to. It would seem as if the Eternal Father fell victim to the naïve illusion common to so many mortal fathers who suffer from a 'baby complex' and have got to have a child at all costs, just for the sake of having one, without thinking about afterwards. It is indeed pleasant to have within reach a living and mindless little thing, made in our own image and likeness, it is especially pleasant to fantasize about it. Fathers stricken by this complex do not, in their creative furor, foresee the sleepless nights they will have to put up with, first because of the infant's crying, then because of the anxiousness caused by his illnesses, and even less do they foresee the more serious and altogether different worries that will succeed each other as the child grows. Such fathers would in fact like to be surrounded by permanent toddlers, easy to satisfy, whose existence is the cause of no trouble, only of delight. For that matter, the first human beings were indeed conceived and created as immutable tots, in need only of a wet-nurse and distractions, and everything was ready and to hand in the Garden of Eden, in the lap of a friendly Nature.

"The Lord Himself did not meet with a better fate than the average father eager to have children for the sake of having children, *l'art pour l'art*: neither did He reckon with the fact that this nursling, who resembled Him in miniature, would someday, perhaps aided by the Serpent, reach the stage of puberty when he would no longer be content just to resemble his Father, but would want to be just like Him. The child engendered by a mortal father aspires only to become a man like his parent, man and father and the adult possessor of power. However, once past the stage of infancy, the first man, perhaps also for lack of another model, decided that he wanted to become, like his creator, God.

"Everybody knows where Adam's stubbornness landed him; and with him the whole of mankind was checkmated in its divine aspirations. But who can doubt that the Lord too failed in His ambitions as creator and parent? The image made in His likeness degenerated into a miserable monstrosity, and—which better than anything else showed what a fiasco the paternal ambitions were— all this monstrosity felt for its Creator was fear, it showed Him only the respect and gratitude it was forced to show, never that enchanted affection a son feels for his father, who is for him the model to follow and surpass.

"The mistaken calculation in the work of creation inevitably influenced the relations between God and man. God's reaction to the first glimmers of human consciousness was dreadful. The punishment inflicted on the sinner, contrary to all pedagogical good sense, was worthy neither of a father nor a psychologist, and in the eyes of the punished person it seemed nothing but an act of despotism. The Creator seems to have been out of His mind, through the infliction of an unparalleled trauma cutting short the normal psychic evolution of His most glorious creature and condemning it to the condition of a hybrid being, midway between beast and God.

"The first punitive act was followed by others no less cruel. One has only to think of the Flood. The idyllic game between father and son had been over and done with long ago, giving way to a veiled struggle which often exceeded the bounds of fair play, and saw the use of guile and ferocity, with punches thrown on both sides—a struggle whose name is History.

"At this point a question arises spontaneously: what with the imperfection of His creature, why did God allow it to survive in wretched conditions rather than destroy it completely? Why did He prefer to continue this perverse game, so complicated and so atrocious for humanity, and not without unknowns and perils for Himself? Why, more simply put, did He decide to take on History?

"Infinite goodness, about which the Archillustrious Personage boasted a little while ago, and which does not emerge altogether unspotted if one considers His way of behaving, is not in itself enough to explain such great patience. To our taste, and to common sense, His infinite goodness would have been much greater or at least much more generous if, instead of letting man survive in this miserable state, He had scrapped him altogether, possibly creating a more perfect and more pleasant being in his stead. And we don't think we are mistaken if we suggest that the source of His seeming clemency is to be sought elsewhere than in His infinite goodness.

"Thanks to the already mentioned book, with whose help we have tried to understand Jesus' divine qualities, we can be brief and concise. It seems that in effect the Lord was forced to accept the new developments which, although foreseen, caught Him off guard. History suddenly stood there before Him, rudely waking him from the sweet somnolence of His Sunday rest. Ah, no, History was not included among the creatures of the six days: it was born the first day of the following week, the day after the expulsion.

"The birth of human consciousness and the birth of History so surprised His drowsy divine prescience that the Lord, obliged to do something about it there and then, first laid a curse on man, then adopted a series of emergency measures so confused and ineffective that, in a moment of despair, He thought of doing away with all of humanity once and for all. Only with the arrival of Noah did He calm down a little, and only when we come to the covenant concluded with His chosen can we properly begin to speak about a divine plan.

"To us, to our puny human reason, it seems obvious that in elaborating His historical plan (foreseen, furthermore, *ab æterno*) the Lord would invest there—perhaps to the detriment of His infinite goodness—His entire capital of divine omniscience. Instead, to our great surprise, this divine plan, despite its grandeur, rather soon proved to be full of flaws and, in the end, as Biblical history attests, showed itself insufficient and even downright disastrous, holding bitter disappointments in store for its Author, and finally nearly costing him the loss of His handful of worshippers.

"An omniscient man, our puny human reason tells us, could have come up with a much more solid and precise plan, which would not have allowed the rebellious creature to get out of control, and would have spared the Lord surprises, fears, and stern interventions. How could the Lord have made do with a plan thrown together in such haste, one that let so few signs of His infinite goodness and His infinite wisdom show through? But now, in a moment of sudden illumination, we remember the third divine quality *par excellence*: omnipotence! Divine omnipotence is the ready-made, though somewhat humiliating, answer to all our anxious questions. Indeed, who besides an omnipotent being may expose himself to enormous surprises on matters which are essential and of vital importance? Who besides an omnipotent being can afford to treat his subjects like so many toys? Who besides an omnipotent being can be capricious and cruel toward man? Who may care not one fig about psychology, pedagogy, logic? Who, in order to govern the human world, can do without any plan whatsoever, or even employ an imperfect one?

"The assumption of divine omnipotence would dispense us from having to assume a divine plan, and in addition it would authorize us to ask the question: why did the Lord, in His infinite omnipotence, tolerate the reality of impoverished and rebellious man and the regrettable phenomenon of History, when with a flick of the wrist He could have wiped all mankind from the face of the earth and all memory of it as well? But our amazement only grows as we discover that this third quality, *par excellence* divine, does not work perfectly either, that it is very prone to breakdowns, just like infinite goodness and omniscience. Leaving aside the reduction that, from the philosophical viewpoint, omnipotence suffers as a consequence of divine prescience (before which infinite goodness itself becomes impotent), it strikes us that the prime cause for the imperfection of omnipotence resides in the perfectness of Creation. To prove that Creation was (or is) perfect, all that is needed is to quote the words God uttered on the last day of the creating, once He had the work completed. But if you think about it carefully, perfect is a way of saying which-cannot-be-different. Those who consciously maintain that with His omnipotence God could have created lots of other worlds different from the one He actually created, are talking without rhyme or reason: if this world is perfect, a 'more' perfect one is inconceivable, and omnipotence, on this score, becomes impotent . . .

"Imperfect man was therefore included and foreseen within the perfection of Creation. The one intelligent question you could ask is this: why does the Lord tolerate this undesirable being who spoils the harmony of His work? And here we touch upon the heart of the matter. For Him the acceptance of man as a reasoning being is a cruel necessity. If He had had another try at Creation, He would again have been obliged to create the man who sooner or later would have ended up wanting to become God. Had He created him differently, this being would not have been made in His image and likeness and, what mattered most or mattered alone, never would He have been able to hope for affection or adoration from this being. And the trouble is that no other creature of His would have been able to worship Him. And a god who is venerated by no one is just plain inexistent. Worship, for a god, is the equivalent, as everybody knows, of your and my daily bread: without worship a god starves to death. This vital necessity for the Lord to be worshipped is the key to the mystery of our existence, and its guarantee also. To exterminate mankind would be for the Lord to commit suicide, to deny His own essence: with the elimination of the earthly image in His likeness, the universe would be reduced to an inanimate mechanical toy.

"You might object that Adam and Eve did not offer the Creator any worship, but this does not contradict our thesis. In mankind's infantile stage, God could be satisfied with the existence and admiration of a thinking being of a level slightly superior to that of the beast, endowed with about the same semi-unconscious intelligence as a not yet pubescent boy. Indeed, the very existence of such beings gives paternal hearts a feeling of sweet plenitude, whereas a son's puberty is a critical moment for fathers too: future relations between them are about to be decided once and for all. The consequences of this destructive period can be much more serious than the mere refusal of affection, of adoration or of admiration; these childish feelings can give way to hatred, to contempt, to the desire to reject one's parents, who thus risk being abandoned, murdered and even torn from the memory of their posterity. The Lord realized He was running all these risks. The unworthy monster His image had changed into had good cause to reproach Him for certain remote and recent acts. To secure even so the worship of these humiliated and tormented beings, the Lord, with His flagging omnipotence, had to show all His mettle.

"The story of the Lord and, reciprocally, that of mankind too is simply a series of desperate attempts to repair the fatal miscalculation committed by both parties in Eden. Humanity tries to return to the paradisial state, God tries to see to it that He is worshipped. Today these two aspirations seem to have reached the limits of the impossible. But it was different at the time right after the expulsion. Man, at least in theory, could nourish some vague hope of getting back into Eden, while for His part God had a firmer grip on the rare human beings about—very rare, for He had had to give up on Cain early on.

"Don't be frightened, my friend, it is not our duty to tackle the problem of Cain, which would deserve a separate discussion—and, moreover, world literature already includes an entire library of works treating this theme. Cain's figure and fate, like those of Judas, beckon to the imagination of writers. And now all of a sudden I have the urge to pass on to you a few of my observations as an amateur theologian. It being very plain that, far from being of a sentimental order, the questions now pending between God and mankind were instead of existential importance, we think that the Lord considered Cain dangerous to His power and His own existence, or to His own future relations with mankind. Cain's punishment came after his murder of Abel, but the Lord already disliked him. It was from the very start and not after the fratricide that Cain was judged wicked by the Creator: He simply seized upon this as as a pretext to curse him and remove him from circulation. But who can say that it did not serve equally to get Abel out of the way, who as the founder of a line might not have turned out to be as satisfactory as Seth looked to be? In as much as Seth's offspring, once it reached the seventh generation, seemed to the Lord worthy of extermination, who can say whether Abel's progeny did not well beforehand appear to Him as a serious threat? And so, at one stroke, God got rid of Abel and of Cain. But whereas He got rid of Abel in a radical fashion, He saw to it that Cain was left alive. This is the most exciting mystery in the Cain problem.

"Nothing better demonstrates the total absence of sentimental-isms at the base of divine history than this concern on the Lord's part to assure life to Cain and his descendants. For Him, Cain was distinctly more important than Abel! The reason why was evident to His divine mind: what apart from its *wickedness* could provide mankind with the necessary incentive to survive the expulsion from Eden? And this statement is not at all cynical or frivolous if we consider that in Biblical language the so-called 'wickedness' of mankind, in those primordial times, meant nothing else than its longing to return to Paradise and become God. To rob it completely of this ambition would have been tantamount to depriving it of the only reason and the only objective on whose account it remained in this world, now become arid and desolate. Cain, as the history of his descendants shows, preserved these sacrilegious and menacing ambitions in all their virulence, and did everything he could to accomplish them.

"There was also another reason why the Lord allowed Cain's descendants to live. The other fraction of mankind, Seth's descendants, resigned to the divine curse and frightened to death by the expulsion from Eden, would never have invented the material and spiritual means that insured its survival. Rather, as we know, it was the sons of Cain who invented the tools with which to brave harsh existence in an unfriendly world. Better still, it was the sons of Cain who invented all the instruments with which the sons of Seth solemnized the worship of the Lord!

"Such were the compromises imposed upon the Lord for having yielded a small part of His absolute omnipotence and acknowledged the rules of the game of History!

"But, naturally, it did not, it could not go smoothly. The extraordinary progress of Cain's line contaminated the pious, just as tares contaminate wheat. The terrorized and the intimidated, in whom primordial rancor survived unconsciously just as it did in Cain's descendants, came little by little to realize that the accursed of God lived better than they, in greater freedom and, in a certain way, in greater dignity. Then, still in the footsteps of the Cainites, there awakened in them too the vague inkling of an astounding possibility, that of a return to Paradise, the land where the trees of omniscience and immortality grew. These unconscious tendencies made the Flood—suppression of the dangerous and indelible *memento* for the survivors—both necessary and unpostponable: one does not trifle with God, everything and everyone are in His power. Man lives thanks to His mercifulness alone, he must therefore be grateful to Him and dread Him. Thus did the good Eternal Father earn Himself the name of *El-shaddai*, which means the destroyer, the violent, the overbearing, and it stuck to Him down through the ages.

"With the passing of time, the Lord's despotism seemed intolerable to a large part of humanity, and the lesser part noted with astonishment that, with the help of other gods, it was able to realize at least a surrogate for that magical garden the Lord's cruelty had driven it from. In ever-increasing numbers men let themselves be courted by kindlier and more affable gods, and this was the worst blow that could be dealt to the Lord: to see men's love go to waste on non-existent or incomplete divinities! To see offerings burnt in sacrifice to beings so inferior to Him! And with the passing of time to see His creatures slip away from Him in ever-growing numbers! Thus did History surprise God with a danger He had not foreseen. He must put up with the rivalry of phantasmagorias created by His own creatures!

"In this humiliating struggle of the One True God with false and unworthy gods resides the origin of the chosen people's history and the covenants made with Him. But whereas the whole of Jewish history lies therein, God's history is not limited to these relations, which were an important aspect of it, but only an aspect. Had God been able to assure for Himself the adoration and worship of all mankind, He would have had no reason at all to choose and bind to Himself the race of Abraham, and perhaps the Jewish nation would have had no particular importance in History. The great honor conferred upon the Jews is owing to the piddling fact that this people alone, among all the nations of the earth, was capable of accepting the idea of Yahweh and of revealing it. But at that extremely delicate moment these virtues were most appreciable, and from one instant to the next Yahweh became a psychologist, interspersing terrifying threats with solemn and pretty far-reaching promises, in order to win the hearts of His chosen.

"Nonetheless we all know how the story of the chosen people went. And whether because God erred through impatience and through over-cautiousness, only doling out with an eye-dropper a few instalments on the promises made to His chosen, or because the Jews were truly unworthy of such promises and gifts, the fact remains that the Jewish nation was periodically decimated, tortured and enslaved, therefore incapacitated from carrying out the mission entrusted to it: and the one true God ran the danger of losing even His *pied-à-terre* opposite the false and unworthy gods. Then, through the mouth of one of those men with long beards and thundering voices, the Lord promised the Messiah. But the most annoying part was that the promise was accompanied by no due-date.

"In this way several centuries went by until the Jews, discontented, energetically demanded of their God that He send the Messiah. But the Lord, in the meantime, had realized the impossibility of sending the Messiah to His people, for History's reality was not in His favor. It would of course have been ideal to send one of His emissaries to earth to settle all pending questions! A Messiah *comme il faut* would have made the chosen people's dreams of national independence come true, the while restoring respect for Yahweh and insuring for a boundless stretch of time His sovereignty over a large part of mankind. But, a few decades before Titus' campaign and the Diaspora, the historical moment did not look proper for trying to lead the Jewish armies to triumph and occupying the throne of Judah. The Lord could not allow the Messiah to come face to face with the Roman legions: a defeat would have amounted to the loss of the chosen people and the total collapse of the Yahwehist reign.

"This situation, until then extremely delicate, evolved in the direction of catastrophe. But in a moment of great lucidity, Yahweh remembered that He still had a card up His sleeve: a kind of joker He would have preferred not to play but which was His last strong card.

"During the period that runs from the last great prophets to

Jesus Christ, the chosen people, following their contact with the gods of their conquerors, manifested altogether extravagant aspirations. While they awaited the Messiah who was to give them freedom, independence and an empire, the Jews conceived perhaps not so much the hope as the desire of obtaining a reward, after their earthly unhappinesses, on another plane of existence, that is, in the beyond. The other-worldly existence would be based upon justice, by virtue of which the good would be raised up and recompensed, the wicked punished, and on the day of the Last Judgment bodies too would be resurrected so as to be reintegrated into Eternity, these in Paradise, those in Gehenna, each according to his deserts.

"Yahweh, we may be sure of it, found Himself in an awkward bind: here on the part of the chosen people was an expectation He had never encouraged, not even by a vague promise to be fulfilled at some unspecified time. The scheme of Creation, like the historical rescue plan, made no provision at all for other-worldly survival, nor for rewards and punishments after death, nor for the resurrection of bodies. All this existed only in the imagination of the chosen people, fostered by the promises of the false and unworthy gods who threatened to dethrone Yahweh. Those perfidious rival gods had made known the way leading to salvation and, unconcerned about the fate of an entire nation, they had won over particular persons, dazzling them individually with the prospect of obtaining in the beyond everything that He would never be able to give the chosen people in this world. What to do? Send down a prophet again and promise something that the false and unworthy gods had already offered to His faithful? Send down a prophet and risk being laughed at? Indeed, the spiritual needs of the Jewish people had not at all put an end to the dreams concerning the Messiah: they were in addition to those needs, but not a substitute. At best, the figure of the Messiah, earthly power and moral force, might coincide with that of the Redeemer, who would have to bring with him the keys to Paradise and to Hell. Promises were no longer enough.

"At that historical moment the Lord, though it was reluctantly, had to play His joker.

"At that historical moment the Word was made flesh."

Dupin paused there, and in the sudden silence the divine revelation echoed for a long moment, solemn even in this not truly orthodox application. Finally my illustrious friend began again, attuning his voice to that triumphant solemnity by whose spell I too had been captivated.

"After this brief recapitulation of God's history, I believe it is clear to you that the dispatching to earth of Jesus Christ was a measure that could not be deferred, adopted as time was running out: the Lord who, appearances notwithstanding, was never capricious, in this instance acted once again at the prompting of History's iron logic.

"To use a very trivial analogy, what was happening in the supernal spheres spectrally resembled a dynastic crisis, where the absolute monarch must yield the throne to the crown prince. Or, to employ an even more trivial analogy, the situation in the celestial kingdom resembled that critical moment when the old capitalist retires to private life, turning the running of things over to his son in order to protect the firm from the workers' discontent and revolutionary impulses. The resigning boss's last wish is always that his son be revered and respected as he was at the start of his own career; in making this move, he bows out with a certain regret, but also as the winner: power, through his children, will remain in his hands.

"Is it possible that this too may have been the fate reserved for the all-powerful and all-knowing Yahweh? It is altogether possible. It is the usual fate of all eternal and immortal gods who, once got entrapped in the cogs and wheels of the machinery of Time, find themselves all of a sudden governed by laws valid for mortals. Only thus is it conceivable that gods marry, have children, and wind up dying a divine death, which, to be sure, is equivalent to eternal survival but at the same time also to a state of powerlessness. They are, in some way, like extinct stars: they no longer warm, they no longer shine, they no longer rule the destinies of mankind, the dim memory of their power hangs on like a dead weight amid the myriads of vital forces of the universe, and yet suffices to testify to their survival. After their deaths, so to speak, they continue to subsist but cease to exist. When he enters History, a god puts his immortality at risk. All this Yahweh realized at the critical period of His existence. The melancholy of 'everything passes away' laid hold of Him with the procreation of His only Son.

"Up until then He had children only 'through grace and adoption,' spiritual sons, whom He subjugated, that they lead rebellious creatures, sons natural and unnatural, back unto Him. He used them as emissaries, proconsuls, functionaries, whom He saddled with unappealing missions, and whom He did not think to spare a bad end. When all is said and done, these adopted sons were only a means to postpone the tragic moment when He would engender His own son.

"History obliged Him at that critical juncture to beget a son, to beget him almost in the standard manner, a son not only in His likeness or adopted by grace, but His flesh and blood. The critical moment became the tragic moment of His existence, subjected to the law of Time, because thanks to His previous experiences with different sorts of sons and thanks to what He knew about the experiences of other gods with their sons, He by now knew only too well what a son of god signified.

"Yahweh, if He took a glance at this world populated by gods, many of whom claimed origins much more distant than His, saw terrifying examples. Indeed, no sooner was he able to walk than the divine son would be plotting against his father, against, that is, the old reigning god, would not hesitate to kill him, emasculate him and, among the several cases, the latter could consider himself lucky if the former were content just to send him into exile. Naturally, the precautions the elderly father-gods took to protect themselves must not have escaped Yahweh's notice. A foresightful father-god, for example, could duly frighten or intimidate his son, cast him, immediately after his birth, into the hostile world of nature or of men, he could persecute him, make his earthly destiny difficult, and he could also simply devour him as soon as he issued from his mother's womb. He must therefore be vigilant, very vigilant: the examples from divine history were not reassuring at all. The one who got short-changed in the end was the father, not the son, who, instead, survived persecutions, devourings and, even, the death inflicted on him by gods and men. On the strength of such examples, Yahweh could not entertain great hopes with regard to His own survival, and at times it seemed to Him that he was marching toward death. But He did not intend at all to resign Himself to the fate of extinct stars: on the contrary, by procreating a son of His own, Yahweh meant to perpetuate His own absolute monarchy until the consummation of time. Indeed, the son would take care of certain delicate matters on earth, but must not dethrone Him in the heavens. Hence He would have to engender a son whose equivalent was not to be found among the various sons of gods since the world began, that is, a good and obedient son who would execute His will without asking for anything in exchange, and whom He could even devour afterwards.

"Out of such resolves was born the most 'infernal' scheme that divine mind was ever able to devise. We might even say that, as he set in motion the peculiar mechanism of His divine prescience, Yahweh, in that moment of great lucidity, came up with Christianity!

"Seen from this astonishing perspective, all the difficulties of the situation vanished in a trice. Bringing to immediate consciousness this basic content of His prescience, He realized that all His insoluble problems arose solely from a fixation on His own part. The one reason why He had got stuck in a blind alley was His unreasonable attachment to the idea of retrieving the chosen people and making them powerful by means of the Messiah. But, Yahweh thought excitedly, is it really so important to keep tied to this handful of men who have obviously become unsuited for their mission, and recalcitrant and unmalleable to boot? What would have happened if He had just dropped the chosen people and demoted them? What mattered the little nation's immense disillusion compared to the enormous advantage that would accrue to Him? Why go looking for trouble with the Jews when, with a skilfully conducted policy, He could win over and conquer the *damned* by the million, men not yet embittered by ill-kept promises and, on top of that, forgetful or ignorant of the punishments inflicted on them at the beginning of time? Wasn't it worth abandoning the chosen in order to win the hearts of the damned? The hearts! . . .

"Indeed yes, it would be an ugly about-face, but what an advantageous one, and, at the same time, a well-disguised maneuver too. The son would win for Him a large part of the world, and He would not even lose the chosen people, since they would not see through the dodge and would keep right on waiting for the 'true' Messiah. Moreover, the new covenant to be concluded with these new faithful would demand far less of Him: it would not commit Him to anything, while assuring Him of everything in return.

"Yahweh's scheme was inspired and farsighted, enabling Him to reduce His many and complicated problems to just one, that is, to the problem of His relations with His son. This problem was no less intricate, and no less important for His very survival. But the son's job would be to handle the complicated matters, while He could concentrate on the family problem. If He succeeded in being acknowledged and reconfirmed in His position as the One True God in the worship and heart of an up until then damned humanity, He would have no further worries except to keep Himself from being dethroned by His son.

"So He took all the necessary measures, and chose the best procedure from the *hieroi gamoi*. History furnished, indeed, some examples of false and mendacious gods whose offspring had not sought the divine throne and had been content with achieving a prominent position among men and a more modest one among the immortals. Why couldn't His son become a hero, perhaps even a demi-god, without someday taking it into his head to get rid of

Him? The danger would already be minimized if He chose a human mother for him. The son, so prudently engendered, would possess enough divine nature and qualities for carrying out his mission on earth, but not so much that he might really be led to covet the father's position. Even if endowed with extraordinary and divine qualities, a son born of an ordinary human mother in a stable, and brought up in exile in proletarian surroundings, would never venture to consider himself God and heir to the heavenly throne. On the contrary, whatever clear intuition he might have of his own divinity, a considerable dose of forever lingering uncertainty would impel him to credit his own greatness only to his Father's goodness, and to be grateful to Him for it. So Yahweh, without giving up an ounce of His paternal tyranny, would modify it in such a way as not to be blamed because of it but praised instead. His old dream of being loved and thanked by a son was finally on the brink of realization! To that son such gifts must be granted that would enable him to perform his mission and to love Him. But nothing more.

"But did everything come out as smoothly as Yahweh had imagined? Two thousand years of history seem to attest to His scheme's positive results, and Yahweh, since then called God, has at present hundreds upon hundreds of millions of faithful who adore Him, worship Him, and, even while struggling against Him, acknowledge Him. Theological speculation and the Church's doctrine assure us that the dynastic question was easily resolved, in as much as it was never raised. The dogma of the Holy Trinity jumps right over all the questions we have grappled with and even those we shall have to grapple with later on. But one of our major preoccupations is, precisely, to do all we can to reduce the number of points of contention with official theology, and that is why we loudly proclaim that our investigations do not by any means call dogma into question, but simply attempt to retrace its genesis.

"However the relations between Father and Son may have been planned, they were bound, at some particular moment in History, to be subject to the risks that derive from involvement with time.

If the Lord could find a certain reassurance in the fact that Jesus was subject to human nature, it was also at times for Him a cause of concern. And Jesus' character included a fine store of essentially human traits, inherited from his mother. Although an instrument in his Father's hands, his viewpoints and his methods, his ideas and his deeds showed the human impress and reflected not only the failings of the human condition, but also its most sublime greatnesses: a moral sense, good will and good faith, courage and purity, and other wonderful characteristics that cannot be found in divine nature, since they are simply incompatible with it.

"Jesus, who carried it out, was not responsible for the scheme thought up by the Father, since he knew nothing about it. Who indeed, even among the fiercest proponents of the essential identity of Father and Son, would dare affirm that Jesus, when he became incarnate, knew he had been sent more to save the Father than to save humanity? Jesus, who, according to all testimony, believed Yahweh to be infinite, eternal and omnipotent, would never for one minute have supposed that the latter's survival depended on the success of his mission. He thought Him so incommensurable that he would never have attributed selfish intentions to Him, and that is why he firmly believed that Yahweh had sent him on earth in a moment of overflowing mercifulness, and for the salvation of the chosen people. Therefore he meant to be of help to mankind and, if he wished to lead it back to God, he proposed to do so not in the Father's interest (a preposterous idea!), but in the interests of the human race. In his mission he saw the concretization of God's infinite goodness, and, more than any other prophet, he made himself the champion of this idea. Indeed, for him, God's goodness could manifest itself daily, even in cataclysms, diseases, destitution and plagues, hence in all those things that according to common sense are unquestionably evil: for it is precisely a life of unhappiness that conducts us unto the kingdom of heaven, where, on the other hand, those who, in this vale of tears, have already profited from divine goodness as it is understood by human common sense, find it difficult to enter.

"Jesus therefore was creating for himself a God the Father in his own image and likeness, attributing to Him his own intentions and his own objectives, as well as their ideal and emotional foundation. In more severe language we might say that Jesus entertained illusions with regard to his mission and to his Father. And if we wished to play the skeptic, we could even wonder whether Jesus, urged by his boundless good faith, did not go and allow himself to profess some rather unreasonable beliefs and venture into gratuitous promises. Redemption, the immortality of the soul, the resurrection of the body, the Last Judgment, Paradise and Hell, were relatively recent doctrines, which had infiltrated the chosen people from neighboring countries dominated by false and mendacious gods, all doctrines and promises never confirmed by the mouth of Yahweh. Nevertheless Jesus, without the least hesitation, became the champion of those ideas and these vague and all too human dreams. The only guarantee for these ultra-terrestrial realities was that Jesus was to end up by becoming God or, to be more exact, that he was to end up occupying the throne to the right of the Father. If these delights had not existed heretofore, it was he who took it upon himself to create them. Unless the Father, on the sly, did not devour him first . . ."

Noticing a shadow of indignation cross my face, Dupin gave me a roguish wink:

"Ah yes, my dear friend, we must also take into account the *hyiophageia* in such vogue in the world of the gods. With that uncompleted sentence—which, after such a long historico-religious introduction, should not strike you as all that frivolous—I simply wish to say that our competence does not extend beyond the threshold of the Kingdom of Heaven, and that we give no guarantee as to the outcome of the work of Redemption. All we wish to do is point out that even if Jesus did finally triumph, there were a good many features of his mission about which he deluded himself. My thesis here is not really very bold: the Old Testament, with its stories of patriarchs and prophets, provides us plenty of examples which confirm that 'walking with the Lord' is never a harmonious and conscious collaboration between God and His chosen, but rather a succession of misunderstandings, tuggings and pullings, and even acts of rebellion on the part of the chosen party, who however—whether he is aware of it or not—ends by accomplishing the mission entrusted to him. As a rule, one walks with the Lord down various and often divergent paths. This is a very understandable phenomenon and it derives from the fact that divine plans are always concealed from men, as, for that matter, they remained concealed from Jesus Christ. And if besides conquering mankind and converting it to worship, Jesus Christ also managed to redeem it, from the Father's point of view this result was of secondary importance, if not completely negligible.

"Thanks to that strange phenomenon of walking together down different, nay, divergent paths, Jesus was convinced he could identify his own program with the divine plan. And so long as Jesus, pursuing his own mission, continued to serve the Father's purposes, the Latter lavished on him all possible gifts and graces. Only one thing worried Him in His Son's personal program: Jesus' tenacious desire to occupy the throne of the celestial Kingdom. On this score the Father had to deny him all help. The divine plan, though it foresaw the possibility of a succession to the celestial throne, could not approve it.

"In moments of discouragement, Yahweh realized that despite all the precautionary measures He had taken, His wise arrangements were not very useful, and that indeed their effect was to incite the Son to pursue his objectives. By denying him the certainty of his divine status, He as good as forced him to seek it on his own and by every means! Despite his having a distinct intuition of his divine nature and many hints supporting this intuition, Jesus, incarnated in the mean envelope of a human being, could not be altogether sure of his own divinity. Just as no human event could disturb in him the clarity of that intuition, so no prophecy and no celestial sign, no paternal message and no miracle was in itself sufficient to give him that certainty: the words of Scripture were susceptible to errors of interpretation, the signs and miracles might be nothing more than acts of grace on the part of the Father. And while these acts might be enough to convince men, friendly and otherwise, they were not enough to convince him: Jesus knew very well that, if he really was the Son of God, this absolute and irreversible fact must, indeed, proceed *also* from the fulfillment of prophecies and the accomplishment of miraculous signs, but it was independent of them, as henceforth it was of the Father's benevolence—to such a degree independent that no circumstance, not even the Father's omnipotence, could have altered it. It was the Father's goodness and greatness that had caused him to be born and sent upon the earth, and it was thanks to divine goodness that he was successful in his mission. But the fact of being the son of God must not itself be dependent on anything and anyone, and must be demonstrated with absolute certainty and with arguments that do not depend on the help nor yet on the approbation of the Father!

"This is why we have ventured to assert that to Jesus his own divinity appeared as a thesis to be proven by evidence furnished by himself. And the New Testament bears witness that his life was dominated by a feverish, unrelenting search for the definitive and irrefutable proof: from his concern to interpret and fulfill the prophecies to the scrupulous observation of the prescriptions of the *iter* for ascending to the Kingdom of Heaven.

"Jesus knew, indeed, that autonomous laws governed the condition of son of god. And he also knew that there existed a well-defined itinerary that all candidates to the various pantheons must scrupulously follow to attain the fulfillment of their divinity. The examples of Tammuz and Attis, of Osiris and Dionysus and other gods pointed to an inevitable destiny: he who was to become god must after an adventurous life fall victim to the forces of darkness, suffer a violent death, and revive to a divine existence. Even the most auspicious date seemed prescribed. The mystery must occur at the beginning of spring, when the sun again begins to rule the sky and heat and light prevail over the cold and darkness of winter. Jesus knew that—as the son of a god—this was the road one had to follow. No one must think that he intended to reproduce what others had done before: simply, just as by nature's law the foetus goes through various phases before becoming a human being, so a mysterious law, which enabled sons of gods to rise to the rank of actual gods, obliged him to take the same road and add to the number of examples by becoming an example himself.

"Yes, unlike the poet who *non fit sed nascitur,* it seems that the gods, some of them at least, are not born gods but must work very hard indeed in order to earn a place for themselves among the immortals. The history of religions calls them 'dying gods,'[*] but the term is not exact, since they die not *as* gods but *to become* gods. I would call them *nouveaux dieux,* if our language had not already reserved this term for those who, starting from nothing or from modest circumstances, have arrived at a lofty social or economic position. As you see, the analogy fits to a T, for these young gods, besides being new in respect to the old ones, appear as *parvenus* in the society of the gods of ancient nobility, if only because they had to toil and sweat seven shirts like so many *self-made men*[*] to obtain what the others have had since time immemorial. If only the term rang a little more prettily to the ear I'd be tempted to rechristen them *self-made gods*, which does perfectly render the idea.

"The Mediterranean and the Near East swarmed with these gods who were 'self-made,' and Jesus belongs in their typology. The fulfillment of the mystery—cruel death and subsequent resurrection—was the absolute and unequivocal proof needed to demonstrate his status as Son of God, and it was the only miracle that did not depend on the Father's will but on an inevitable higher law, superior to the world of the gods themselves. If He was truly the Son of God, this mystery must be accomplished independently of the Father's approval, nay, even against His will . . .

"Convinced as he was that in its every aspect his life was the

---

[*] English in original.

fulfillment of the Father's will, Jesus never felt that the Lord might not be completely in agreement with his personal program. That is why it he was bitterly surprised each time he sensed sudden interruptions in the Father's warm protection, especially during the concluding phase of the mystery's consummation. And it is sure that a tragic face-off occurred between Father and Son, a moment all the Gospels evoke, but until now seldom taken as irrefutable proof of the conflict between Jesus and Yahweh. That conflict was to come out on the Cross and to coincide with the moment of mankind's Redemption—for at that moment the mystery of the Son of God came about also. At that instant a painful realization flashed through Jesus' mind: the Father had abandoned him! No interpretation has yet succeeded in satisfactorily explaining the meaning of *'Eli, Eli, Lamma sabaktani!'* This despairing outcry would have been completely meaningless had Jesus ascended the Cross with full paternal approval, and would have been almost blasphemous had it at that moment still been his belief that he was doing the Father's will. It would really be romanticism to reduce its significance to an everyday cry of despair from an atrociously tortured man at the point of dying. At no moment of his life had Jesus ever been more God than now! We believe that his exclamation must be taken in its strictest literal sense. Jesus, at the moment of his death, must have discovered a painful truth he had never suspected before: the Father, by whose side he had thought he had walked his whole life long, was rejecting him in the final moments of his mission. He understood that the Father had abandoned him. But he did not understand that, on the contrary, it was He who had abandoned the Father—that is, had somehow outstripped Him in accordance with a law more powerful than the gods themselves. The Father no longer had any power over him . . .

"If we are sufficiently without scruple to be willing to employ our Lilliputian mental categories to evaluate divine attitudes and qualities, and if we do not shrink from calling upon the criteria of human common sense and good taste to judge divine matters, we can say many unkind things about our One True God, but we can in no way lay upon Him the blame for Jesus' death. He had every reason to dread this death, which for the son was the prelude to resurrection but which for Him could signify the hour of decline.

"Even if we agree with theology and proclaimed dogma, and accept as beyond argument that in the Kingdom of Heaven the dynastic question was settled in the best of ways, we must affirm that Jesus' death was not well received by the Father for another, no less important reason. For Jesus violent death was not only a phase prescribed by the mystery of those famous new gods, it was also, at the same time, a sacrifice He offered to the Father in the name of mankind. And we do not think we exaggerate when we declare that on that account too Jesus' death produced in Yahweh a disagreeable sensation: He was forced to admit that it was the one sacrifice worthy of Him.

"One has but to think of the significance of all the sacrifices that human beings offered and offer to their gods, and to cast a retrospective glance at Yahweh's analogous demands upon the chosen people. The truth is that at the present stage of psychological-religious studies we still do not have a very clear grasp of the meaning and essence of the sacrifice, but even so science has been able to isolate a number of constants in this complex problem. One of the most important of them is that to every god the sacrificial offering is the god himself, or else a victim who is identical or at least equivalent to him. If we accept the dogmatic conception of the Trinity, the Christian sacrifice of Holy Communion is no exception to this rule either. In fact, daily, millions upon millions of times each day, Jesus Christ is sacrificed to God, which is to say God is sacrificed to God. In other terms, the sacrifice on Golgotha is continually re-enacted, the violent death of Jesus Christ offered to Jesus Christ and to the other two indivisible persons of the Trinity. And it is no different in other religions and in more remote times. Sacrifice was and is the only effective means enabling man to put himself in communication with his gods. The meaning of divine sacrifice eludes modern man, but, in primordial times, for our distant ancestors, it was indisputably, almost palpably obvious that the best way to thank, coax, worship and get the attention of a god was to kill him in accordance with precise and solemn norms. By consuming the non-volatilized remains of the sacrificed victim, man ate god and perhaps believed that he became somewhat god himself, or assimilated some small scrap of his strength. Or else he thought that, by killing him, he would make felt his ephemeral power over the supreme being. Whatever the case, the attitude of sacrificing man implied the pre-logical intuition that God was in some way affected by the sacrifice. And why wouldn't He be? To be killed, even for the immortal gods, is at the very least a rousing sensation . . .

"Upon this point, also, Yahweh's position was very particular. For since the creation of the world no fitting and worthy sacrifice had ever been offered to Him, and those who think Christianly can only lend their support to our thesis: the one way to sacrifice properly to God is to sacrifice Him, that is, Jesus Christ, on the altar of the Mass. But to arrive at this thousands of years had to pass, because the One True God, absolute spiritual being, had never explicitly declared Himself on the subject and had left mankind in the regrettable state of not knowing what holocaust it should offer Him. Most obviously, nothing worthy of Him existed on the face of the earth: no product of the soil, no animal, bird or reptile had the stature to replace Him on the sacrificial altar. Yahweh was not at all a pantheistic god, He was not contained in the Creation, a miserable speck of dust compared to His incommensurability. The Jews naturally had offered Him sacrifices even so, following the prescriptions of the Law, which taught them what and how they must sacrifice in order to please Yahweh. Who knows, though, whether any sacrifice of the Jews had ever pleased Him! Calves and rams reminded Him of those primordial, rather humiliating times when He had not yet revealed His purely spiritual being and was identified with a totemic animal. To His palate, more refined with the passing of the centuries, the taste of these sacrificial viands was rather irritating than pleasurable.

"It is very sad to imagine how this improper treatment at the hands of His faithful may have distressed Him over the course of so many centuries. More, it is frankly terrifying to think that for so many centuries the chosen people made the wrong sacrificial offerings and that their sacrifices could not be fully appreciated by the Lord: in fact, instead of putting Him in a favorable mood, they sometimes enfuriated Him.

"And here a question spontaneously occurs to me: why did Yahweh fail to reveal His true tastes to the chosen people, thus condemning Himself to vegetate miserably and the Jews to forever offer Him incorrect sacrifices? Since theology and the history of religions never have and, I believe, never will phrase the question in these terms, I myself have the right and duty to venture a reply. I would say that a twofold reason lay behind Yahweh's attitude. Perhaps He didn't play fair. He may not have been on the up-and-up. While it is in men's interest to offer the gods the best possible sacrifice, at times it will be in the gods' interest that the sacrifice not be completely irreproachable, and therefore not put them under too great an obligation. Since a sacrifice implies some sort of coercive power—even though upon the gods it may perhaps only have the effect of a nudge—we can well imagine that our Yahweh, the absolute monarch, did not take well to the idea of being subjected to the effects of man's will and strength, even if it only amounted to a faint prodding. Perhaps that is why He gave up rich fare and made do with ordinary dishes.

"But I wish to tell you right away that He could have had another, far more serious reason, which—what a coincidence!—turned out to be profitable to His faithful. Now, what could He have asked the chosen people to sacrifice to Him instead of rams and calves? What sacrificial victim could have deservedly replaced Him on the altar of the holocaust? Who or what was the terrestrial equivalent of His essence as pure spirit? Well, we know, and He too knew it and yearned for it, the Jewish people knew it and feared it: Yahweh was entitled to human sacrifice. What other sacrificial victim would have been more ideal than man, who,

though not being God, is the only other at least partly spiritual
being, the living image and likeness of God. But why did Yahweh
refrain for so long from explicitly saying so? His repugnance for
such sacrifices is clearly proven by the Old Testament, and as for
ourselves we are of course too cautious to attribute it to His infinite
goodness or philanthropic dispositions. In our opinion, the acceptance of human sacrifice on Yahweh's part would have been
tantamount to recognizing that, through the sin committed in the
Garden of Eden, man had become, or almost become—be it for one
fleeting instant—God, or a divine being, thus giving him reasons
to go on indulging in the dangerous dream of divine aspirations.

"That there is some foundation for this line of thinking we
attribute to Yahweh is shown by the Biblical episode of Jephthah,
who never for one instant considered offering the Lord a ram or
some other pure animal. Thanks to the examples provided by
neighboring peoples, his enemies, he was the first and only one to
hit upon the right choice and offer a sure-fire sacrifice. Jephthah's
state of necessity was also a state of necessity for Yahweh: it was a
matter of the chosen people's life or death, hence the offering could
not be turned down. But the sequel convinced Yahweh of the
cogency of His misgivings concerning human sacrifice, since a cult
was dedicated to Jephthah's daughter and since every cult stands
upon the experience of a divine epiphany. Human sacrifice would
easily have led to the creation and spread of further false and
mendacious gods. Doubtless, the modest competition represented
by Jephthah's virgin daughter could be put up with, but if you
consider the potential such sacrifices have for developing into cults,
Yahweh, it seems to us, was being especially sensible when, at the
last moment, He stayed Abraham's arm in its murderous intent:
who knows what sort of complications the rivalry of a divinified
Isaac would have introduced into Yahweh's relations with the
chosen people . . .

"The prophets were perhaps the first to sense the uselessness of
the sacrifices offered God by the chosen people. They claimed,
indeed, that the Lord was more fond of prayers than of sacrifices,

no doubt performed according to the rules but without an uplifted heart. And who knows but that it was Yahveh Himself who suggested this idea to His prophets. The prayers of mortals put Him under much less obligation than their sacrifices, in particular when they were well carried out.

"That is why the Lord, to begin with opposed to the death of His son because of the unforeseeable dynastic complications, after that could not approve of it because of its character of a sacrifice offered on behalf of the human race. Under the pressure of this twofold threat, the Lord had to condescend to a new covenant with humanity, a covenant entitled the New Testament, whose guarantor was His Son Jesus Christ. The compromise, which turned out to be so brilliant on Yahweh's part, also opened the door to a human victory, modest though it was: we are no longer at El-Shaddai's mercy if we put ourselves under His Son's protection, the Father's tyranny weighs less heavily if we make our lives into an *imitatio Christi*, and our primary aspirations also attain some satisfaction, if only in a transcendent manner, in a celestial Paradise after our corporeal death . . .

"For us it was important to show, with our modest means, that the Father's plan and that of the son were not in perfect harmony, and that between these two plans the contact was only superficial, since on the essential points the son was in the dark about the Father's projects and the Father had no way of scenting out the projects of the son. For us it was important to stress this unavoidable disagreement between Yahweh and Jesus, a disagreement which at critical moments took on the colors of a life-and-death struggle where the two combatants risked their divine existences, one of them through the possibility of losing it, the other through failing to conquer it. For us it was important, finally, to bring out that if Jesus managed to achieve his personal goals, he owed this to his own human-divine resources, and not at all to paternal aid.

"Had the Most Illustrious Personage we called to the witness stand not preferred to repeat the banal words in catechism, He would have been able to untangle the whole complicated business we have just talked about. But given His reticence and the skimpy or worthless contribution theological science offers for clarifying the mystery of the true situation in the supernal regions, this arduous sacrilegious task fell to us. Let the excuse for this incursion into the higher spheres be the fact that it was not an exercize for its own sake and did not aim at uncovering secrets not meant for profane eyes or ears: it served simply and solely as a preliminary step to doing justice in the Judas Case.

"And it was Judas we were talking about," Dupin went on, raising his voice. "One thing now stands out with glaring obviousness: to wit, that the Lord, having no responsibility for Jesus' death, logically has none for Judas' betrayal either. And as from our earlier discussions there came out, among other things, that the responsibility for his crime cannot be unreservedly pinned on Judas, our attention turns again to the protagonist of the human-divine adventure, to Jesus Christ, whom, as long as we were able, and even to the detriment of his Father, the One True God, we tried to keep free of any shadow of suspicion."

"So there we are again," I exclaimed in a voice made faint by weariness. "Do you hold Jesus responsible for the betrayal of Judas Iscariot and, consequently, for the twelfth apostle's desperate end and damnation?"

"You cannot deny," replied Dupin, rising to his feet, "that in the course of the preliminary investigation new elements have appeared in whose light we are duty-bound to re-examine the position of the Son as well. But the matter is not so urgent that it cannot be put off until tomorrow. The sun stands at the horizon and admonishes us to retire for sleep . . ."

... and behind the infernal ones

THE EVENING OF THE NEXT DAY AGAIN FOUND US TOGETHER AND MY FRIEND
Dupin immediately got down to business.

"Our investigation in the celestial spheres," he began without
waiting for me to settle into my chair, "has given results that,
curious though they are, cannot be set aside if we wish to find our
bearings amidst the divine things and the human things in that
marvelous labyrinth, the evangelical moment of History. Shall
modesty or dread of Heaven's ire prevent us from declaring that the
New and Old Testaments take on another aspect, meaning, and
import once we have understood that divine nature is full of
shortcomings, and that the Lord Himself is subject to the laws of
History? Or from affirming that, instead of having before us a
single divine plan, we must clearly distinguish a plan of the
Father's and a plan of the Son's, concordant or parallel on many
points, but divergent and even opposed on points that are

essential? And, finally, how can we not take into account one of the most interesting results of our investigation into the celestial backstage, that is, that Jesus Christ, only Son of the One True God, was in his day one of those whom, for lack of a more felicitous term, we have dubbed the self-made gods of the Mediterranean and Near East?

"To call this a 'result' is rather presumptuous, for, in reality, we have done no more than underscore a fact which, having lost all its importance and relevance over the centuries, has been forgotten. Precisely as happens with our own homespun *nouveaux dieux*: their success once consolidated, after a certain while no one is interested in knowing how they got to where they are or from where they started out. To remember this in Jesus' case is neither degrading nor humiliating for him. It is strange only to his present-day faithful, who are born into Christianity, live with it and in it, breathe it the way they do the air, with the greatest naturalness. And it is right that it should be so. A religious person does not also have to be a theologian, philosopher, or historian; just the contrary, I should say. But there's why the immense majority of good Christians do not realize that religion, part of their daily experience and behavior, is the result of a long and troubled historical process; that the verities of faith, today condensed inside slender catechism booklets, were not always thus; and that if they could go backward in time, they would come to periods where they would be hard pressed to recognize even God Himself and His Son, so different would they appear from the image, imprecise yet customary, that is almost innate among today's believers. They do not know, all these good Christians for whom there is only One God, namely the True one, with His Son Jesus, he too being God, unique and true in the mysterious equality and oneness of the Most Holy Trinity; they do not know that these truths were not always so evident and that theologians such as Augustine, Tertullian, Origen and many others had to work like Trojans to support them and insure their triumph. A good Christian nowadays does not realize that not even two thousand years ago for millions of men there existed *true* gods, in the same way our God exists for us today, and that the great Fathers of the Church in combatting them had willy-nilly to allow them a certain reality. It required fierce battles to affirm the truth of Jesus' Word against that of the other gods! Have you any idea of the difficulties in trying to demonstrate a truth of this kind in the teeth of other identical truths? There were crucial moments in the history of dawning Christianity when it came near to being overthrown and annihilated. And if that had befallen? Would you care to exercize your imagination a little? In that case, we today, faithful worshippers of Attis or Mithra, would not easily remember, in the everyday practice of our religion, that at the beginning, two thousand years ago, our Church Fathers fought the (false) doctrines of a certain Jesus (of mythical existence) who (mendaciously) claimed that he was the son of a (false and mendacious) god. And perhaps these faithful worshippers, modeled by who knows what theology, would consider their god Attis diminished and offended by the fact that a poor private detective has the brass today to say that in the beginning He too was a self-made god, like so many others, among whom a certain Jesus . . .

"I know, this is only an essay in historico-religious fiction," Dupin exclaimed. "But I feel that it is advisable to take precautions so as to be protected against your usual right-thinking people, the mere thought of whom gives me goose flesh. With them you can't ever be too careful. To set them at ease, after Peter's Credo, after the hypothetical Credo of Judas and the historical Creed of Trent, I shall even go so far as to solemnly pronounce Dupin's Creed. I maintain this and only this: that since even to this day Jesus is born, dies and arises again every year as others did and would do, promising redemption, individual salvation, a life after this, justice, resurrection of bodies, as the others promised, thus replying to the spiritual demands then in fashion in those areas where, with the same aims, the others were operating—yea, I for my part maintain that Jesus was one among ever so many other self-made gods! Though bias shows in this part of my Creed, I believe that Jesus, among them all, was the only true God. Obviously, it is not for that reason he had to go down the exemplary road of his colleagues and predecessors: the only God, the true God he would have been and would have remained regardless; but if he had to do so, it is because he was a son of god, the Son of God, even though, or despite the fact that, he was the only true god. Don't expect me to be able to tell you why a son of god degraded to the human condition must follow the *iter* of the Passion, of cruel death and of Resurrection in order to attain divine status and, at the same time, to redeem humanity. That's how it is, and it's not I who invented it. Can you imagine some other way to save the human race than the one Jesus employed? I don't suppose you can. And get the idea out of your head that it's my fault if this mythological path that Jesus chose was taken before him by so many other false and mendacious gods!"

My friend Dupin seemed quite carried away and I stared at him in amazement, for this was not his wonted state.

"But did I say anything?" I ventured to put in. "Why are you getting after me?"

He continued to glower at me.

"At times you too behave like one of those right-thinking people," he grumbled and huffed. "I very well remember that shocked expression on your face last night. Whatever, I am going to have to turn my scrutinizing eye on Jesus in his role of self-made god, since the mythological *iter* foresees a well-determined place for Judas too: indeed it is Judas who prepares his violent death for him, without him Jesus would not have ended up on the cross: and when all is said and done, without Judas there would have been no Redemption. Now do you begin to glimpse the importance of the betrayal? And for whom it was important? Important that it occur? And that it be carried off to perfection? Everything is leading us back to the Son of God.

"However, one thing—fundamental, I'd say—distinguished the position of Jesus Christ from that of the other sons of gods, his exemplary predecessors: instead of living exclusively in myth, as did, for example, a Mithra, an Adonis or a Dionysus, he lived almost exclusively in History. His parents were not a Zeus or a Rhea but modest Jewish artisans, his deeds did not take place in limitless mythical atemporality, but rather in the limited space of three years, and his tortures were not witnessed by an Io, a Hercules, or a chorus of Oceanides, but rather by Roman soldiers and a frenzied populace. Facing his destiny, the mythical hero need not have any worry: he himself is the myth, he himself is the mathematical axiom, on the basis of which all that comes to pass will turn out true and consecrated. For the mythic hero there is no risk in allowing the forces of chance to act upon his destiny, since the events of his life will become the mythic paradigm. But it is quite another matter to realize a myth within the context of historical reality, in banal and necessarily hostile circumstances, in a world which is gradually losing the sense of myth and is being regulated by reason. In this case the hero cannot afford to let things take their course, rather he must be more than ever conscious of his own objective and act resolutely to make reality and chance fit the paradigm. Scrupulously distilled everyday reality becomes the instrument of his mythic action, and this precisely was the case with Jesus Christ.

"Handicapped vis-à-vis the other major Mediterranean gods because he had not lived exclusively in myth, Jesus had to secure the foundations for his cult through public teaching and by leaving on earth behind him the small but solid bridgehead made up of apostles. This aspect of the problem did not seem too bothersome to him; the dwindling number of his disciples during the critical period of his wanderings left him indifferent: he certainly knew that he could attend to the consolidation of his 'church' at a later time, after the fulfillment of the mystery. Indeed, it was after the resurrection that he created the foremost of his apostles, Paul. Nor must he have been worried about the resurrection itself. When a son of god dies according to the rules, he is bound to come back to life, owing to his divine nature. The crucial point of his problem, strange though it may seem, was to die his violent death at the right moment.

"In the life of ordinary persons death is an ever-present possibility, and only the calculation of probabilities affords us a certain assurance of reaching the natural limit of our earthly existence. But in an adventurous life, as Jesus' undoubtedly was, the statistical probability of a sudden and violent death steadily increases. Now, while Jesus divinely foresaw or consciously insisted upon a violent death, humanly he feared its unseasonable occurrence. We have alluded to the Master's prudent avoidance of a premature end: with that in mind he took every precaution and did not hesitate to resort to miracles. Death threatened him not only from the side of the authorities but from that of the populace which, exasperated by some of his declarations, could have made him undergo the same end reserved for so many prophets. Certain details of the Good Tidings not only shocked the representatives of the official religion but even at times appeared to be upsetting to his disciples, who, furthermore, after the Master's initial successes, deserted him en masse. Teachings and life-style contributed to earn him the nickname prophets so easily won for themselves—that *me-shuge* which meant something close to 'idiot' and could compel the indulgence of the assembly, but could also excite the crowd to the point of pelting the hapless 'man of God' with stones, and killing him on more than one occasion. Jesus, of course, did not aspire to such an end. When the situation became threatening, the Master, using his miracle-working faculties, faded away like a mist. John, not knowing how to account for these successful get-aways, supposes that the audience, almost in a hypnotic state, unwittingly promoted Jesus' inner plan: 'Therefore they sought to seize Him, but no one laid a hand on Him, for His hour *had not* yet come.' This explanation, short on logic, is nonetheless correct: Jesus continued to elude their grasp because he so willed; and he was caught when he wanted to be, because—and for no other reason— his hour *had* come.

"Keeping out of the way of an unlooked-for death was the

simplest aspect of the problem, and for that it sufficed to proceed with a certain care and to bring one's divine or miraculous qualities into play. Much harder was to prepare a death that was correct from the historical standpoint, a death that was to take place at the propitious moment, that is, during the feast of Passover and at just about the mystical age of thirty-three, a violent death following a trap set by the powers of darkness. It is difficult to elude death; yet—as is well known—death also eludes him who seeks it. It is obviously easier to avoid an ordinary death than to die a death conditioned by so many circumstances and specifications: it must be prepared with circumspection, and not left to the whims of chance. And we know from the Gospels how this subject preoccupied Jesus.

"We know now, thanks to our inquiries behind the celestial scenes, that the source of Jesus' uneasiness must have been a vague feeling—I would dare call it the unconscious certainty—that he was not always nor perfectly in agreement with the Father, and specifically on the point which for him mattered most. Deep down he is always afraid of overstepping the bounds of paternal patience, and that is why when he sees a prophecy become reality he is thrilled in his heart and his self-confidence takes a giant step forward. Only towards the end of his life, almost reassured by the proximity of his mystery-death, does he venture to look upon himself as equal to and identical with the Father, as the one without whom nothing is accomplished, neither on God's behalf nor on men's. Up until that period of reinforced self-confidence, which will turn into certainty only on the Cross, he is ceaselessly oppressed by the anguish of being enslaved to the the paternal will. How often had Yahweh left His prophets to take care of themselves, just when they needed the backing of a sign!

"One easily understands how, in such a situation, Jesus could not just let things go their own way, but had to come forward and actively lead them to their proper destination. We do not believe that Jesus would have been less successful in proving himself to be the Son of God had he, on the occasion of his triumphant entry into Jerusalem, ridden the she-ass herself instead of her foal. But, as John explicitly states, he tried to adhere scrupulously even to those most minute details which were destined to confirm his divinity in the eyes of others. How then could he not meticulously prepare the essential details that were to prove to himself that he was not laboring under a delusion?

"Only a Monophysite extremist could compare Jesus' life to a simple mathematical equation, where you arrive at a satisfactory solution once the unknowns contained in the prophecies have been replaced by facts and events carefully chosen from everyday reality. Obviously, for a god one hundred per cent pure everything is easy! But Monophysitism does not stand up and the Gospels testify that among the unknowns of this equation some truly did not take to any kind of replacement by real quantities.

"Indeed, often enough it happened that prophecies *were loath* to come about, that reality was in no hurry to meet them halfway; sometimes reality seemed to differ from what was foreseen, sometimes to be the exact contrary. The prophets' prophesying had been inspired by God, therefore could not be mistaken: its eventual non-fulfillment would have been an error on the part of reality!

"There existed two irrreproachable ways of getting out of such embarrassing cases: either adapt the prophecy to reality, or, vice versa, adapt reality to the prophecy. In the first instance, it was necessary to *interpret* the prophetic predictions in such a way that they should appear to fit in even with those facts that were not absolutely pertinent. And this is standard procedure. All divinations, of course, have to be interpreted if you want them to adhere to reality: sometimes by taking them literally, sometimes, conversely, by addressing only their spirit.

"When however the difficulties arise from reality, the only solution is to make reality adhere to the prophecy, whether by *modifying* it if it proves rebellious or inelastic, whether by simply *creating* it if it refuses to come forth on its own.

"I am not being one bit ironic about the Old Testament prophecies and above all about Jesus' attitude towards them. For him, who regarded prophecies as divine truths, and was convinced that 'what is' must concord perfectly with 'what *must* be,' to make arrangements was neither sleight-of-hand nor sophistry but, at the most, an act of delicacy toward the Father. To give a little nudge to the unfolding of events foreseen *ab æterno* was like giving the Lord a helping hand.

"Interpreting prophetic phrases is far easier than altering a given concrete reality, but we know that Jesus never hesitated to confront obstacles of all kinds in order to demonstrate the validity of whatever prophecy. The most patent example of creating a totally absent reality in order to make a prophecy come true is the already mentioned episode of the she-ass's foal. Obviously, no she-ass's foal would ever have come into Jesus' possession, even if it had been so written a thousand times over in the prophecies. But, without being fazed in the last, Jesus sent two of his disciples to a nearby town and borrowed the prophesied animal. And in this way, against all anticipation, he entered Jerusalem in the manner forecast by the prophecies.

"Reality, by its nature somewhat rigid and indifferent to human desires, did not this time anticipate Jesus' intentions, who wanted it to be such as it had been forecast. This one example among many others would be enough to prove that Jesus took an active part in his drama. True, some of the unknowns in his equation were automatically replaced by real factors, but others required impromptu adaptations, as is shown by the episode just mentioned.

"The most critical unknown in Jesus' divine-human equation must nevertheless have been the figure of the betrayer—this latter, obviously enough, was not as docile a reality as the indifferent beast which, once located and identified, without objection performed what was expected of it: it let itself be saddled, mounted, and, with Jesus on its back, it headed down the road to Jerusalem as naturally as you please, just as if this were a routine transport of freight and not an event of universal significance, foretold, moreover, since the earliest times. We may be sure that Judas Iscariot did not set off on the road to betrayal with the same naturalness and the same docility as the she-ass's foal set off for Jerusalem. Expressed in other terms, the unknown was a human being, not only illuminated by free will but subject to the abrupt and startling changes of the human psyche which could make it into a qualitatively different *quantum*, therefore unfitted for mathematical operations. Despite all the certainty he was assured of by his divine prescience, in Jesus there must still have remained a good deal of uneasiness and anxious curiosity about the future developments of this unknown in his divine-human equation. The question here was to see whether and how 'a vessel of innocence' would turn into a 'vessel of iniquity.' For what if Judas persisted in his state of innocence?

"To be sure, even with regard to the other apostles, Jesus had to allow for the unknowns in human reality, but there the risk was negligible. All that was needed was that they be equal to the demands of the apostolate during his earthly life; after that, they would be the beneficiaries of divine favors and the gifts of the Holy Ghost. But it was impossible, for this wicked deed, to provide any such celestial reinforcement to Judas, not only because of the profound contradiction but also because Jesus himself didn't dispose of much: during his lifetime he was not and could not be a dispenser of divine favors.

"On the other hand, Judas' task had such importance in his divine-human career that Christ could not entrust its outcome to pure chance. In his relations with Judas, Jesus must more than ever have experienced the resistance put up by Reality to the ambitions and aspirations of the Spirit, a resistance all the more complex for it being a matter here of a human will opposed to interests of a higher order, but sustained by psychological laws of a natural order. All things considered, a Judas who persisted in his state of innocence and his good intentions would have been entirely logical. Since things took the turn they did, we must posit the coercive intervention of an outside force that exerted a deforming effect on his character. This mysterious force has not been identified up until now, but—given the entity of the resistance it had to combat—it seems logical to us that it was of a supernatural order.

"Last night's conversation," and Dupin leveled his forefinger at me, "led us by other paths to suppose that Jesus was not altogether a stranger to the damnation of his twelfth apostle. I believe that you will now feel even more shaken by this suspicion and that your horror will grow as you see the Savior's direct responsibility take shape before your eyes. Let me hasten to assure you, however, that this so dreadful supposition will completely vanish as our untiring investigation digs deeper.

"Yes, among all the realities Jesus had to 'adjust' so that they meet the demands of the prophecies and of his own foresight, the hardest nut to crack must have been the Judas reality. This reality must have been thoroughly worked over in order to make it consonant with Judas' unnatural task. The great difficulty did not have to do with the final outcome: this was as good as in the bank, guaranteed whether by foresight or by the mythological schema of the mystery of the sons of god, and from the standpoint of the final outcome any intervention or direct action on Jesus' part must be considered as an *adiaphoron*, an act that cannot be judged morally. The true difficulty—in which the Master's moral responsibility becomes an issue, and the dreadful suspicion strengthened— consists rather in the fact that Jesus had actively to intervene in order to turn this reality, at first indifferent and passive, then more and more reticent and unwilling, into a reality conformable to higher, metaphysical exigencies. Hewing a path out of the rock to get across the mountain is not a human act one can condemn. But to transform, to deform a human being for one's own purposes, bringing down upon him eternal damnation and the contempt of posterity as well—this is certainly something else again. Jesus, source and example of all morality, would be definitively compromised had we to resign ourselves to so dreadful an idea.

"Jesus' active collaboration in the betrayal perpetrated at his expense by Judas is, indeed, the most highly charged and the most delicate problem in the whole of Christology: having to acknowledge it does not render it any the less incredible or unpleasant. But we propose to get the better of this execrable problem; and just as we dared refute the gratuitous charges brought against Judas, we shall take even greater pleasure in giving short shrift to any supposition or conjecture that would compromise the moral integrity of Jesus. Just as we have no right to introduce any gratuitous novelistic element at all into the character of the traitor or into his relations with the Master, so we do not have the right, and even less the desire, to attribute to Jesus characteristics and attitudes incompatible with his historical figure and with the image handed down to us by two-thousand-year-old tradition. Of course, everything would be taken care of were we to allow that Jesus, in one way or another, forced Judas to betray him! But no, we rule out any form of constraint on the Master's part, from the little stratagem to diplomacy in the grand style, that would have enabled him to trap the innocent one; and we also decidedly rule out Jesus revealing his own objectives to him with the purpose of inducing him to sacrifice himself for him.

"Such complicity between Jesus and Judas, sensed by a certain order of writers and thinkers, not only verges on the gratuitous, on the novelistic, but is downright absurd if not farcical. Complicity presupposes common interests and a common perspective. Well, only Jesus had an interest in being captured, and only Jesus saw the final results of his sacrifice. What advantage could Judas have expected from lending himself to a game of this sort? None, obviously. He could, possibly, lend himself to it out of innocence or naïveté, but it is precisely this arrangement that we must at all costs exclude: Jesus could let an innocent bring about his death, but he could not drive him to damnation: at most he might not stand in the way of a disciple becoming unworthy of him, but he must not become unworthy of himself! The complicity theory presumes that Jesus advised the twelfth apostle of his aspirations. An appeal by Jesus to the goodheartedness of the most infamous of human beings smacks too much of the fictional and, basically, as an idea in itself, is rather grotesque. Judas in that case would no longer have been the most infamous of human beings, but, on the contrary, the greatest and most generous in all of Creation; furthermore, Jesus, morality incarnate, would never have been able to accept the sacrifice of a magnanimous being, compared to which his own sacrifice would have seemed like child's play. Jesus' personality also excludes the romantic fantasy according to which Judas would have sacrificed himself in a surge of boundless love for his Master. This absurd hypothesis would spare us the search for the advantage accruing to Judas: generous impulse and blind love sometimes operate at a capital loss.

"But the proponents of this poetic theory of a sentimental drama altogether lose sight of the very essence of the work of betrayal. In fact, within the mythologico-mystery framework, the program followed by candidates for divine existence calls for their undoing by the power of Evil. A strange incarnation of Evil—a Judas overflowing love and kindness! And stranger yet a Jesus who, with the complicity of his affectionate Judas, made the world's most generous man pass for the wickedest, just to take in posterity! Anyone accustomed to thinking in terms of myth must underscore that Jesus was not improvising a theater piece to convince his contemporaries and posterity: he followed the path of his tragic destiny in order to convince himself and to vanquish his Father. And it is from this angle that we must consider his relations with Judas, who before being an apostle, before being a man, in his eyes had to appear to be the symbol of Evil."

"Forgive me for interrupting, my dear friend," I stopped him at this point. "It may be that your ideas are too far over my head, though I am still struggling to follow you. You have persuaded me that on the plane of historical reality Judas' betrayal was a useless act, superfluous, as you called it; that Jesus himself and the divine Father too could have done without it. You have demonstrated that in performing his infamous gesture, of scant or of no importance, the betrayer had to overcome uncommon difficulties to induce the high priests to move, and that, to boot, he didn't even have a

personal motive. A short while ago you described Jesus' preoccupations and his efforts to make the unwilling man he had chosen
fit for the part which, in the end, had little or no importance for
anyone. Would you mind telling me clearly, why then so much of
a fuss over nothing?"

"There's no harm in clarifying things from time to time,"
Dupin replied grandly. "I'm ready to admit that Judas' betrayal
did little to affect the development of events, and am even ready to
go one better and state that it is a jarring detail in Jesus' history,
with something artificial about it. But since for Jesus himself it
meant so much, I obviously cannot deny its importance; I ought
even, on the contrary, to attribute enormous importance to it.
From many angles, this famous betrayal was indeed of only slight
consequence, even in Jesus' plans, and now I shall enumerate for
you all the reasons why he did not need to have a betrayer.

"Surely not in order to found Christianity—that's certain.
Nowhere is it said that the founder of a religion has to be betrayed
by anybody at all, and I believe that, from the most ancient
religions down to the latest ones, you'll not find another example
of this. Furthermore, I see nothing that suggests that the sacrifice
on Golgotha would not have had the same value from the Father's
standpoint, or that it would not have entailed the redemption of
mankind in the same way. If we go by the teachings of the Church,
all the good we reaped from the sacrifice of Jesus Christ would have
come to us even without the betrayal, which was no doubt an
infamous gesture, but whose importance consisted only in handing
the Redeemer over to the authorities. It seems to me that in the
Church's view Jesus Christ would have redeemed mankind even if
it had been on their own initiative and without the intervention of
a betrayer that the Jews had arrested him and the Romans killed
him. On this chapter let me remind you that the Creed of Trent,
which immortalizes the name of Pontius Pilate, makes no mention
of Judas Iscariot and does not enjoin us to believe in the betrayal
as a condition for the Passion, the Descent into Hell, the
Resurrection, and the Ascent into Heaven! And if it does not

oblige us to do so, you may be sure that it does not see it as necessary or important that we do so. And thereby it places itself profoundly at odds with Jesus himself, who was of a different opinion and had gone to great lengths to make certain of his betrayer and the perfect unfolding of the work of betrayal.

"Jesus felt very particular about this, and that lone fact justifies Judas' presence in Sacred History and merits more attention than do the hypotheses on the real importance of the betrayal as an indispensable contribution to the fulfillment of the Redeemer's earthly destiny. But why did Jesus so want to be betrayed by Judas? Which of his objectives could he not have attained without the man's perfidious act? Before being put to death by Roman law, what need had he to get himself done in by his twelfth apostle— having to surmount all kinds of psychological and material obstacles to accomplish this in a manner that, in the terms of the story, is so imprecise as to become almost improbable? For his earthly death, what reason had Jesus to demand the useless, evanescent, almost symbolic intervention of Judas, which after-wards made such an impression on the imagination of posterity? I believe, *cher ami*, that with these questions we have reached the heart of the problem and that we are about to penetrate to the essence of the work of betrayal.

"For you the problem's solution should be within reach and not very surprising. You should already have understood that Jesus, even if he had been able to attain most of his goals without the help of Judas, to attain one of those goals, the supreme and fundamental one, he absolutely needed Judas' existence and assistance. Precisely that which his heart was most set on, the fulfillment of the mystery of the sons of god, would not have been accomplished without the collaboration of Judas, the figure of whom, even for the most simple believer, takes on a much broader significance than that of a faithless apostle and represents the very incarnation, the personi-fication of Evil itself. And, indeed, in the earthly destinies of those who beset by a thousand miseries and dangers marched toward the various Olympuses, it is a role of capital importance that is reserved for the destructive and annihilating force of the powers of darkness. In the *agraphos* rule of the *iter* it is expressly stipulated that in order to ascend to godly rank, the aspirant to celestial existence must be smitten down by Evil, whether it go by the name of Set, Mot, Jotunn, Maenads or Boars. Jesus could not afford not to hold rigorously to the prescribed route. He too must have his assassin . . ."

"His assassin? This is where your seductive theory wavers," I rejoined. "Judas did not kill Jesus, he simply betrayed him, having almost to be forced, and without it serving any useful purpose, as you have pointed out several times."

"What you see here is more of the disagreeable interference between History and Myth," Dupin answered calmly, "or else of the unavoidable compromise Myth had to strike with History. Don't forget that historical facts are what they are, Jesus was put to death by Roman executioners in accordance with the laws of Roman justice. But Myth also has its exigencies. Do you believe that people, accustomed to conceiving of certain events only in mythological terms, would have divinified a man condemned to crucifixion by the Roman political authority, at the request of Jewish religious authorities, when aspirant gods in neighboring regions got themselves killed by divinities, or at least by mythological beings? The laws of the *iter* for becoming god have nothing to do with those of historical reality, and they need only the consecration of Myth. Myth, in its turn, required that the violent and annihilating action of Evil put an end to the new god's earthly destinies. It had to be this mythological Evil in person that caused the death of the Son of God, and not ephemeral earthly powers, transitory religious and civil authorities, insignificant Jews and Romans! For the sake of mythological authenticity, and solely for its sake, next to Jesus there had to be the historically evanescent and unsubstantial figure of Judas! Judas ought personally to have killed him, that's true, but it is just as true that History compelled him to kill the new god through intermediaries.

"Thus, through History's fault, Judas, instead of becoming a

cruel, brutal, blind destructive force that kills, rends, hacks to
pieces and devours, was demoted to the rank of infamous betrayer.
It would be asking too much of me were you to try to get me to
tell you what would have happened if Judas, as a good mythological
character, had killed the divine Master with his own hands. Far
from preventing, that would rather have guaranteed the Passion,
the Descent into Hell, the Resurrection, and the Ascension, but I
don't know whether Christianity would have lasted beyond its first
centuries of existence: it might very well have known the same end
as the other religions of its day and in its area, its competitors, in
which the aspirant gods had been killed *only* by mythical beings.
I who reproach the fathers at the Council of Trent for not having
designated in Judas the *conditio sine qua non* of the work of
Redemption, should perhaps praise them for perspicacious realism
in mentioning Pontius Pilate: the survival and triumph of Christianity owes more to History than to Myth. But let us not forget
that Jesus would not be part of the Holy Trinity without the
mythological intervention of Judas Iscariot.

"Instead of this 'anti-historic' would-be objection of yours, you
might ask me a more pertinent question: that is, why was it
betrayal that mythic murder was replaced by, and why did this
substitute satisfy the demands of Myth just as well? My answer
would be that the mythological imagination couldn't find anything
better. Actually, the betrayal directly provokes what it replaces,
the murder, and *grosso modo* amounts to the same thing. In other
myths as well the murder is often preceded by falsehoods, traps,
deception. But I don't think we need to go far outside Jewish
tradition. Just take that predecessor of Jesus, the Master of Justice
in the Dead Sea Scrolls, who was also captured and put to death
following the about-face of a former companion of his. I could tell
you further that the sacred texts and the great prophets, whence
Jesus drew his quotations to confirm the authenticity of his own
mission, never alluded, even in the vaguest and most obscure
manner, to the possibility that the Messiah be killed by one of his
faithful. Ah! no prophet, even the most inspired, would ever have

had imagination enough to foresee a genuine Son of God appearing
on the chosen people's horizon! Jesus, burrowing in the ancient
texts, was unable to find anything more than a confused allusion to
some betrayer . . . But perhaps—and I don't claim I'm right—
betrayal more nearly corresponded to the character of supreme Evil,
such as the Jews had imagined it, than did brute violence. For the
worst enemy of God and man, the Satan of the Old Testament and
the legends, the cunning serpent of the original sin, the subtle
theologian of Jesus' temptation, scheming betrayal probably
seemed a more suitable instrument than a dagger in hand. Perhaps
the *forma mentis* of the Jewish people, source of myths, would have
preferred betrayal to murder even if historical reality had not
imposed it . . ."

I declared myself satisfied with my friend's explanations. "So
according to you," I concluded, "the figure of Judas at Jesus' side
is more mythological than historical."

"Historically vague, evanescent, elusive and almost superfluous," Dupin acquiesced, "but mythologically indispensable."

"Another question, if I may! Could you explain how posterity,
but above all Jesus himself, managed to find analogies between
that wretched human being, little aware and perhaps innocent,
and the terrible destructive force of mythic Evil?"

"Because Judas was that Evil, *cher ami,* that's what he was!
Morphological analogies with the adventures of other gods would
be enough to convince me that, in the history-myth of Jesus
Christ, Judas was not only the betrayer and the most infamous of
men, and the incarnation or the symbol of Evil, but he was plainly
and simply identical with Evil, he was Evil itself. What mythological analogies teach us is that the powers hostile to new gods are
in the same class with them, not only as regards strength but also
as regards divine origins: they themselves are deities, on the same
grounds as their triumphant victim. Continuing on the plane of
Myth, we could *a priori* attribute a divine essence to the wretched
betrayer, an essence and origin that do not seem to show through
the historical outer layer that covered his figure.

"But is it after all really so true that this historical 'outer layer' is impenetrable and that on the other side of it the higher reality of Myth does not show through? Used as you are to my theological disquisitions, you are perhaps readying yourself, dear friend, for further wonderful performances. But this time your thirst for fireworks shall be disappointed. Instead I don the gown of the dullest teacher of history and drily quote an exceedingly reliable and well informed source. That Judas was Satan himself is no longer a hypothesis advanced by me on the strength of mythological analogies, but rather the assertion of Jesus Christ himself. 'And one of you is Satan'—are they not the words of the divine Master? What has remained an enigma for scholars over twenty centuries was for Christ something so obvious that he declared it *expressis verbis*, unhesitatingly; and we, for our part, express deepest astonishment before the fact that such a declaration by Jesus was never taken seriously enough and all its importance for an understanding of the complicated affair we are dealing with never recognized. Our astonishment but grows when we consider that the foregoing declaration is the Master's only direct reference to the betrayer. And if we remind ourselves of the fact that not one of the evangelists has handed down to us any information about Judas' person, and that all the other data concerning him are uncertain or refutable or susceptible of various interpretations, our astonishment reaches its peak. Why is it that for two thousand years scholars have not deigned to notice the one piece of evidence coming from an undisputed and indisputable source? How is it that so many illustrious minds abstained from seriously examining these particular words of the Master which, with their absolute lack of ambiguity, are alone able to shed light on his relations with Judas and explain the betrayal's role in his divine-human drama?"

Dupin stared at me for some time with the look of an accuser, then he continued, gripped by strong feelings.

"Without bothering to enumerate the possible reasons for this incomprehensible negligence, which certainly include the rationalists' dislike for the figure of Satan and theologians' unfamiliarity with his machinations, let us look at the attitude of the theological manuals toward this declaration. To our amazement, Jesus' perfectly straightforward words do not catch the attention of the theologians, who treat them as though they had been uttered only in a figurative sense. And this seems so natural to them, that to not one of them has it occurred that they might be taken literally. The opposite, I would never dream of taking them in a figurative sense, something I have never permitted myself to do with anything the divine Master said. The theologians would very rightly spit fire and flame if someone thought to interpret figuratively other of Jesus' statements. Those in the figurative camp might maintain, for example, that Jesus was the Son of God and identical with the Father only on a symbolic plane, while in reality he wasn't any more than a man of genius. These heretics also quote from Jesus' statements, and it would be difficult to persuade them to attribute a more real content to the term 'Son of God' than to that of 'Satan.' For us who on the basis of his declarations truly consider Jesus as the Son of God, it is altogether obvious that the term 'Satan' has to be understood in the strict sense of the word.

"The first indirect proof of our thesis is almost as surprising as our 'discovery.' Indeed, only if Judas was Satan can we exculpate Jesus for his ambiguous, not to say immoral behavior toward the twelfth apostle. To be more exact, in this case alone is there no need to exculpate Jesus, for his attitude ceases to be immoral: it is always fine and good, always logical at least, for a god to vanquish, destroy, crush the representative of Evil, be it by the use of trickery. Thanks to our discovery the most delicate problem in all of Christology is finally overcome, a problem that until now Christology did not even dare to face with the necessary frankness, preferring to keep still about it or tiptoe around it. Overcome in addition is the need, felt by every theologian when he sees himself in a corner, to 'exonerate' Jesus with gratuitous affirmations, such as, for example, the one according to which the Master, out of the infinite goodness of his heart, supposedly tried to 'warn' the wicked apostle and prevent him from committing

the fatal act. Jesus' alleged warnings can thus remain just what
they are: obscure threats addressed to the future betrayer. No one
with any common sense can imagine that Jesus would throw a
monkey wrench into the works of destiny by hindering Satan in
the accomplishment of his functions, for himself so important.
Our 'discovery' confirms our thesis on Jesus' active participation
in his own betrayal, but now with the risk removed of
compromising his morality. To Satan, in Jesus' eyes, not the
slightest consideration was due. Those who wish may now go
ahead and imagine a Machiavellian and jesuitical Jesus: a Jesus
able to use Judas—that is, Satan—as a mere instrument for
accomplishing the mystery of the sons of god. The Devil, of
course, does not *deserve* any consideration.

"Judas was Satan—there you have the authentic truth from
Jesus' lips, the truth which at once seemed so startling and
unbelievable that none of the apostles appreciated its seriousness.
Only John among the four evangelists reports Jesus' words, but he
too fails to allow them their true significance, for later on, to find
a motive for Judas' betrayal, he ventures the hypothesis—put
forward also by Luke—that Satan had *entered* into the hapless
twelfth apostle. Surely, Satan could not enter into Judas if the
latter was Satan himself. But for the apostles, who were acquainted
with Satan through hearsay, it was absurd to imagine him in
flesh and blood and, what's more, as a colleague. And the scholars,
in so many ways heirs to the apostles' obtuseness, have made
the same mistake: their ears have remained deaf to the Master's
perfectly explicit words, only because, acknowledging them, they
would have been forced to understand them also! Nevertheless, we
freely grant that acknowledgment of this reality would have
hampered rather than helped them in the pursuit of their
theological investigations. True enough, minds preoccupied with
hair-splittings and cavils have not much worried about the
enigmas surrounding the figure of the betrayer and his betrayal;
but a Satan incarnate face to face with and alongside the incarnation
of God might have seemed too awkward a *novum* to be taken

seriously into consideration: they would have run the risk of having to revise theology from top to bottom!

"The difficulties that may result for theologians because of our 'discovery' in no way lessen its validity or the extent of its implications: thanks to it, we have found not only the one way to 'exculpate' Jesus for his ambiguous behavior toward his twelfth apostle, but at the same time also the only path by which to approach this character Judas, to come to know him, understand him, make him in some way tangible. We have, in fact, but to investigate Satan . . ."

Dupin produced his resounding laugh.

"Yes, *cher ami,* strange to say, we have far more abundant and better documented information on the Devil than on the betrayer of Jesus Christ. However, you must not suppose that our task will be easy. For, just as strange to say, although more is known about the Devil than about Judas, we do not know the truly essential things about him either. Thanks to various mythologies, to sacred texts, to pious legends and, perhaps, to everyday experience too, we possess an enormous amount of data concerning the infernal powers in general and Satan in particular, but to make you understand how insufficient this abundance is, let me suggest to you how confused, contradictory and inconsistent our knowledge about God would be if we knew Him only through the Bible, popular traditions, and His presumed interventions in our everyday life. I should note that if the things we know about God are more precise, it is owing to a special science, theology. Well, even if a rich literature has concerned itself with him, the Devil has not been honored with a particular science that can match theology for seriousness and profundity. And I find this curious. As though the meaning of Evil was so obvious and unambiguous in relation to supreme Good! Yet this special science alone will be able to make clear what role Evil played in the Creation and in the destinies of gods and men. Until such a new autonomous and organic science sees the light of day, all the elements on the Devil that we dispose of will be mere tesserae for a mosaic, scattered about hither and yon, and whenever we speak of him we shall have to confine ourselves to the vague and the general.

"Although feeling most keenly the want of this appropriate science, which I could very well call *satanology*, I cannot create it *hic et nunc* and *ex nihilo*. I fear indeed that I have already taken the first steps upon the *terra incognita* of this inexistent science— brashly exceeding the bounds of a private investigation, even though impelled by it—when I showed that the function Judas performed in Jesus' behalf was identical to the brutal and destructive work that conduced to the death and therefore, indirectly, to the resurrection of other young gods in the Mediterranean zone and Near East. But as for what in its essence this mythic Evil may be, that it play this role in the destinies of new gods, it is not for me to say. I believe that for our purposes we may be content with the familiar old generalities, and along with them refer to some terrible dark force, it too of a divine nature, but belonging to a fallen world vanquished by the reigning gods, for future gods an ominous world bristling with dangers. This obscure force, called diabolical, titanic, infernal, identified with destructive and deadly elements, with winter, with night, with the *tenebrae tenebrarum*, and located in awful places, such as the underworld and hell, is always represented by divine figures, by infernal gods and demi-gods who, despite their apparent triumph, are doomed to a fatal defeat.

"*Mutatis mutandis*, this schema also fits Judas. Earlier on we alluded, in passing, to the possibility that certain merely formal and even non-essential differences, which distinguish him from the deities of Evil belonging to neighboring peoples, may be imputed to historical reality, to the traditions and the *forma mentis* of the prevailing ethnic and cultural environment, for which Evil personified itself in the figure of Satan.

"Consequently it would seem logical that, in our wish to know more about Judas, we try to investigate Evil within the framework of Jewish mythology, but, alas, up until now the Jewish Satan has not been the object of an in-depth examination conducted with up-to-date methods of study; and so, rather than risk committing inaccuracies, about him as well we must repeat the things that are generally known, from his legendary cooperation in the work of Creation to the Revolt of the Angels led by him; from the role he played in the original sin, to his descent upon earth and his marriages to the daughters of men; from his limitless power in the underworld realms, to the power he exercizes over the lives of men in his capacity as Prince of that world. We might repeat that his name means Adversary or Opponent, and that the name Phosphoros, or Lucifer, perfectly befits him, and that he is, according to Genesis, 'one of the divine.'

"As you see, Judas has no apparent connection with the Jewish Satan, and should you still have any doubts on the subject I shall dissipate them by reminding you that the feature which distinguishes Satan among all the powers of Evil is that of leading men into temptation. The Devil of the Jews, and ours as well, is the tempter by definition! This fact is both a decisive argument against identifying Judas with the Jewish Satan, and an argument important enough for me to continue to demand that science of satanology. It serves me as an occasion for showing you the extent to which vagueness characterizes our talk about the Devil, and how we accept certain clichés as proven truths merely because they have been repeated for hundreds and thousands of years.

"According to a traditional belief, the Devil is man's number one enemy, he leads us into temptation and does his best to bring about our downfall. But for me, new in these studies and coming to them with fresh eyes, this belief does not appear to have any basis at all and I would easily arrive at diametrically different findings. Satanology will have the last word, of course. But so long as it does not declare, as it perhaps might, that the Devil is a totally indifferent and passive entity, and that he has nothing against anybody—something I intuitively wouldn't rule out—, it seems more logical to me that his grudge is against God rather than us, who simply serve him as a battlefield: even when he harms man, this is not his primary purpose, but rather the secondary, almost accidental consequence of his eagerness to thwart the Lord. When he apparently turns himself inside out to wreck things for man, he is actually only trying to make the divine scheme go awry. In the last analysis, so-called 'temptations' can be traced back to those aims of his: through trouble brought to human persons he seeks to defeat the order established by God.

"To entrap man he has recourse to the most various means, and only exceptionally does he employ what would seem to be his apanage, that is, outright and ordinary evil, as in the case of Job, an inveterate and unshakeable defender, whatever the evidence, of the goodness of the divine order. Satan prefers to suggest to man extraordinary ideas and deeds, which become so many unforeseen and surprising moves in his great chess game with the Lord. And before human eyes he dangles seductive rewards and gifts, unfailing in their effect, always producing the anticipated response in the souls of the tempted. His snares, always set at the right moment, are in fact cut to measure. And of course: to him man readily displays his own vulnerabilities . . .

"This seems to me the right moment to say a few words about the temptations of Jesus. No other example more clearly illustrates the Devil's method and the objectives of his game. Oddly, Christology devotes little attention to this episode and does not register the gravity of the moment, when the Master's entire mission was endangered: at that moment Jesus could complete the first stage in the direction of his chosen goals, or he could *a limine* bungle everything, our redemption, his own glorious ascent to the celestial throne—and, what Satan wanted most, compromise the Father's intentions. The tempter set his three traps shrewdly, and with an insider's knowledge of the case.

"Think a moment of the insinuating form he gives to his apostrophe: 'If thou art the Son of God . . .' Can you imagine a more formidable temptation for someone who, certainly, is convinced in his soul that he is the Son of God, but who at the same time knows how much it is going to take before he has proven it to himself beyond all possible doubt. And now, just as he is about to start on his long and dolorous journey, here is the opportunity to produce the irrefutable proofs regarding the point he cares about most! What wouldn't he do for that certainty? After forty days of fasting and physically exhausted, the first temptation is enormous, even humanly so: possibly to change a stone into a bit of bread and, at this difficult juncture, to eat one's fill, could seem to Jesus the most wonderful of all dreams. But he realized that to utilize his divine nature to compensate the weakness of his human nature would have signified the subordinating of the one to the other, something that must never occur. Also, this would have been his first miracle: well, being without experience in regard to prodigies, what guarantee would he have had that his was not the ordinary jugglery of any ordinary magician, assisted, on top of it all, by the Devil? And Jesus had the strength to decline this dubious proof that would not have proven anything.

"Going on to the second temptation, we encounter a slight difficulty: we do not actually know the chronological order of the last two temptations, and we are free to accept Matthew's version or Luke's. I can think of reasons for preferring either one, and could justify my choice in both cases. But in as much as the question has no importance for us, let's follow Matthew, if only because Satan again opens his speech with the mightily seductive 'If thou art the Son of God . . .'

"This temptation was even more overpowering. By yielding to it Jesus could find out for sure whether he was or was not the Son of God. To cast himself from the pinnacle of the Temple and to have angels prevent his fall would be an irrefutable proof of his divine status. Of course, everything could go wrong: the angels might not appear and he might wind up smashed on the pavement. This too would be a decisive proof, but in the opposite direction: proof that he had been deluded about himself. It was obviously not fear of death or of disappointment which held him back; it was, to the contrary, fear of certainty! The Father, yes, would have saved him from corporal death, and for that matter he might even have saved himself through his own divine powers; but a premature epiphany deprived sons of god, who were not born upon an Olympus, of the possibility of ascending to it, for only a god subject to human nature, and not a manifestly divine god, could conquer the Kingdom of Heaven and presume to impose his will there. During this critical moment Jesus personally experienced the well-known dilemma arising from the heresy of the *iota*, seriously deliberating whether it were better to risk showing himself to be *homoiousios* (of like essence) to the Father, or to keep patient until the moment when he would reveal himself to be *homoousios* (of the same essence).

"In his third temptation (or the second for the evangelist Luke) Satan does not make an issue of Jesus' divinity: he simply offers him the kingdom of this world, the realization of the dream of the Messiah and of the Jewish nation. Had Jesus yielded to this temptation, he would have best responded to the expectations of his people. We, from today's perspective, see no chance for a Messianic venture succeeding at that moment in history, but we do not know how Jesus himself judged the situation in its concrete political reality. The mere fact that he was tempted by the idea in itself shows that he had sufficient reason to take such a mission into consideration. Perhaps, to succeed in it, he needed but remain the good and obedient Son of the Father, to be God's condottiere and lieutenant on this earth. Perhaps, this may actually have seemed to him the easier path, compared to that other which at this point he had already decided to follow. But the apparent oneness of the presumed divine intentions and Satan's desires aroused his suspicions. To fulfill the Father's wishes and what an entire people was waiting for, would this amount to worshipping the Devil? Oh yes, worshipping Satan often consists in forsaking the 'true' path, arduous and risky, and opting for the easier solution: to run away from destiny—this is, sometimes, the very greatest temptation for the chosen! And that was when Jesus made his definitive choice: he renounced once and for all becoming the Messiah in the current meaning of the word, and struck out resolutely along the hazardous and painful path that all the sons of Mediterranean gods had to travel. Satan no longer had any power over him . . .

"At least the Satan of Jewish tradition no longer had any. Jesus, through his choice, entered another order, where Evil took on a different aspect too. Rendered incompetent in the matter, the Jewish Satan was obliged to yield to one of his near relatives, to one of those dark powers, horrible and brutish, which employ more drastic methods than his, heaping obstacle after obstacle in the path of the candidate god and, if that does not suffice, eliminating him physically, murdering him, tearing him apart, cutting him into pieces, nailing him to the cross.

"A Devil of this kind was not compatible with the idea of the one omnipotent God of the chosen people, although Evil conceived of in this way was not completely outside their ken in that age so rich in contacts with the spiritual, religious and philosophical currents in neighboring civilizations. Those who in spite of everything managed to accept such a Son of God also ended up getting used to such a Devil. Everything fitted together perfectly.

"Well, dear friend," said Dupin, shrugging his shoulders, "our timid venture upon the terrain of the satanology to come has indeed led us somewhere, in as much as we've been able to establish that Judas physically embodied the annihilating Evil of Mediterranean and Near Eastern mythologies, whereas he did not have much in common with the traditional Devil of his own environment, as would have seemed natural; but we have progressed very little toward our primary objective, that is, to find out something more concrete about Judas through extending our knowledge about the Devil.

"And yet I am loath to believe that the incarnation of Supreme Evil did not bear some telltale, plainly diabolical mark, whether physical or spiritual, and if we are unable to discover it, I lay the blame, for the nth time, on the absence of the science I wish for. If, for example, there existed a kind of satanalogical catechism, we would simply open the booklet at the page that contains questions such as 'What does the Devil look like?' or 'What are the special features of Satan?' or else 'On the basis of what signs can I recognize the Devil?' and from among the spelled out characteristics we would choose and examine those which must or might be present in the figure of Judas.

"Since no such booklet exists, we are once more left to our own devices before an avalanche of data which instead of enlightening us confuses us. Nevertheless, Judas being the Devil, I am convinced that at least one of our imagined catechism's answers must fit him like a glove, and that is why I have decided to dig through this avalanche of information until I turn up a clue. Let no one try to get me to believe that the mythologic way of seeing in those days would have accepted a Judas about whom one would not in one way or another have *seen* that he was the Devil. But, mythology aside, doesn't it seem logical to you that, were it only to the extent that from the shape of him one sensed there was something 'divine' about Jesus, Judas too would have exhibited about his frame or in his character some traits of his diabolical nature? Doesn't it seem right to you to picture him with a sort of mark of Cain on his forehead, which, to attentive eyes, to those of the Master, would have revealed and confirmed his true identity? A perhaps imperceptible mark which, while it might go unnoticed by his colleagues, sufficed to reassure the Master that he had Satan at his side?

"With the courage bred of desperation, let us review some of the Devil's characteristics, such as they are handed down by our sources, hoping to hit upon one useful for our purposes. In desperate cases, even a detective has the right to resort to guesswork.

"Nobody could reproach us if we were to let ourselves be influenced by the various images which over the ages have represented the Devil as a monster. Even though we have little trouble rejecting the idea of a Judas with a long tail and cloven hoofs, even though it is hard for us to imagine him with certain mysterious protruberances at the temples, the signs of incipient or hidden horns, and leaving a sulphurous odor in the wake of his steps, we are nevertheless tempted, easily, to imagine him as ugly, exceptionally so, 'ugly as the Devil.' Thus would the iconographic tradition have Christ's betrayer, and for centuries painters and sculptors vied with one another in making him into a Lombrosian type. Be that as it may, it is a recent tradition. On the strength of older traditions we could picture Judas as actually very handsome, for the legend explicitly says that he was 'attractive,' at least as a child. But on the basis of the oneness of Satan and Judas we could also suppose Judas endowed with uncommon beauty. According to traditions much more ancient than our pious legends and our medieval frescoes, the Devil, a fallen angel, retained the divine beauty of those celestial creatures even in his state of decadence, and then there are the miniatures from the early Middle Ages which depict him as a comely youth and, what's more, with a halo around his head. In Christ's epoch it did not seem necessary that Satan be incarnated in a particularly ugly guise, for good taste was part of his patrimony. Let us not forget that they were indeed the fallen angels who taught women the use of cosmetics and the art of pleasing! Only in the disordered imaginings of the late Middle Ages was it the standard thing to couple evil with the ugly, the somber, the unhealthy, the vulgar and even with the stupid, the figure of the Devil being the symbol for all those inferior qualities. And thus, through this psychological process, the Devil finally became a comic figure, abject, ridiculous, little to be feared. The figure of Death was subjected to the same simplifying or reductive process. All this was probably a rather crude and obtuse attempt, on the part of the medieval psyche, to exorcize frightening phenomena, so many dreadful nightmares impossible to dispel otherwise than by de-dramatizing them.

"So it was that the Christian of the Middle Ages reworked the handsome Devil into someone necessarily ugly, and Judas, his incarnation, became ugly too; had we so wished, there was nothing to prevent us from picturing him as beautiful. But, proceeding in the same direction, he was also able to become foolish, comical, ridiculous, like the power he incarnated. Judas, however, did not suffer the Devil's fate: nobody, indeed, wished to imagine Christ's betrayer as an idiot, perhaps so as not to grant him that extenuating circumstance in the indictment against him. Judas was someone responsible for his actions, and a Christian must think of him as such so as not to have to absolve him. Neither would he want to imagine a Judas diminished in his mental and volitional capacities, for in that case, despite Jesus' explicit words, we would see his oneness with Satan seriously compromised. Hence, none of us must forget that Judas did not incarnate the 'poor devil' of the Middle Ages, but a kind of cross between the brute, blind, devastating Evil of the Near Eastern religions, and the refined Satan of Jewish tradition. While his historico-mythologic role relates him to the former, through his essential characteristic he resembles someone whose image was more familiar to his people: the Devil capable of carrying on a *dialogue* with God and men.

"Satan, who in the Jewish people's prehistory retained a close kinship with marine monsters, in the same sense the Almighty did with sheep, also, like God, with the passing centuries underwent a process of spiritualization. And while the Bible gives us no piece of particular information about God's physiognomy, it gives no physical description of Satan either: no, whereas in emergencies the Lord appears in the guise of a wayfarer, a burning bush, or a column of smoke, the Devil, outside his memorable apparition in the form of a serpent in the Garden of Eden, never takes shape. On the basis of traditions which are very ancient but not reported by the Old Testament, he continues to live in the imagination of the Jewish people as a fallen angel, but of resplendent beauty, a beauty which, still more than that of the body, is a beauty of the mind: the beauty of intelligence and wisdom. If we translate the secret language of the Old Testament, it was precisely Satan who made a gift to the first men of the human race's distinctive quality, the vainglory and curse of consciousness, and according to some presumedly apocryphal writings, it was precisely Satan along with his rebellious companions who taught mankind the sciences and the arts, treasures until then guarded by God under seven seals and considered by Him so dangerous in the hands of man that, to deprive him of them, He ended up deciding on the extermination of his entire species. The name Lucifer proves that in ancient times Satan was considered to be the source of light; not the creator of day, but of another light, which for human existence is just as important as that of the Sun: naturally, I am referring to the light of reason, commonly called intelligence. And intelligent the Great Malcontent must have been, haughtily intelligent in order to be called Satan, Adversary of the Lord and Opponent *par excellence*. This intelligence, still more than beauty, is probably Satan's essential attribute, and this is probably the reason why human intelligence also is viewed with great disfavor by the Lord. For the salvation of our soul, the Church does not indeed demand intellectual efforts: faith and religious observance open the gates of Heaven even to the simpleton or the dullard.

"Intelligence being, for Jewish tradition, Satan's chief characteristic, you will therefore not be surprised if I seek in Judas be it only a glint of that mysterious diabolic wisdom, which would render his identity with Satan evident even to our eyes and which—and this is much more important—would have convinced Jesus himself that near to hand and standing there before him was the one who was to undo Him. I hope you will shortly be in agreement with my thesis that intelligence was the unmistakable 'mark' that set Judas apart from the other apostles and from all other men in the world. However, you must understand right now that Judas' was an intelligence *sui generis*, totally different from what we mean by intelligence.

"That preamble was to relieve you of the fear that in my discussion of Judas Iscariot's intelligence I am about to fly off in the direction of the fictional or the fantastic. Rest assured, I have no intention of making Judas into a kind of superman, nor, influenced by the pious legend, am I thinking of attributing to him a cultural background different from that of his fellow apostles. History does not exclude that in this respect too Judas may have been different from his companions, since he was the only one not from Galilee and one of the few about whose origins and trade we know nothing. (Iscariot may simply signify 'man from the city,' and if that were so it would surely sharpen his dissimilarity!) But these problems are without importance for us. Seeing him surrounded by the other apostles, we would probably never have thought we were in the presence of a phenomenon without equal. Certainly he did not stand out among them as a genius does among run-of-the-mill mortals, nor even as the brilliant pupil among dunces. Still, if I dwell on the theme of Judas' intelligence it is because I wish to forewarn you, I want to tell you that it must have been somehow extraordinary, in the etymological sense of the word, that is, outside of the ordinary. What was special about his intelligence resided in the fact, precisely, that it belonged to a *different* order, in a word, a *diabolic* order.

"Until the ever-absent science we have called satanology defines it with some precision, we will remain unable to describe diabolic intelligence. However, Satan being 'one of the divine,' our introductory inquiries into divine omniscience may come to our aid. Satan must have had an intelligence, a cognitive mode similar to that of the angels, and not very unlike that of the Lord Himself. We know by now that the omniscience of God bears no relation to the intelligence and mode of cognition that men have, and, even if Satan's wisdom were inferior to divine omniscience, it must also differ enormously from man's wisdom too. As a tempter, he proves that he is also able to reason humanly and understand men's reasoning better than the Lord, but, in a parallel fashion, he must be very gifted as well in the Lord's way of reasoning, which to us average mortals sometimes seems illogical, irrational, at any rate humanly inconceivable. Were this not so, he could not have been the Adversary by definition, and all his opposing of the Lord would amount to a farce. True, in our human view, Satan lost all his battles with God because he was doomed *a priori* never to win. And yet, despite his defeats, never did he give up the fight against the

Lord. This fact might incite us to be somewhat more modest, and to suppose that, with our limited human wits, we judge Satan's high feats just as erroneously as we do those of God. Perhaps in that superlogical realm where God's thoughts and those of His Adversary evolve, the contest is not yet over and Satan still has his reasons, or his super-reasons, to hope for a final triumph."

Dupin heaved a deep sigh and with his hand traced some vague figure in the air:

"I do not claim, *cher ami*, to be either a theologian or a satanologist, and you can't ask me to define the Devil's intelligence. But I can tell you one thing with absolute certainty: there's one hundred per cent documentation for it: *he knows God*. He is able to recognize Him at a glance, he can make Him out from miles away.

"Even when visualized as the ludicrous dunderhead of legend, no one has ever thought to deny the Devil his acquaintance with God. And that's not something to be sneezed at! Satan is the only one in the world who knows Him personally, for him therefore there is no question of His existence and He can unfailingly recognize Him, anywhere, anytime. And this is the point we had to come to in order to give its full weight to my earlier question about some special feature that would give the Devil away. Actually, we can get by without knowing anything at all about Judas, since his identification with Satan has put us in possession of an inestimable piece of knowledge: *he knew* that Jesus was the Son of God! The twelfth apostle could be a great deal more intelligent, more refined, more knowledgeable than the others, or he could be like them, could even be more simple-minded and more ignorant than all of them, but whatever the case, he was sharply different from the others through the mere fact that while the others *believed* in Jesus' divinity, he *knew* the truth. That the Master was God's son was for him an established fact, something that went without saying, a piece of fundamental knowledge, the most natural idea in the world. When Jesus met him, he must have been struck by this man who regarded as a certainty what he himself saw as a thesis to be demonstrated. And, at that instant, he could not help but understand that this disciple must be the Devil. But what about Judas? . . .

"This seems the right point to ask the following question: was Judas aware or was he not aware of being Satan? While the Gospels furnish enough evidence to give us an idea of how the problem of his divine nature presented itself to Jesus, we don't of course find any allusion to Judas' possible problems in respect to his diabolical nature. Considering how all his colleagues remained without any suspicions about him down to the very end, I venture to say that he exuded no overpowering odor of devilishness. Besides, in order to notice it, the apostles would have had to know what diabolical qualities consist of, at least in what way they outwardly manifest themselves. Nor are we ourselves in a better position: as I have already said, our information about diabolical nature amounts almost to nothing, even in comparison to the very scant and very sketchy information that we have about divine nature. And practically speaking this means that we cannot even vaguely suggest by what unique and indisputable token Judas could have been made aware of his identity with the Devil. As an amateur satanologist my intuition is that such a nature may not have any perceptible outward signs and that it comes out only in diabolical behavior.

"Though as regards Jesus we know that in addition to his faith, nourished by the upwellings of his divine nature, countless other signs, premonitions, miracles and so on combined to buttress him *humanly* in his 'purely divine' certainty of being the Son of God, nothing of the sort can be asserted as regards his twelfth apostle. Support for our hypothesis on the ebbs and flows of Jesus' divine qualities can be found in evangelical accounts; but nothing authorizes us to suppose that diabolical qualities appeared in Judas following some resurgence every rare now and then of his diabolical nature. And I can tell you another thing, *cher ami*. To Jesus, to the human nature in him, the proofs of his divine nature were the cause of enormous satisfaction!

"Now, that a man should try to prove to himself that he was not mistaken in believing himself to be God is perfectly understandable; but there is nothing to indicate that Judas, animated by the same fervor, sought to prove to himself that he was Satan. In this regard his position is very much like our own: aside from Jesus' damning statement, he had no evidence on the strength of which he could define the essence of his true nature, and were he ever to try to prove something, he would have gladly shown that, concerning him, the Master was dreadfully mistaken. If my intuitions as a pioneer in satanology are worth anything, I would be tempted to say that Judas was not conscious of being the Devil; I would almost go so far as to say that he took Jesus' word for it, and only little by little resigned himself to the idea.

"But while Judas would have gladly avoided proving himself to be Satan, Jesus could not be satisfied simply to have him at his side. Even if during a high tide of his divine knowledge he had succeeded in convincing himself that his disciple was the Devil, during the low phases he was anxious to have from him some actual proof of it or at least some clues. And then, even though he was sure he was right about the true identity of his apostle, that he was the Devil wasn't enough: he had to behave like the Devil! Day after day he must provide further new guarantees proving that he knew what was expected of him and was able to bring it off. If, Jesus knew, Judas was truly Satan, then Satan would do his duty even in the event Judas were to resist. As well, it was only through Judas that he could keep abreast of what Satan intended to do: only Judas, with the anetennae of his peculiar diabolic intelligence, could receive his silent, desperate questions, and give him the appropriate responses, likewise silent and desperate. Only Judas, with the *sui generis* intelligence of an Old Testament Devil, could understand and perform the incomprehensible and the unperformable.

"Thus, between them, was born a dialogue which, by its very nature, was conducted wordlessly from beginning to end, under constant tension, accompanied at all times by a tormenting mutual uncertainty as to the other's ability to understand: neither of the two was ever sure he had really understood or been understood. And this right up to the words brought forth at the Last Supper. 'Do as you must'—the only sentence spoken aloud was the first and final line in this wordless dialogue—and it brought the certainty that they had understood each other perfectly, without the shadow of a doubt!

"Very well, dear friend,"—and Dupin stretched his arms and exhaled slowly—"I believe we may adjourn. The results we have obtained are only modest, and we have no way of going farther. It is true, we have learned no more than we knew before about why and how the Judas of historical reality betrayed Jesus Christ, but on the other hand we have penetrated and grasped the transcendental workings of one of the most significant moments of our History. My aims never went beyond that, and I feel I have done what I set out to do. I may perhaps have disappointed you; but for my own part I could leave it at that, and put the word 'finished' to our meditations.

"I have several reasons for not doing so, however. The first is that for quite a while now I haven't heard a sound from you and it seems to me impossible that you should have nothing to say or ask. But this is not the main reason why I wish to devote another evening to our subject. You know that detective stories usually end with a stereotyped assemblage in the course of which and in the presence of all those concerned, injured parties, suspects, witnesses, et cetera, the private detective, finally in possession of all the elements needed to solve the case, relates it from start to finish in all of its details, putting the tesserae of the mosaic back together to form a skillfully reconstructed picture. It would be truly masochistic of me were I to deny myself this satisfaction; and in addition I believe that for you too it would provide some well-earned relaxation after so much theologizing and satano-logifying."

With a nigh to furious gesture he relit his pipe, long since gone out. "Tomorrow," he resumed, "I will try to give you an un-interrupted account of how Judas became aware of his thankless task. If there is a shred of truth in what we have said up until now, what we shall say tomorrow shouldn't prove entirely false either."

Dialogue without words

THAT EVENING WE SKIPPED DINNER, FOR AS SOON AS I WALKED IN THE DOOR Dupin had me sit down in my armchair and he started the conversation immediately.

"Imagine a Jesus, the Son of God, who knows that that is what he is, and who yet stands a long way short of certainty; imagine a Judas who is Satan but does not know it at all and, above all, does not want to know it; finally, imagine in the background a God who knows everything, but who wants and at the same time does not want what He knows: there, in a nutshell, you have the highly disconcerting traits of the three protagonists at this historical moment, when the destinies of mankind were modified in this vale of tears and, possibly, in the Kingdom of Heaven also.

"There is no further need to emphasize that, under such circumstances, the relations between the future betrayer and the future victim of betrayal must have been most unusual. Having identified the Devil in Judas, Jesus had to confront two tasks. First of all, he must convince himself that this intuitive recognition of his was not an error but the horrifying and withal comforting truth, and therefore accumulate probative signs, hints, clues in order to acquire the certainty that at his side, within reach and at his disposal, he had the fundamental pillar for his work. Oddly, this was a relatively easy task compared to the second one, to which he attached as much if not more importance: he must awaken or reawaken his apostle's sense of duty, the duty incumbent upon the Devil, that being to lead him to his corporal death. Could he confine himself to hoping in a reasonable manner, even in the mythological or transcendental manner, that sooner or later Judas would all by himself wake to his diabolic duty? Did that virtuous countenance, ascetic and penitent, promise a spontaneous illumination? Well, gnawed by his human impatience, Jesus absolutely had to have palpable, human guarantees!

"How was he to obtain them? Owing to his constantly ebbing divine qualities, Jesus would have had to reason humanly. Also, from personal experience he knew all about Satan and the traditions concerning him. He knew that Satan is endowed with an intelligence *sui generis* that gives him a grasp of 'divine things.' When with such astonishing ease he had recognized in him the Son of God, his disciple had provided a wonderful indication of a possible identity with the Devil. If he were the Devil, he would have to be endowed with that exceptional diabolic intelligence, even though it were buried deep under the vestures of a wretched human shape. And there was a very simple and foolproof way of checking on this: if Judas responded to the provocations of 'divine things' in a different way from the eleven other apostles, if Judas also understood words unsaid and inconceivable to the human mind, then yes, he could be sure that his twelfth apostle was Satan! If Judas did indeed possess the Devil's extraordinary intelligence, all one had to do was uncover it and awaken it and, once brought to light and duly guided and instructed, it would drive the unfortunate apostle to understand and impeccably carry out the task he had been assigned by the mystery of the sons of gods. To that end he had but to be treated the way a good pedagogue treats his disciple: without using any coercion, develop in his soul and mind his personality's most precious and characteristic tendencies and qualities, those very ones thanks to which he would succeed in building and achieving something important in his life. Training Judas came down, in effect, to refining and rendering ever more sensitive in him his unique diabolic quality: his exceptional intelligence.

"To be chosen as an apostle may have left Judas perplexed, with the feeling he was not worthy of such an honor. But a little after, something else the Master did convinced him of his importance, which in the view of the others seemed limited but which to him at once appeared in its ambivalent aspect, halfway humiliating, halfway honorable. I refer to the bestowing of the purse, which was Jesus' first pedagogical act in the training of the twelfth apostle and the first line of the wordless dialogue that was to unfold between them.

"The fact (the only one that was never questioned among the elements relating to the betrayer) that Judas was responsible for the purse containing the common funds was several times and variously commented upon, but never, in our opinion, gone into as thoroughly as it deserved to be. In the eyes of the exegetes, it is a determining factor in the betrayal. Greed for money supposedly generated the first criminal thought in Judas' mind and drove him to the fatal step. To these gentlemen it seems natural that a trusted steward burn with an unholy desire for money and be—latently, at least—a thief.

"But others pose the problem this way: how was it possible to entrust the funds of the little community to a person who, in the end, turned out to be a thief as well as the worst, not just of all the apostles, but of all the men in the world? And, the rationalists add ironically, if no one had ever noticed anything suspicious in Judas' character, Jesus at least, with his presumed divine foresight, would have been able to tell that the steward, in whom he had from the start identified his own betrayer, was a dishonest person, the least suited to hold such a position. And if Jesus, though knowing his man through and through, entrusted the purse to him, it was altogether consciously and with a specific purpose. According to these blasphemers, in handing over the purse Jesus laid a trap for Judas . . .

"By now we are well beyond reducing the mystery of Judas to the episode of the thirty pieces of silver, and we agree with those who have absolved the betrayer of this minor offence. Nonetheless it remains that Judas was responsible for the funds, and this fact merits closer analysis. For us who resolutely reject the thesis of the ill-intentioned, the problem presents itself in these terms: why was it indeed to Judas that the purse was entrusted? It is not enough to repeat with John that 'Judas held the purse,' for it was certainly Jesus who entrusted him with it.

"If Jesus did not mean to ruin Judas by entrusting the purse to him (as he did not) and if Judas was not a dishonest steward (as he was not), it becomes more interesting to find out why the Master entrusted the administration of the little community's meager resources precisely to his future betrayer. A number of answers (some already given and discussed) come spontaneously to mind. There are those who say that Judas was given the job of steward because he was not fitted for higher offices; there are those who affirm, to the contrary, that to manage the community's modest patrimony called for a little practical sense and experience, qualities the twelfth apostle was supposed to have, but not the other eleven. A wide-awake scholar now asks a question: why wasn't the purse entrusted to Matthew, a former tax-collector and therefore more qualified for such a role? But to us, and we are not the only ones, it seems obvious that handling the funds should have required no special experience and, from this point of view, the purse could have been entrusted just as well to Peter, to James, to the other Judas sometimes also called Thaddeus, or to any of the other apostles worthy of better tasks. Parenthetically, none of our sources claims that our Judas was less fit than the others for strictly apostolic functions!

"An impartial person could also say: there was a purse and this purse, of necessity, had to be kept by one of the apostles; if Judas was neither a thief nor dishonest, neither more nor less intelligent than the others, neither more nor less gifted than they in the strictly apostolical activities, the question of the purse loses all importance. And the person following this line of reasoning would be almost right, if he didn't forget that the purse was a heavy burden. Heavy, of course, not in a physical sense: the purse and the handling of the money were a moral burden, and not because of the responsibility they entailed, but because of the humiliation they tacitly inflicted on the person put in charge.

"It is not necessary to cite the Master's invectives against wealth and the miserable goods of this world, nor to recall that money, when it appears in the Gospels, is always connected with something unpleasant, annoying or repellent, from the coin to be paid to Caesar to the three hundred pieces of silver wasted at the Bethany supper and the famous thirty pieces of blood money. Money, for Jesus and his disciples, not only had no value, but was an object of scorn, the source of all evils and a major obstacle to entering the Kingdom of Heaven. To follow the Master, the apostles had in fact left everything behind, giving no thought at all to the future problems of their material lives. For them money stank, and caring for this execrable object, which belonged to their former life, would have meant not having cut all one's ties with it. How was Jesus able to persuade a single one of his apostles to surmount the disgust and disdain he himself had inculcated in them, so that the household funds be somehow looked after? It is significant that the community's economic life was not administered by Matthew: the former blood-sucker did not, of course, even want to hear the mention of money.

"Jesus' choice was therefore not necessarily determined by any particular capacity of the twelfth apostle, but by the total inaptitude of the other eleven. Their strength lay indeed in their conviction that everything must be taken literally and in their promptness to reject everything that appeared doubtful or unseemly. And, along with all that, each of them wanted to be at the head of the class, to accumulate merits and honors and assure himself of advantages for the hour of triumph, to the detriment of the rest. To act as keeper of the money during the years of preparation would not have been to get off to a very promising start. The apostle in charge of those matters could have hoped to become minister of finance in the Messiah's kingdom, but he would no longer have dared dream of becoming the 'best' among his companions, or of sitting beside the throne of Jesus, the crowned King of the Jews. And it is well known that, thanks to a series of misunderstandings, they all let themselves bask in such dreams.

"Even if they had all understood that some one of them had to take responsibility for the purse, that one would have been greatly let down and would have gone on asking himself: why am I the one to have been chosen? Obviously Jesus took their foreseeable reactions into account, and chose not to puzzle their simple minds to no useful end. His apostles, all worthy wholehearted people, for the time being were good only for the fishing of souls, and it was to be desired that they make further progress in this activity. It was therefore preferable to avoid any situation that might interfere with their one-track pursuit of perfection.

"But, with our perspicacity, we can claim that the presentation of the purse to Judas was also determined by far more important considerations. In our opinion this was the first testing of Jesus' clairvoyance, the testing of the rightness of his choice. The twelfth apostle's reactions must confirm the presence of that intelligence *sui generis*, the telltale mark of diabolic nature. Had Judas reacted as the eleven others would have reacted, that is, by being upset and feeling humiliated or by giving way to rancor or resentment, he would obviously not have been Satan, or at least, in his present incarnation, he would have failed to give proof of a minimal amount of the exceptional intelligence Jesus expected from him. Had this happened, he would have been in a very awkward situation: he could have made Judas his betrayer in order to accomplish the work of Redemption, but he couldn't ever have transformed him into Satan, without whose aid the mystery of the sons of gods would have been compromised.

"But Judas' reaction did not disappoint Jesus' expectations. No one should imagine that the twelfth apostle welcomed the humiliating task with particular relish. But he understood and, what was important, understood in his own manner, in keeping with his 'extraordinary' intelligence, what none of the other eleven would have been capable of understanding. He understood that Jesus' mission could not go forward without his specific contribution, even though offered from a lowly and humiliatory position. He understood that it was possible to promote the Master's work indirectly too, and, finally, that the choice conferred upon him a position which in the eyes of the Lord was unique.

"We do not know to what extent and in what manner Jesus aided him to attain this illumination. We have every reason to suppose that instead of humiliating the twelfth before the others, he tried to present the arrangement in its true light. He certainly did not tell the others that he had chosen Judas because he was not suited for higher offices. Rather, he stressed that, in his view, the twelfth apostle was a man of quality who, besides performing his regular apostolic duties, had sufficient energy and flexibility left to undertake various chores, humiliating but indispensable. And the others, who would not have understood and forgiven if the choice had fallen upon them, became understanding in regard to Judas and ended by considering him very well suited to his money-managing duties, perhaps even better suited to them than was Peter to being 'the rock.'

"Jesus certainly did not want to expose his apostle to his colleagues' contempt. From humiliation hatred could be born, and though hatred is an excellent spur to crime, in Judas-Satan it might have begot consequences contrary to those he desired: to get back at him, Judas might not have betrayed him!

"With a psychological deftness worthy of him, Jesus played upon Judas' self-esteem, which, since we are in the satanic sphere, might more correctly be called pride: far from being humiliated, the twelfth apostle should be made proud of the inherently humiliating task. It took Judas Iscariot's singular, his diabolic intelligence in order to psychologically digest this inversion of ethical values, to bear with this reversal in the moral realm. When he placed the purse in Judas' hands, Jesus saw to it not only that Judas' prestige vis-à-vis the others remained intact, but that the importance of his future functions was presented in its true light. We do not know how Jesus went about clarifying things for his disciple. He must at any rate have come right out and told him that for this particular purpose there was nobody else he could rely upon. The Master, certainly, would have praised the virtues of the eleven others, but at the same time emphasized that in some cases faith, honesty and zeal are not enough, and that what was needed was a superior intelligence, whose care was not for appearances, and which, as well, understood the unsaid. Now, Jesus would have explained, such intelligence was possessed only by Judas, unique among the twelve; he ought therefore to understand and to forgive him if in this business about looking after the money he was obliged to turn to him. Sometimes, as in the present instance, mean tasks cannot be entrusted to simple souls, in whom they would give rise to disgruntled and rebellious feelings; instead those tasks require minds of a higher order, who understand how the obscurest task can be quite indispensable to the sublime purpose that is conditional upon it. And so it happens sometimes that the simplest and most modest task, mean in the common judgment, must be entrusted to superior persons: they alone can afford not to care what the others think. It's in some such style and with arguments like these that Jesus must have persuaded Judas to accept, with a light spirit and with a proud heart, the contemptible job of handling the accursed money. Only thus was Judas able to draw the greatest honor and the highest spiritual good from his humiliating position. Next to the Master's personal opinion, of what weight and of what account could the opinion of the others be? He, Judas, *knew* certain things, things the others didn't even dream of, and he also knew exactly what the Master thought! And no one would ever penetrate into the secret they shared!

"That the purse was kept by Judas is therefore important, but only from the angle it has been discussed here. The purse was really Judas' ruination, not because it made him into a thief and betrayer, but rather because it deluded him into thinking that he understood the Master and was his most trusted collaborator. Anyone who has eyes to see and ears to hear must perceive that the act of handing over the purse contained *in nuce* the entire formula for the relationship between Jesus and Judas. From that moment on the future betrayer felt himself the person closest to the Master, almost his accomplice, and from that moment on he did nothing but strain his attention to intercept the most recondite thoughts of the one who honored him with the meanest charge, but in the most flattering fashion.

"With the handing over of the purse began between them an unexampled dialogue, for the speeches were composed of gestures, looks, hints, obscure allusions, but never any spoken words: words were not suited to the terrible 'divine thing.' So theirs was a dialogue full of anxieties, uncertainties, trepidations, and did not want for highly dramatic moments when two opposed wills and two desperations in search of salvation met headlong; it was a fierce struggle which took place in perfect silence, without a single question being asked or a single confirmation being given. None of the eleven discerned the tremendous storms that rose in both their souls during that long mute conversation, which had inevitably to lead to the surrender and total defeat of the one or the other.

"But this dialogue without words could not proceed without leaving traces which, elusive and almost imperceptible though they sometimes are, seem to be milestones for the gauging of its course and progress. From Judas' behavior, from his suddenly going pale, from a fleeting glint of terror in his eye, Jesus surely succeeded in finding out whether one of his dissimulated communications had roused the hoped-for echo in his interlocutor's soul. Judas who, from the moment of the handing over of the purse, realized that the Master's gestures and words had, beyond their obvious meaning, also a hidden meaning intended exclusively for his ears, became used to looking for it and discovering it behind even the simplest utterances; and the more incomprehensible the hidden meaning seemed to him, or, if he understood it, the more dreadful, the surer he was that he had understood aright. And how natural it was to persuade himself that the meaning of certain words was reserved for him alone, since to the others they made no sense at all!

"The evangelists testify that the apostles very frequently did not understand the Master's words, especially on the occasions when he spoke about the most important things. The eleven were not much given to reflection: they took note of certain statements, and continued to strengthen themselves in their faith. And if something too far exceeded their mental capacities, and at the same time caused their hearts sorrow, they opposed it energetically, even to the point of refusing the painful words. Jesus who in the course of his public teachings often alluded to his passion and his violent death, and at least four times predicted them clearly and in the minutest detail, did not succeed in winning his disciples' belief: the allusions escaped their attention, and the fourth explicit declaration made no more impact upon their minds than the first. For them these were absurd things, contrary to all common sense and all expectations, and Peter, instead of realizing that it was a serious matter, the most serious matter in the history of the world, behaved like any old granny who supposes a few affectionate banalities will dispel her little grandson's nightmares. Rarely did Jesus become so angry as on that occasion, confronted by so much ingenuousness. He ended by calling it devilishness on the part of his Peter-the-Rock, who scarcely a moment before had pronounced his solemn Credo. So much for what these people understood about 'divine things'!

"To be sure, he knew what they were like when he chose them: simple, straightforward men, imbued with faith, dominated by it and by zeal and a stubborn determination to reach the objectives they attributed to the Master. But the mental sluggishness of his closest collaborators—what it must have put him through! It could only have been a joy to have someone there who reacted intelligently to his revelations. Judas' different kind of intelligence, sprung from metaphysical roots, was almost a projection of Jesus' own psychological need. Spirit beckons to Spirit, the creative intellect needs the receptive intellect, needs at least one glance, one nod of the head, one frown revealing that the idea has been perceived, and not fallen on stony soil.

"It is not possible to say to just what extent this degenerated Lucifer understood 'divine things'; but he did at any rate perceive their existence and presence, and allow for them. Jesus never looked for anyone at all to grasp the innermost meaning of his words: the most secret spring of his actions was knowable only to himself and to the Father. For him it sufficed that someone, the one he elected for Evil, submit to the magic of 'divine things' impossible to express with human words, and obey the orders given by him, no matter how absurd and senseless they might seem.

"From the wordless dialogue Judas grasped no more than what concerned him, to wit, that the Master ardently aspired to a death determined by numerous conditions and prescriptions, and which only he, Judas, could and must make possible. The proof thereof is that while the eleven others even down to the Last Supper were still not aware of the imminence and necessity of the Passion, Judas had already made his arrangements for it. For a long time he had given thought to what had to be done, and he may have been launched into his anguished meditations by the Master's very first obscure and startling allusion. He had no need to know the passages in the Scriptures relating to the Messiah's earthly destinies, nor the analogous adventures of the other sons of gods. It was enough to understand that Jesus' prophecies in regard to the Passion also implied an ardent desire, a fervent prayer addressed to him—the exalted if timid appeal of a person whose fate lay in his hands. It was enough to understand that the Master needed him in connection with an essential point, the crucial point of His life, and that apart from him there was no one who could help him.

"The twelfth apostle, of course, did not suddenly give in to his Luciferian pride. He made great mental efforts to convince himself that he was wrong and was misinterpreting the phrases of this dialogue without words. When Jesus made his first allusion to his betrayer, Judas had even then felt a shiver run down his spine. And the apparently unmotivated start his twelfth apostle had given was certainly noticed by Jesus. Judas' sudden agitation was the answer to his allusion, proof that he had hit the mark.

"To attempt to reconstruct the stages of the wordless dialogue would be risky; nevertheless we have enough elements to provide an approximate idea of how it unfolded. The Gospels have conveyed to us some striking episodes that we may properly see as marking the stages of this dramatic conversation. Who could deny the fantastic importance of that memorable scene sometimes referred to as the Eucharistic Promise of Capernaum? In accordance with John's testimony, the specialists in the life of Jesus judge that the criminal idea's first appearance in Judas' mind dates, precisely, from the events that transpired in front of the Capernaum synagogue. We too see in this strange episode a decisive stage in Judas' painful wakening. As we all know, the Jews who are there respond indignantly to certain statements by the prophet of Nazareth, the disciples and sympathizers are also ill at ease and many among them feel the moment has come to part ways. Jesus, probably in favor of a weeding out of the fearful and the hesitant, is little daunted and brusquely addresses his chosen in a challenging tone: 'Will ye also go away?' Peter, as usual, comes forward as spokesman for the apostolic college and hastens to make a declaration of fidelity in the name of all his colleagues. But in spite of what the Master said a moment before, he does not realize that he is in the presence of the Son of God. He hails him as the Messiah and as the Holy of God. For him, just as for the majority of the Jewish people, the figure of the Messiah is not necessarily identical with that of the Son of God. Jesus, in any case, rests satisfied with such an answer: for the moment it is enough for him to know that he has well chosen his elect. 'Have not I chosen you twelve,' he says proudly; but then immediately adds: 'and one of you is Satan.'

"This addition, connected to the earlier sentences not by an adversative but by a copulative conjunction, would be truly out of place and perfectly useless if Jesus were not by now sure of being understood by his twelfth apostle and of being able to put his fate confidently in his hands. The ground-plan for the sons-of-gods mystery is now in place: alongside the new God, here is Satan, identified; alongside the light of the world, here is the very night of darkness.

"John, alone among the evangelists to recall this episode, does not describe the effect that the Master's astonishing words had upon the apostles. Luke, forever pointing out how reluctant the apostles were to believe in the prophecies and how unwilling to comprehend even the simplest things Jesus said, would probably have harped on the bewildered looks they exchanged upon hearing such strange words. Indeed, a declaration like that came out of the blue, and for long afterward continued to seem an exaggeration, far more surprising, for instance, than the third or fourth prophecy concerning the Passion, which the apostles were likewise not disposed to heed and believe. The first moment of stupefaction once got over, they considered what they had heard to have been, so to say, an auditory hallucination; it was dismissed as an absurdity, with the result that, aside from John, nobody remembered it. On the other hand, the favorite, who scrupulously sets down all the facts which tend to denigrate the betrayer, gives great prominence to the episode, whose meaning did not become apparent to him until later. At the time he too was probably one of those who stared dumbfounded at each each other.

"Judas too must have looked at the others, taken aback and upset; but none of the eleven noticed that he had gone deathly white and that a cold clammy sweat glistened on his brow.

"For Judas this declaration of Jesus' came like a bolt out of the blue; and in the course of the dialogue without words it was what told him most about the role he had to play. A bolt out of the blue it indeed was, for only a few instants before he had been thinking that, despite the purse he was entrusted with, he could consider himself as one of the twelve faithful who, in the midst of the general flight, had not abandoned the Master, that *enfant terrible*. But a few instants later he was snatched from his sweet dream and forced to take cognizance of his own identity—of being nothing less than the Devil.

"That was the tragic moment in the career of the apostle Judas, that was the tragic moment in the life of Judas the man. The Master's words had struck the mark. Going back to the terms of the pious legend, the time had come for Judas to recall the augury his bride-mother had thoughtlessly disclosed to him in the nuptial bed: 'Thou shalt be the opprobrium of the world, the downfall of our race . . .' The man who, after having been especially hounded by divine malediction all his life, now hoped to find the way to salvation at the Master's side—for how many reasons was he thunderstruck at hearing himself called the Devil! Is there then no saving oneself through good will? Cannot even the Son of God save those whom Yahweh has chosen for Evil? Must he who is born a devil die a devil?

"But even if we dismiss as idle chatter all that the pious legend contains, even if we allow that Judas had never yet committed any crime, was no more than 'a vessel of innocence' or, at least, an ordinary starry-eyed apostle, we would say that he was quick indeed to acknowledge that the Master's thrust had struck home. For us it is a revealing fact that, with the exception of John, the evangelists attributed no importance to this statement of Jesus'. But then, we venture to ask, why would Jesus have come out with those words the moment after his apostles' profession of faith? To sow in their breasts the seeds of doubt, of fear, of confusion? Surely not: he simply hoped that his words would reach the one they were meant for. And that one, thanks to a sudden illumination, instantly reacted to the thrust. Making an enormous effort, he looked at those about him, not to see which one among them might be the Devil, but to cover up his having recognized himself as such.

"I like to imagine Judas reacting instantaneously, but the situation does not much change if we grant him a brief lapse of time to think about it. Warned by the shiver that ran down his spine, he quickly realized that the Master's words bathed in the same ambiguity that surrounded the matter of the purse. Doubtless, to act the Devil is a much weightier task, more absorbing and 'infernal' than taking care of the purse; yet if the Master requires Satan's presence at his side, this dignity and the terrible honor and the honorable horror proceeding from it—to whom could they be assigned other than to him, the only one capable of bearing their weight? If the Master wanted the Devil at his side, it meant that he had *need* of him for some mysterious reasons, and his task consisted not in ferreting out what that signified but in acknowledging the fact and giving the Master a helping hand without demanding explanations.

"Did it not require an exceptionally strong spirit and an extraordinary intelligence not to seek for explanations? The good, the zealous, the fanatical—the Peters, the Andrews, the Jameses, those destined to glory and to martyrdom—would they have submitted themselves to a senseless or unreasonable wish on the Master's part without wanting to know why? Would they have taken on the role of the Devil in order to help Jesus fulfill his destiny? Of course not; the ignorant, the honest, the cautious always ask why and at the most will die only for the revealed truth. Only a generous and 'extraordinarily' intelligent soul is capable of believing, unto self-sacrifice, in a person who has yet to reveal the truth and bring salvation. The eleven others had followed Jesus because of the Messianic promises, and to the cause, for them become the sole reality, they remained faithful, but not to the Master, whose Word they manipulated and re-manipulated in the interest of the cause. As for Judas, from the moment he accepted identification with Satan, or perhaps even from the moment he resigned himself to looking after the purse, he ceased thinking of the cause and until the end remained faithful to Jesus' person. It was precisely this personal attachment that made him so odious in the eyes of John, who never succeeded even vaguely in understanding its meaning.

"It would be fascinating to know the former life of Judas Iscariot in order to better grasp the effect of the blow he sustained. If he was, as the pious legend describes him, a man upon whom God had pronounced a curse, it must suddenly have dawned on him that there was no escaping accursedness and that he, who was seeking salvation, was headed for perdition. If, on the other hand, he was the 'vessel of innocence' that we cannot totally rule out, he would have been utterly stupefied and would have thought about all the aspirations and ambitions that had led him into the Master's orbit. During this tragic moment of illuminating certainty he must have realized that henceforth he could no longer pursue *his* end, for it had become inexorably and irrevocably subordinate to the Master's.

"In reality, the Lord's stupefying command: 'Judas Iscariot must be the Devil!' was more terrible, more annihilating than any bolt of lightning. Or was it no command at all? It was worse. If the twelfth apostle was not a vessel of innocence, but the wretch described in the legend, the Master's astounding words must have struck him not as a command but as an observation. The Master had all of a sudden realized that he was one of God's accursed, one of those elected to Evil, and he had done no more than let him know that he knew this: 'Judas is the Devil!' The revelatory words were a straightforward communication, untinged with reproach or aversion. It was in fact perfectly clear to Judas that the Master was not saying to him anything like '*Apage, Satanas!*' On the contrary! If the astounding words were anything at all beyond a simple declaration or definition, they needed to be seen as implying the Master's secret desire to keep this devil in his company. 'Let be that which is,' he seemed to be saying, 'the Devil is in our midst, and let him stay, since he too was chosen by me.'

"Obviously, if he had taken to his heels five minutes before along with the dozens of scandalized disciples, he would have avoided hearing himself identified with the Devil. But, unfortunately for him, he was not scandalized at all and remained steadfast with the eleven others, determined to follow the Master. Was it worth running away now? Whatever version we were to accept of the figure of the twelfth apostle, accursed of God or vessel of innocence, in neither case do we see why he ought to have run away. That hour of illuminating certainty was tragic precisely because it revealed that for him there would be no way out, Devil he would remain wherever he might take his wretched existence. And Judas did not run away. He remained at his post and this solution seemed to him the best. If in his desperate situation there could be a speck of consolation it was indeed the idea that Jesus had elected him to be his Devil because he evidently needed him, even if he was unable to make out why.

"The temptation is irresistible to try to reconstruct the twelfth apostle's state of mind prior to that subsequent line in the wordless dialogue which brought confirmation that he had rightly understood. During this interval, in which the craziest ideas alternated with the most hopeless resignation, Judas withdrew into himself, since there was no one he could turn to. Beset and distressed as he was, he sought solitude, in so doing of course taking care not to draw attention to himself, and settled into his definitive place at the tail-end of the line of apostles. To be sure, given his functions and his material preoccupations, the steward would in any case have found himself ranked in the rear of the band of apostles, in a perpetual ferment over spiritual matters. But it was by no means unwillingly that he assumed this rearward position, and it was in no way synonymous with humiliation or humility. By thus keeping to the rear he remained clearly within the Master's view, distinctly separated from the eleven others who, given their identical activities and concerns, all blended into a single face. The Master too kept himself at a remove from his bunched together disciples and Judas liked to imagine that he was pleased to behold him at the antipodes. And the instinctive habit became a conspicuous one when the incredible feeling that the Lord regarded him as the Devil became a certainty. Does not the universal order require that God and Satan occupy the two extremities of the axis around which the lives of mortals revolve? Over the faceless heads of mortals they thus looked at each other, watched each other, pitted one against the other in an unending struggle.

"At the outset, however, poor Judas was not at all at ease in the Devil's role and, despite the lightning bolt of illuminating certainty, he still hoped he had been mistaken. One of his wildest ideas during that critical period was to draw the Master aside and say to him, 'Tell me, Lord, am I the Devil? And if I am, what do you want from me?' But Judas knew very well that the Master would have answered evasively. One cannot tell someone, looking him straight in the face, that he is the Devil. Especially if that person is at the same time a chosen apostle. Certain incompatibilities can subsist so long as no one speaks about them: become explicit, everything constructed upon them is bound to collapse. Cornered, Jesus would have had to accept Judas' resignation from the dignity of apostle or from that of Satan. On the other hand, were it true that one of the apostles had to be the Devil (and how could it be otherwise, if the Devil *was* a chosen apostle?), then the second part of the question would have been an absurdity. An odd sort of Devil he would be who, even in his capacity as apostle, offers his diabolic services to God, or to the Son of God! And, finally, how could God, or the Son of God, communicate his instructions to the Devil concerning those fine services?

"It was impossible to challenge the Master on the subject, and the dialogue had to continue wordlessly.

"One thing is truly worthy of note," Dupin went on. "It is that Jesus Christ first made sure he had a betrayer and only afterward attended to the rock on which to build his Church. Not until he had laid the first stone of the mystery of the sons of gods did he then get to work on his cult. This happened some time after, in

Cæsarea Philippi, when Peter pronounced his Credo, was solemnly awarded his charge and authority, but also received his formidable reprimand from Jesus who for an instant was irritated enough to call him a devil too.

"This emotional episode was very instructive for Judas who, by now in an impasse with respect to his personal aims, strove to fathom those of the Master. This scene, it seemed to him, replied to a number of never formulated questions. He persuaded himself that he was on the right track to discover Jesus' secret.

"Like everybody else, he too had listened to the Master's curious declaration, to wit that he 'must go unto Jerusalem, and suffer many things of the elders and chief priests and scribes, and be killed, and be raised again the third day.' This declaration, more like an impassioned vision than a prophecy, shook Judas as much as it did the others. They, as was their wont, exchanged speechless glances, and the newly glorified Peter stepped forward, with an at once preoccupied and protective air, in order to protest. No one would have expected the rush of anger with which the Master reprimanded him. All felt their blood run cold. Crimson with shame, Peter backed away and the others remained so perplexed that, after the brief silence during which Jesus recovered his self-control, they merely heard the ensuing words, but did not grasp them.

"Iscariot too was taken aback, not knowing what to do before the anger that had shone with divine brightness upon the Master's countenance. Nothing so subjugated him as these fits of anger. It seemed to him that at such moments the divine in the Master proclaimed itself irresistibly and, though imprisoned within a human shape, became intransigent before the inferiority of other human beings. Neither was he at the time able to understand what was so irritating in the good Peter's solicitude, and he too, though he kept his head, was affected by the unexpected scene. In line with his recently adopted habit, he kept in the background, well behind the others, and then all at once a sudden light seemed to enter his mind. That sudden light began to penetrate the dense shadows of his brain and, as though by the wavering glow from a feeble oil-lamp, he discovered the existence of unexplored vistas of thought. With an hallucinated attentiveness he followed the words of the Master, who in the meantime had completely calmed down, and those words became engraved not only in his memory but also in his soul. He again had the honorific and terrible certainty that the Master was addressing him, and only him, so completely unconnected was the previous thought with the one he was now giving utterance to.

" 'If any man will come after me, let him deny himself, and take up his cross, and follow me. For whosoever will save his life shall lose it: and whosoever will lose his life for my sake shall find it,' said the Master. And the twelfth apostle, who stood off at a certain distance from the others, from everything that had occurred and could occur, at a certain distance by now from himself and from his own life, felt that these startling words were addressed to him, to him alone, in order that his doubts be answered and his suspicions confirmed. In the light of these words he understood the essence of his relationship with the Master, who had explicitly enunciated what he desired of him: that he renounce his own self and follow him, even at the cost of his own life. And to whom would he have said this if not to him, who had asked this of him? But what the Lord explicitly desired, could it fill him with horror and despair? No, surely not. And, in a trice, Judas' heart was overflowing with hope. Never would he have won salvation by pursuing his own insufficiently clear ends; but by serving the Master's ends he would find life again, the lost meaning of his life. Had not Jesus himself said so? And who could renounce his own life more completely than he, who had sacrificed his own personality to assume that of the Devil? To act the Devil out of love for him was the greatest sacrifice one could make for him and the greatest guarantee of finding salvation through him . . .

"Judas all of a sudden felt pervaded by a feeling of happiness mixed with anxiousness and excitement. He was ready for anything. But what exactly did the Lord wish from him? Did he mean to tempt him? Lead him to damnation? Stupid questions! Formulating them, he felt merriment take possession of his heart. What role would the Master assign to him? But whatever he might have to do, he would always be acting in accordance with his will. Is not the Devil a function of God? Is not their relationship a cooperation along two different but convergent paths?

"Proof, all this, demonstrating how ill-prepared Judas was for playing the Devil's part!

"But, got started on a fair path, he opened his eyes and his ears. In addition, the Cæsarea Philippi episode had produced plentiful food for thought, and in his aroused state thinking led inevitably to further knowledge. Though he had not succeeded in closing in upon the Master's secret, he had arrived at the conviction that this secret really existed. The upbraiding of Peter furnished him with a precious clue. At first, naïvely, he had wondered how Jesus could have roughly and even ferociously rebuffed the apprehensions of a gentle heart. Was it not understandable and altogether appreciable that the good Peter's faithful heart had sunk upon hearing the cruel prophecy? But, by dint of thinking it over and over, the meaning of the scene appeared to him in an unexpected light: he all of a sudden understood that it wasn't Peter's affectionate concern that had irritated Jesus, but rather the immense disproportion between the enormity of the coming event and the naïve, all too human emotions of the apostle. And without recalling the exact words Judas did vividly recall the meaning of what the Master had said, which had landed thunderously upon the poor 'rock.' '*Apage Satanas!*' the Master had cried, with the terribly irritated mien of an irascible god: 'Get thee behind me, Satan; you offend me, for you have no sense of the things that are of God, only of those that are of men.' That's what he had said, or pretty close to it; or 'no sense of the thoughts that are of God, but only those that are of men'—a slight variant which expressed the same idea, and to the twelfth apostle's attentive heart provided the key to the secret. For the Master, Judas concluded, there existed two orders of things: the things of God and the things of men, and he was capable of thinking with the mind of God and with the mind of men. The human mind determines the way men reason about the things of God, but the only court competent to pronounce the final word about the things of God was indisputably the divine mind, where the human mind's arguments were not even taken into consideration. Everything the Master had said, the terrible statements concerning his Passion, death and resurrection, were evidently divine things, comprehensible only to God's mind, dread things, that even the human heart's most spontaneous compassion could only diminish.

"Had Judas been present at the Transfiguration, he would have moved ahead more rapidly in the dialogue without words. He would have understood that besides being 'things of God,' the Passion and the Resurrection—which to the others appeared liked the Master's latest fixation—were also, though for a mysterious and inconceivable reason, extraordinarily important things for Jesus, who harped upon them so frequently.

"But a few days later, while the little band was shifting from Judea to Galilee, the Master repeated the prophecy about his death and resurrection. The apostles gathered round him listened in dismay to the feverish and upsetting words, but, mindful of the outburst at Cæsarea Philippi, dared neither protest nor ask questions. Judas, however, who was bringing up the rear and was following the Master's footsteps as though he were his shadow, was horrified to hear the mysterious prophecy repeated, and only now drew from it the conclusions he would have come to sooner had he been present at the Transfiguration.

"For Judas the months preceding the entry into Jerusalem were marked by intense cerebral activity, with dramatic phases which brought him near the brink of madness. They were restless months, full of changes of abode, preachings and miracles; but the Master drew smaller audiences that were sometimes even hostile ones, going so far as to throw stones at him or to try to lay hands on him. He might employ his wonder-working powers, he might repeat that his strength came from the Father—it was to no avail: he did not correspond to what the people were in hope of, who would have liked to have found in him the Messiah such as he had been promised by Yahweh through the voice of His great prophets. Assuredly, Jesus hardly had the appearance of that King of the Jews who, putting himself at the head of his armies, would have reconquered his people's independence. He never uttered a word on this subject, he always spoke about other things which, unconnected with grand practical objectives, seemed of only very relative value. The public ended by viewing him as one the many prophets and Messiah-candidates the villages and synagogues were teeming with. The general discontent affected even the disciples and apostles. For them there was no possible doubt that Jesus was the Son of God and, consequently, the Messiah as well, but they might perhaps have preferred a Messiah who, though not the Son of God, would, through the general features of his career, have given more guarantees of attaining terrestrial glory. Notwithstanding the total absence of promising signs, they would not give up on this and right up until the Master breathed his last they awaited his elevation to temporal power.

"When Jesus called them together, telling them that he was to go to Jerusalem, and describing to them in detail how there he would die on the cross and would rise again, the apostles refused to believe their ears and disregarded the prophecy, their minds taken up with the same ruminations upon the messianic triumph—to such a point that right after the tragic declaration, John and James, those two fire-eaters, went up to the Master on the sly and tried to get him to assign them the most prestigious posts in the messianic regime. Sermons, parables, the most explicit statements in the discussions between the Master and the scribes failed to win the apostles away from the grip of their ambitious dreams. It was as if during the three years of his public ministry Jesus had talked to the deaf!

"But fortunately—fortunately for Jesus and for mankind too—one of the twelve apostles, indeed the Devil, kept alert, watching and listening attentively. During the months that preceded the final journey to Jerusalem, he whom the Master had chosen for his ability to understand him accumulated evidence, abundant evidence, that prevented him from sharing any such fantasies as those his colleagues entertained: the exegetes presume that during this lengthy period Jesus must have spoken about his sufferings, his death and resurrection much more frequently than we are told by the Gospels, so that his obsessed predictions must have seemed to Judas like that many indirect speeches in their very special dialogue. In him, who had long since understood that Jesus would not become the Messiah in the going sense of the word, with every passing day there grew a horrible and absurd suspicion that the Master not only desired his own grim end, but that this was his one true preoccupation: to reach Jerusalem, fall into the hands of the high priests, get himself killed and rise again after his death! And towards the end of the long months of migrating from place to place the suspicion changed into certainty. Judas already knew what the others were far from having even imagined.

"But during those long months he was unable to figure out *what* Jesus expected of him.

"When at last Jesus told the apostles that the last journey to Jerusalem was imminent and described in awful detail the suffering that awaited him there, the twelfth apostle, unlike the eleven others, had a further illumination. Seeing that his colleagues remained impassive as ever at the announcement of this prophecy, Judas again had the impression that the Master had addressed himself solely and directly to him, who as usual stood behind the others and facing him, at the other end of the imaginary axis. The detailed description of the impending peripeties had an intense impact upon him and he was unable to escape its wicked spell. The more he thought about it all, the clearer these surprising circumstances became to him.

"The most surprising was the prediction that, having condemned the Master to death, the high priests would hand him over

to the Gentiles who, after mocking and torturing him, would end
by crucifying him. Above all else it seemed impossible to him that
Jesus could commit anything defined under the law as a crime and
that the civil authorities punished by crucifixion, the maximum
penalty reserved for the worst offenders. At first sight it even
seemed to him improbable that the high priests, as the supreme
religious authority, could take any measures whatever against
the Master. He was the cause of no political unrest, and could
reasonably have hoped to pass unnoticed amidst such a throng of
prophets. The worst that could befall him was to get himself killed
by his own auditors, in the grip of a sudden furor or, it could be,
incited to revolt by the high priests' agents. Such was the end that
logic would have foreseen for him, but in no way did it resemble
the prophesied one.

"The farther he progressed in his reflections, the more it all
seemed absurd to him, beginning with the Master's dwelling on
the images of his atrocious death. Even though the Scriptures, and
in particular the prophets Isaiah and Daniel, had said something
about the Messiah's suffering and death, one came to see that not
everything truly squared with the circumstances of the Master's
life: to begin with, the fact that Jesus was not the Messiah in the
sense promised by the prophets. And since he was not a Messiah
comme il faut, and plainly never wanted to become one, it was
incomprehensible that, while rejecting earthly glory and power, he
considered himself duty-bound to accept the indecent end of
someone who had pretended to such power and glory. Nothing
warranted his prediction; indeed, everything contradicted it.
Using caution, a perhaps more vigilant caution than that observed
up until then, the continued dissemination of the Good Tidings
did not seem threatened by any danger, and should some danger be
expected in Jerusalem, then one ought not to go to Jerusalem, or
else go there in a strictly private capacity, as had already been done
in the past.

"For the simple human mind these were all problems that could
be dealt with somehow. Ever in Judas' mind, however, was the

upbraiding of Peter and the words the Master had employed on that occasion. He well knew that Peter's mind was only capable of understanding 'human things,' whereas in the case at hand—as Jesus himself had said—it was a matter of 'divine things.' So there was no point in arguing about it: he must simply take note of the Master's determination to go to Jerusalem in order to die there at Passover. The 'divine things' were known only to him, and only he knew why they mattered so much to him.

"Such was Judas' opinion on the objective aspect of things. But, unquestionably, these also had a subjective side for him, for, according to his unshakeable belief, they involved him too. The more firmly this inner conviction rooted itself in his mind, the more he felt himself affected by the Master's personal affairs. He could not get rid of the thought that it was above all to him, better yet, exclusively to him that Jesus had addressed his revelatory words. Recollecting the scene over and over again, he seemed to remember that from the Master's eyes a sort of silent supplication had gone out toward his, something that in his memory of it resembled an impatient entreaty. And by dint of re-thinking and re-evoking, Judas persuaded himself that he had not been mistaken. But what was the Lord beseeching him to do? What did he really want of him?

"Judas arrived at the conclusion that, rather than real prophecies, the Master's predictions about his end were closer to anxieties or desires because their roots in reality were few or none at all. For a time he was unable to distinguish the reason for the anxiety from that of the desire, but, little by little, he came ever more distinctly to see that the desire bent in the direction of death while the anxiety or, more precisely, the tormented anxiousness was fed by the fear of not attaining it. At least not in the manner foreseen by the prophecies. Was that not the point! Into Judas' mind stole a ray of light. Ah yes, the Master stood an excellent chance of winding up like so many prophets who had provoked the indignation of their auditors. But, obviously enough, this style of death wouldn't have satisfied him. Perhaps the 'divine things' or

'the thoughts the divine mind thinks' excluded *a priori* that he die
wherever it might happen to be, at whatever time of day and in
whatever haphazard manner: indeed, these 'divine things' seemed
to prescribe rigorously that the Messiah, or the Son of God, or
simply Jesus of Nazareth had to die in Jerusalem, during the
Passover feast-days, and had to die crucified. Perhaps one couldn't
come back to life after an everyday sort of death! The minuteness
of the description, the obsessively repeated details of the end made
such an impression on the disciple that in every look the Master
cast his way he discovered an appeal for help.

"But what need had he of these prophecies? He again felt
impelled to go up to the Master and ask him the question, flat out:
'Tell me, O Lord, what do you want from me?' But if it were all
a misunderstanding—what then? and what if his theories were but
the elucubrations of his over-excited brain? And in the way of
answer what kind of a look would he have had from the Lord?

"But what of the annihilating look that would smite him were
he actually to await aid from him and were he, Judas, not to lift
his little finger? His feverish thoughts were unable to hang on even
to that fine thread of truth which he had sometimes managed to
catch hold of during the acutest stage of his rationalizings. The
most absurd ideas assailed him, mainly at night when, consumed
by insomnia, darkness obscured for him the evanescent boundaries
separating the possible and the impossible. Now and then one
aspect of the problem would predominate over the others and one
of his bizarre ideas would sound forth obsessively from the confused
orchestra of his soul, deforming the uncertain significance of the
ensemble. Thus, for example, starting from the idea that the
Master wished to die in order to be able to rise again, by dint of
reasoning and deducing he succeeded in overlooking other truths
that he had discovered and clearly perceived in daylight, such as for
instance that Jesus wished very precisely to die in Jerusalem,
during Passover, on the cross. Such essential particulars, clearly
glimpsed during the day, escaped him in the tormented dreams of
the night, and as he lay tossing about he would think of the

possibilities of a different end. Back into his mind came some
things the Master had said which, in the misleading light of false
premises, assumed extraordinary importance and a sinister accent.
Had he not said that 'No one shall take my life away from me, it
is I who shall take leave of it'? Judas shivered, for an unexpected,
macabre-sounding word had come into his mind: suicide. And for
some time, what with the overwrought state he was in, he was
unable to banish it. Indeed, what is the way out available to
someone who wants to die at all costs, but whom no one wants to
kill? Perhaps the Master needed his collaboration in suicide? Was
he perhaps fated to hand him the weapon or the poison? Or,
perhaps . . . had he been chosen to kill Him?

"For a long time this fantastic idea obsessed the unhappy
apostle. Completely dominated by this fixation, he saw himself as
potentially a murderer and he suffered profoundly in anticipation
of his guilt. Because of his state of mind, and contrary to his wont,
he sought to avoid Jesus' eyes and glanced at him only covertly and
from out of his colleagues' midst, but even so he constantly had the
painful sensation of being scrutinized by the Master. The latter, so
it seemed to Judas, had even tried to catch his attention.
Sometimes, inevitably, their glances did meet, though it would be
for only the barest instant, for the disciple's worried and unhappy
gaze would slyly steal away. But those instants sufficed to upset
him still more. Indeed, it seemed to him that the Master's ever
dreamy eyes were staring at him, as though endeavoring to sound
his very depths; and in their expression was something interroga-
tive, curious, almost ironic. All this augmented his terror, for it
was the confirmation of his fantastic conviction: the Master's
strange look seemed to say yes to his desperate questions.

"To where may a man wander who loses the light of reason! The
terror of having to kill stifled the voice of logic. It took a moment
of extreme lucidity for him to be able to discover the contradiction
between his fixation and the Master's desires. It was an ordinary
sort of moment, no different from those he had spent in agonizing
reflection, but with the slight difference that during it he beheld

his nightmares vanish as if in a puff of air. All his torments, all his anticipatory remorse suddenly appeared ridiculous and shameful to him. How could have got himself going on such nonsense? How could have imagined that he might have helped the Lord by killing him with his own hands when he had foretold that he must and consequently wanted to die in Jerusalem, during the Passover holidays, on the cross? Alas, into what a hell will a man's thinking plunge him that madness has entrapped, he told himself as he wiped the sweat from his brow, and felt his chest nigh to bursting with triumphant joy.

"Let no one decide that we are arbitrarily imputing thoughts and emotions to Judas Iscariot—since he was Satan, such ideas had perforce to occur to him. Never would Judas have believed he was so close to the truth as when he was in the state of mind his fixation brought on. He came within a hair of being damned by posterity as the murderer of Jesus; it was the same hair's breadth that separates History from Myth! But, thanks to the fact that he was to perform on the stage of History rather than of Myth, Judas was spared from having to commit the most appalling crime. In the world of mythology—of this we can be absolutely sure—it would have been Judas Iscariot's diabolical hand that extinguished the divine life. In his deicidal transports he would perhaps have savaged the Master's corpse, perhaps would have torn it asunder and thrown its pieces to the human jackals.

"According to an ancient legend, Judas as a child, accompanied by his mother, went to visit Mary's son, but instead of doing him homage, he struck him. Popular imagination hence saw the figures of the Son of God and his betrayer as linked from the start, and in the child's innocent gesture saw the homicidal intent of the born criminal. Had both of them grown up in the world of Myth, Judas would not have escaped steeping his hands in the blood of God. But, so to speak, History rescued him. Thanks to its specific exigencies, History demanded its own altogether particular form of deicide, a more complicated, more civilized and more ignoble form, carried out with administrative and bureaucratic means. The historical character of this eminently mythical event was of especial concern to Yahweh, Who was eager to put His historical relations with mankind in order. Jesus could only accept the parental point of view, since for his part he was deeply interested in the future of his 'church,' the custodian and guarantor of his future cult—an eminently historical problem. Being killed by Judas would have been sufficient to allow him to rise again and ascend to celestial glory. The mystery of the sons of gods would have been just as well accomplished this way, but nothing would have assured the spread of the religion of the Father and the Son. The right thing then was to stop just this side of perfect fulfillment of the mythologic scheme so as not to risk duplicating the premature end of the rival religions of Attis and Mithra.

"At any rate, in this moment of mental lucidity, Judas beheld his wild fixation of having to kill the Lord give way and, with a relieved heart, he laughed at the danger that had menaced him from so close on. In a mood of quite uncharacteristic euphoria he resumed the distinctive place reserved for him behind all the others, at a certain distance from the always compact group of apostles, and once more set to observing the Master, who stood opposite him and seemed to stare at him over the heads of the elect. No longer did he shun Jesus' eyes. On the contrary, proud of the crisis he had overcome, his eyes glowed with happiness and towards him expressed faith, love and hope, which did not however efface a lingering hint of indulgence. Oh yes, the fault for all those unnecessary emotions in a certain sense lay with the Master. And Judas forgave him with all his heart.

"But, a short while later, Jesus gathered his disciples together and once more (the fourth and last time mentioned in the Gospels) announced to them the march on Jerusalem as well as the terrifying program for the sojourn in that city. The communication put an end to the twelfth apostle's barely acquired peace of mind. Again he had the impression, but this time with incisive clarity, that this program wanted desperately for some foundation to stand on, and that alongside the prophetic fervor shining in the Master's eyes one could make out a childlike confusion, and even a look of prayerful supplance! For the twelfth apostle there was no further doubt that the Lord awaited his aid, and that his words were addressed to him since the eleven others seemed once again not to be listening to him. And, once again, Judas plunged head first into his tormented cogitations.

"Like something recollected obsessively, in his memory there kept rearising the inquiring gaze of the Master, who had seemed to be wondering why his twelfth apostle had rejoined the ranks and mingled with his companions. But wasn't there a gleam of hopefulness in that gaze? During all those days, while the prey of his fixation, Judas had interpreted that gleam of hopefulness as an exhortation, an incitement, a virtual appeal to murder. The mad idea that the Master might be looking for death at his hands had definitively left him, thanks to his inward reasonings and to the Master's recent communication; but, alas, he had never been able to get entirely rid of its memory, which continued to poison if not his mind, then surely his soul. He had of course been mad to think that he must kill him with his own hand or provide him with the suicidal weapon. But was it so mad to think that he must help him obtain death, the death he so yearned for, and in the manner prophesied by him?

"Six days before Passover, on the road that led from Ephraim to Bethany, while the apostles went ahead in a group around the Master, Judas, who was walking behind him, following him as though he were his shadow, realized exactly what the Lord wanted from him. And at that instant his heart filled with bitterness and overflowed with fierce hatred for him to whom he'd come in quest of salvation and who, instead of that, had appointed him to the role of the Devil. By now he did not doubt that it was for him who walked behind all the others, for Judas Iscariot, to see to it that, in every last detail, exactly, faultlessly, the Jerusalem program became reality. Only now did he understand that Jesus' strange declarations were indeed prophecies, but prophecies *cum grano salis*.

They weren't even desires! They were straight-out orders! Orders given to him, to Judas Iscariot the Devil. See to it, Satan, that it all works out beautifully! These aren't things you leave to chance, nor yet to luck! It's up to you, Satan, to make sure that my plan, this 'divine thing' of mine, comes off without a hitch!

"And what if these were altogether genuine prophecies? If they were the fruit of divine prescience? If the Master actually knew that everything would take place as he had foreseen and desired? But in this case, how did he, Judas Iscariot, enter into the picture? What need was there for his help? He shuddered—and what if his collaboration too were foreseen? If nothing could transpire without his help? From tormenting himself with these desperate thoughts of his Judas ended up before two equally terrible possibilities: either the Master, thanks to his infallible prescience, had *known* from the outset that his twelfth apostle would provide the help needed for the perfect fulfilment of the Jerusalem program, and so there was nothing he could do but shut his eyes and submit to his fate; or else the Master knew nothing, only ardently, wildly, desperately wished that what he had prophesied would come to pass—but, in that case, everything depended on him, Judas Iscariot! And if everything depended on him, he would say no!

"No! No! A thousand times no! he mentally shouted toward the white-clad figure that was walking ahead of him and to which he was linked more inseparably than if he had been its shadow. But the terrible thing was that in that dialogue without words there was no answer to his cries of terror and hatred. Straight ahead went the white back, erect and proud, indifferent and unconcerned. In vain did he hurl his mute cries after those unhearing shoulders! And Judas suddenly understood that that white figure was imperturbable only because it felt protected and covered by the man who had been following it as though he were its shadow. The one to whom that indifferent and proud back belonged did not fear being left in the lurch: he was sure, not of Judas Iscariot, his twelfth apostle, but of Satan . . .

"And in the end Judas did indeed surrender unconditionally,

putting himself body and soul at the mercy of the will of Jesus Christ."

I had listened with vast pleasure to my friend's winged speech, noting with satisfaction that his poetic vein was as remarkable as his keenness as an investigator. However, with our arrival at this point what seemed to me a logical and essential question arose in my mind. Could it be that Dupin, so perspicacious and so scrupulous, had nicely slipped past a delicate item without whose clarification all his feats of wizardry would have collapsed? Taking advantage of the spontaneous pause that followed the last and highly dramatic sentence of his narration, I turned to my friend:

"Allow me two questions, one of them of a purely preliminary order. Working from the meager store of data, upon whose importance you are the first and only person to insist, you are to be congratulated for having attempted to reconstruct the psychological process through which Judas arrived at the betrayal. But do you really claim that things actually happened this way?"

Dupin laughed. "That would be too wonderful for words! Not even in the case of the mysterious death of Marie Roget did I dare affirm that things transpired exactly in the manner I indicated: I confined myself to proving that the hypotheses of the professional police all lacked foundation, and to offering a plausible reconstruction whose strength derived solely from the weakness of the others. I must stress that I am not and never have been a policeman, but only an analyst. And still less am I a theologian. I seek only to point out which are the wrong paths so that they will not be fruitlessly pursued in the future: but finding the right path is a job for the professionals. As for my reconstruction, it possesses, in my view, a relative value. In the best of cases, it could turn out as it did with the reconstruction of the murder of the *midinette*: to wit, that it be excellent. But I am almost sure in the case at hand that things went otherwise, if by 'things' we mean recorded events. Personally, I place the accent on the substance of things, on that transcendent reality which hides off-stage but leaves its stamp on historical reality and guarantees its likelihood. My attempts at reconstruction are based above all on the results of our investigation into the divine spheres: if they show a certain solidity, I'm truly very pleased and for the rest I declare myself satisfied if things took place *just about* as I have reconstructed them."

"It is in this same connection that there is something I'd like to point out to you," I broke in. "Enraptured by your unusual and ingenious fictional-historic reconstruction, you seem to be forgetting your goal and to be neglecting metaphysical reality which—according to your claims—underlies the whole thing. While there exist mysterious transcendent relationships between realities 'as thought by the mind of God' and those 'as thought by the mind of man,' one cannot accept that Judas Iscariot would have put himself at Jesus' service to help him realize his aims. Judas, the disciple, the apostle, the man, Judas the great unknown, could have had a thousand undiscoverable reasons for serving his Master, and if your fictional-historic reconstruction comes close to what really was, fine. But I for one did not forget for a single instant that Judas Iscariot was the Devil, and I long to know why the Devil gave Jesus a helping hand."

Dupin cast an almost sorrowful glance at me.

"I was expecting that question and dreading it. In this regard I have been behaving a little in the manner of the Lord when He does not approve of situations which He has nonetheless foreseen: He forever puts off resolving them, in the hope that He finally won't have to put Himself to the trouble. I was hoping in the same way that over the course of our long sessions together you would have acquired a mastery of the mythological idiom and become so well acquainted with Satan that there would be no need for subsequent clarifications. But perhaps it is in fact those minds accustomed to conceptual reasoning that have a hard time penetrating the luminous obscurities of myth, which with an image and a few phrases neatly expresses everything it wishes to say, whereas modern man, in order to arrive at the same result, must engage in exhausting disquisitions or write treatises or invent new sciences, always with the risk of being poorly understood. You, *cher ami,* are asking for nothing less than a translation of myth into modern terminology. Now if I were to declare straight out that in my opinion the mythologic term *divine order* expresses an important and lengthy phase in humanity's journey; that the emergence of Satan corresponds to the period in whose course man becomes aware that he is due to perish if he does not radically change the situation he is in, that is, change the divine order currently in force; and that Satan himself is nothing else than the inevitable though rebellious act through which man chooses among the new existential possibilities hitherto excluded from his order but to which he is now implacably driven in the interests of survival— well, what would your response be to all that? You would be justly taken aback or shocked, not very convinced or frankly skeptical, you would come up with a lot of objections and all sorts of embarrassing questions some of which I would be only barely able to answer and some not at all, to the extent they are outside my competence, which does not go beyond the field of investigation and analysis. Worse still, we would find ourselves in unknown territory, indeed in the domain of the science of satanology, still lacking and ardently wished for by me, and which mild but steady pressure being exerted unrelentingly by you is constraining me to found."

My friend unloosed his resounding laugh.

"It is not possible to 'translate' a myth faithfully," he went on. "The only thing one can do is 'reduce' to anemic rationalistic concepts the rich, concise and unequivocal content of biblical language. Give some thought to my already expounded 'prologomena' to a future satanology, and all this will perhaps seem clearer to you now.

"In primordial times myth was the form through which man succeeded in grasping the universe and the multifarious aspects of existence in order to orient himself among them. He found the world so wide and so marvelous, and the conditions of his life so predetermined and inescapable, that he ended by requiring a supernatural being, the creator and organizer of everything. He came thus to conceive of God, the divine order and the iron laws established by Him, which regulated the phenomena of nature and human society. God and His perfect immutable order were the guarantee of mankind's life and survival. Everything outside this order, everything that threatened to disturb and undo it, the very precariousness and the transitoriness of hunman life, were person-ified in the figure of Satan.

"The figures of God and Satan, such as they appear to us in Genesis, are already the result of a long historical evolution: like all discoveries, they were fated to become more profound, more refined, enriched with more significances, not, of course, because of some congenital tendency in the human mind to theologize, but because of the desperate need to give a meaning to the inevitable changes in the human plight. When in the Garden of Eden, at the moment of original sin, our first encounter with Satan takes place, his figure has already reached full flower, he is 'one of the divine,' a spiritual being, God's adversary, subtle bearer of ambiguous gifts to men: he is the Satan of the Old Testament; in short, our Devil.

"But anyone who fails to take this figure's origin and past into account, who fails to remember that it is a compendium of multifarious millenial experiences, who is bent on seeing it as different *toto cælo* from the similar personages in other mythologies, commits irreparable errors. The most glaring of them is to view him as a person, endowed with intelligence and will. And you too let yourself be caught, forgetting that myth, by its very nature, *personifies* powers, principles, laws, phenomena, sensations, emo-tions, intuitions, non-concrete realities, that is to say everything that is the opposite of what characterizes a face. The mythical figure which materializes immaterial and impersonal realities is hence conceived of as a person. Now, a person who does not think and does not want is inconceivable; yet everything the mythological figure personifies remains an abstraction, which does *not* think and does *not* want. To be sure, that would also apply to the figure of God. But God is a person in the belief of billions of men and for a pluri-millenial doctrine: to suppose that behind the miracle of the harmony of nature and the universe and behind the miracle of the phenomenon Man there is a creative act and a Creator who thinks—this, on the part of the human unconscious, is logical enough. But the same cannot be said when we examine the Devil's position.

"Have you ever heard tell of a 'diabolic plan' as the alternative to 'the divine plan'? Obviously not, and this fact by itself proves that Satan is qualitatively different not only from God but also from men. At the very most, just as myths and legends attest, he is an improviser who puts in his wise appearances in order to sabotage the Lord's good relations with His favorite creature. But if we go back to the reality he represents in his 'person,' we immediately understand that it is not possible to attribute shrewd plans to him, nor even a scrap of will nor any of that intelligence with which, as God's interlocutor, the mythologic way of seeing invested him. As a consequence, he cannot even be cunning. He simply exists. And he exists in a curious manner. By that I mean to say that his manner of existing is frightening: Satan *is he who is not* exactly as God *is he who is*!

"This thesis of mine will appear plausible to you once you take cognizance of the Satan-Chaos identity. Without bringing in the analogy of Hades, at the same time god of the nether world and place of punishment and existential dimension, you have but to think of the ancient legends and Judeo-Christian myths. If you keep in mind that God created out of chaos (and not out of nothingness) and that Satan witnessed and opposed the Creation, it will cost you no particular mental effort to discover the validity of my equation. Effectively, whereas nothingness is pure non-existence, chaos is disorder, confusion, indefiniteness, one might say existence without existence, something that at once is and is not: and this—by the merest chance—is also Satan's mode of existence. Only when in possession of this fundamental notion will you be able to understand the names, such as Adversary, Opposer, Slanderer, Despiser (so many meanings of the Hebrew word *Satan* and which Greek tries to translate with the word *Diabolos*) and understand also the role of the Devil in Creation, his relationship to God and to Creation. Out of chaos God created the magnificent universe, to do this using but an infinitesimal part of the material at His disposal, and through the act of Creation He at the same time left to neglect all his unutilized infinite possibilities. God created out of Satan, and at the same time excluded him from His order. But He was never able to annihilate him.

"I doubt whether you will find any contradiction in the fact that Satan both lends his body to Creation and is at the same time excluded from it: just think of the little block of marble out of which Michelangelo created the *Pietà* and of the enormous amount of marble lying in the quarries of Carrara: the first is sculpture, work of art, creation, order, equilibrium, beauty; the second is raw matter, crude, amorphous. Yet it is still the same marble, containing within it the possibility of innumerable other sculptures, just as from out of the small block used to fashion the *Pietà* one could have created innumerable other sculptures just as perfect! But watch out: the masterpiece still remains something of marble, hard, white, gleaming, throbbing with life, yes, but at the same time fragile, subject to the wear and tear of the centuries and also to certain mysterious maladies to which marble is prone.

"This somewhat too 'plastic' comparison should make it easy for you to understand Satan's role in the Creation. He is enchained within the created order since a minute portion of his immense forces were turned into principles, laws of nature, balanced tensions, functions of a system, while the overwhelming majority of those same forces, plus there's no telling how many others which proved unnecessary for the Creation, were relegated to a state of inactivity, condemned to serve no purpose. In his primordial mythic figure, Satan perhaps expressed the resentment of the not-created towards the created, the mute rancor of infinite possibilities against realization's oneness. And if you keep in mind the two other signal components of our metaphor, that is, the erosions of time and the inherent susceptibilities of matter, you will perfectly understand how Satan comes to be God's number one Enemy, without this requiring that he be conceived of as a 'person.'

"I believe that what I have advanced will become still clearer if we now take the courageous leap that brings us to the Devil's first appearance in the Old Testament, which coincides with Man's first appearance in History. Much has been written about this great moment, in particular in the recent work I mentioned to you in connection with divine omniscience; therefore I can be brief. With his first intervention in human destiny, inducing Adam and Eve to eat of the forbidden fruit, the Devil bestowed upon mankind the gift of omniscience and the knowledge of good and evil. In other words, that wonderful myth recounts the birth of human consciousness, which, as everybody knows, was in reality not born but developed, possibly through a series of prodigious bounds. What interests us is to understand why in the mythic vision that incomparable, fateful moment was connected with the Devil. How is it that the brute force of Evil begot in him Man's supreme pride and joy, that Intelligence which qualitatively sets him apart from all other creatures?

"Only take into consideration what we have said so far and you will have no difficulty in answering this. The very first day after the Creation, the Devil, who until then had existed only for God, became reality also for the new being endowed with reason, a reason scarcely superior to that of the beasts, but sufficient to have the intuition God. Everything that in nature and life was disagreeable, harmful, deadly for the human world was condensed in the figure of the Devil: night, storms, famines, diseases, death. All these ills were the dark aspect of marvelous existence, its negative side that had to be put up with, and for a long time man considered the Devil simply as a part of Creation, completely contained within it, himself a creature.

"But once man reached the point of *thinking* that instead of enduring all the ills that befell him he could perhaps avoid them, or eliminate them outright, by manipulating or by employing against them the natural forces up until now the exclusive property of God, Satan changed aspect: Evil revealed itself to be an independent entity, a force existing even outside Creation, capable of shaking the hinges of the divine order itself, but capable too of improving man's situation. All the expedients man had resorted to in order to change the face of Creation were condensed in this new image of the Devil. Most often it was not a matter of looking for new *comforts*, or of swaggering defiance of God, but almost always a matter of self-defense, of the necessity of surviving in the various stages of evolution, of a desperate struggle against a divine order which from time to time showed itself hostile to existence; and by bringing about new living conditions not foreseen by the Creation, by reproducing and provoking natural phenomena and processes or by simply creating new things, creations of his own, with which to control those created by God, man had the ever more distinct impression of going against the Creator's will. Since Satan was everything that had not been created by God, man soon realized that he too was creating out of Satan and with Satan's approval, against the Lord's will.

"The ambiguous position of man in regard to God was expressed through the ambiguous figure of the Devil and through man's ambiguous relations with him. In primordial times man did not even ask himself whether his gifts should be accepted or refused: they were existentially necessary; but all the while taking advantage of them, man felt he was wrong. The Devil was at the same time the only Friend and the most terrible Enemy: he was Lucifer and he was the Prince of Darkness . . .

"In all mythologies, I believe without exception, if it is not actually a god (most often in opposition to other gods) who gives man the gift of new conditions of life, they are generally rebellious beings, Titans, demigods, heroes who, with a defiant gesture and without thought for the consequences, make away by force or cunning with the greatest assets, formerly the jealously guarded patrimony of the gods and little by little become the basic elements for human progress. In this connection we need only recall the myth of Prometheus, who stole fire from heaven for the benefit of human beings, but we could cite countless other examples drawn from the mythologies of the entire world in order to demonstrate how hostile the gods were to all of man's great conquests and how often they imposed the heaviest punishments on man's benefactors. According to Hebrew myth, it was the fallen angels, Satan's companions, who introduced men to the sciences and arts, and if to this you add the fact that the founders of the earliest civilizations were the descendants of the abominable Cain, you will easily grasp the close connection between Progress and Evil, between History and the Devil.

"While all mythologies abound with myths about the origins of the great—and also of the little but no less important—human conquests (and of this we find examples and traces in Hebrew mythology too), only the chosen people—so far as I know—succeeded in condensing into a single myth the essence of all the others: I refer to the myth of original sin. Indeed, not one step in the direction of progress would have been possible had not human consciousness first been born—the Devil's superb gift, the source of all of our weals and woes.

"I perhaps do not need to admonish you anymore not to see in Satan a *person* who greatly wanted to spite the Lord and to that end hit upon a stratagem. But since the authority considered most competent in the matter is still capable today of upholding the existence of the Devil and of lesser devils enveloped in an odor of sulphur and provided with horns, tails and cloven hoofs, no amount of prudence seems excessive to me! Little wonder if the Church—as it reduces the forces of Evil to a joke in very bad taste on the part of the Lord and showing, consequently, that it understands nothing about either the mechanism of History or the psyche of man—proves less and less able to influence the course of events and less and less able to be of any use to the souls it claims to have in its care. A consternating undertaking it was, doomed *ab ovo*, and in which even papal infallibility was bound to fail—that reproposing of some thirteenth century theses, verbatim, without the support of arguments more adapted to modern sensibilities, heedless of the void left by seven centuries of indifference and that no one nowadays has been in a hurry to fill. An undertaking we cannot but disapprove of. While our Pope gets credit in my book for having exhumed a long-forgotten problem, I am concerned however that he has done so in a manner that may produce the opposite effect: it is to be feared, indeed, that after the pontifical allocution people really begin not to believe in Satan anymore. But the ways of Providence are inscrutable . . .

"But Satan exists, all right, and now perhaps you will better understand his mode of existence. Man, at the 'moment' of the birth of consciousness, represented in the Bible by the acquisition of omniscience or the knowledge of Good and Evil, realized that he had to take his fate into his own hands, detach himself from nature so as to confront and control nature, oppose the divine order which was becoming dangerous for his survival, consequently act against God's will. What in the myth takes the form of the expulsion from Eden was in reality man's departure—at once spontaneous and forced—out of the natural order, which had become intolerable and menacing: an ascent, painful and fraught with risk, from the rank of a more or less reasoning animal to the human condition. Incidentally, do you remember Jesus' last words on the cross? For the myth it is God who seems to abandon man, while in reality it is man who abandons God. But this ambiguity is direct proof that along mankind's path there now and then develop critical situations which are pleasing neither to God nor to men: they might at best be pleasing to Satan, were he able to feel emotions.

"And now remember what we said previously about the infirmities of marble! Magnificent Creation was subject from the very start to the laws of the matter out of which it had been constructed, to the intrinsic and indestructible properties of chaos. God, in creating, was obviously mindful not only of the virtues of His material but of its flaws as well: the great geological cataclysms, the glacial eras, the extinction of entire animal species, everything was foreseen and calculated in the perfection of the

Creation! Isn't the world just as beautiful and marvelous without the dinosaurs? But who could maintain that the world would be the same without the one being capable of conceiving of and worshipping God? God first and foremost would be unable to maintain it. Yet divine omniscience foresaw from the outset that this precious species, in order to survive the crucial moments of its existence, must ally itself with Satan against Him, building for itself a world exclusively its own out of the material of the divine order, pulling it apart and reshaping it, just as He Himself had done with chaos, against chaos.

"But to oppose the so very hurtful divine order man first had to *understand* that this was *possible*: and this, in my view, is what the magnificent myth of the forbidden fruit and original sin comes down to. Man, at that magical moment, grasped Satan's true essence. He overcame the prejudice that had Satan constituting only the dark sides of marvelous existence, and suddenly everything that was unpleasant, stifling, threatening seemed to him closely connected with the divine order. Man, at that magical moment, understood that Satan's more important part lay 'outside' the created order and that it was luminous! At that magical moment man rounded out his ancient experience of Satan, the being who is not. The great contradictory mystery cleared up prodigiously. Who actually *is*, what actually *is* the one who *is not?* The answer came spontaneously: he *is* and at the same time *is not*, he is the one who *could* be!

"To man, at that magical moment, was revealed the realm of Satan, the infinite wealth of chaos, the power of rendering existant that which does not exist, the capacity to choose the one that pleases from the welter of possibilities. From a little bit of omniscience, from the knowledge of good and evil, was born the formula of human intelligence; within the world a world was born, within the universe a microcosm.

"The myth of original sin explains the Devil's function in the history of humanity and in each of our lives. When man comes into conflict with the divine order, Satan appears offering a new gift that it is dangerous to accept, but impossible to refuse. In our modern language, based on rational concepts, we would have to say that Satan enters the fray whenever man prepares to take some outrageous step to conquer for himself new living conditions which would facilitate his survival. To detach oneself from an already existing and consolidated order so as to then set forth in quest of a new, never experienced one always seems blasphemous and sacreligious, but above all it entails risks; and if this statement applies for some profane order or other, it is supremely applicable for the divine order. Here the risk is twofold: man's choice among the various possibilities offered by the Devil may turn out to be bad and lead to failure; or it may so anger the Lord as to incite Him to decree mankind's extermination.

"But humanity has always managed to survive, and this proves that Satan's gifts and advice have always been positive, or, in other words, that from among the various possibilities for radically changing or modifying its conditions, mankind has always chosen the right one when the chips were down. But could it have been otherwise? If you think about it carefully, man, even when he thought he was turning the divinely ordained world upside-down, remained inevitably inside it, for not even the boldest effort of intelligence, the wildest flight of imagination is able to conceive of an order *toto cœlo* different from the one in we live in, and the greatest conquests (even the gratuitous and therefore most 'sacreligious' ones) end by being included in the divine order, ultimately making it broader, richer, more human, but leaving it fundamentally identical. What previously had seemed to be a rebellion, a challenge, an inspiration of Satan's, very quickly becomes part of everyday routine, and the horripilating *novum* which yesterday seemed to be heading everything toward cataclysm is on the morrow perfectly integrated within the jolted order. In the Bible these recovered equilibriums take the form of compromises between man who, filled with fear and feelings of guilt, does the Creator an injury, and God who, though angry, does not annihilate him, but dictates to him the conditions of future peaceful cohabitation: and these are called covenants, alliances, testaments. Through these compromises the Devil, his ambiguous work once accomplished, sees himself again excluded from man's history for a certain while, until the next existential crisis.

"At the historical moment we are concerned with, man and God were again at daggers drawn: endangered was not only the survival of the people who were the defenders of the One True and Living God, but the survival of God Himself. Imagine what would have become of the Lord had there been no new testament for mankind! The chosen people, due to be dispersed throughout the world and to vanish from the scene, would not have imposed the worship of the Lord on the other peoples of the earth, and the One True and Living God would have wound up forgotten in one of the cupboards of History, which would have set off on a new tack under the aegis of Attis or Mithra. Truly, this was no laughing matter: if He wanted to survive, the Lord must concede to humanity at least what His rivals had been promising and giving for quite some time, and which it would never have entered His own head to promise and give: free will, in the true sense of the word, free will upon this earth, and immortality and justice in the hereafter. It is not our job to try to find out to what state a great part of humanity must have been reduced that it aspire so fiercely after such impalpable and altogether unverifiable benefits. But it was a demand so widespread and so imperious that the Lord could not pretend deafness to it.

"In the historical moment we indicate through the term Redemption I for my part like to see a phase which in mankind's career had to be gone through, and to compare it—somewhat airily, I admit—to a point of arrival in the physical and psychical evolution of the being Man. It seems to me that the latter, having started from the unthinking state of the child in Eden and then undergoing the severe pedagogical regime of the Law, finally arrived at the crisis of adolescence, in the course of which the desire to get out from under paternal authority and acquire an adult autonomy hides beneath sublimations appearing as more authentic aspirations. During this period of crisis relations between father and son change radically, and this applies even when the son is mankind and the father is God. I believe that we may yet be hearing a great deal more from psychology on the significance and importance of the Redemption in mankind's story. I wish merely to point out that, in any case, it was Satan's moment! Present as he was at the birth of consciousness, could he have been absent at its reawakening?

"You understand perfectly now that when we speak of a diabolic intervention in history, we intend a critical moment in the existence of mankind which, after having courageously chosen to detach itself from the previous order, also runs the risk of going under. And what I am saying to you is that never since his expulsion from the earthly Paradise had man run a greater risk: he was about to repudiate the values of earthly life and assume an existence of hardships, burdened as he already was by the hatred of the Lord Himself: staking everything on the card of the next world, he risked waking up empty-handed—risked, that is, never waking up again. Still in all, rebirth demanded the sacrifice of earthly life, even at the risk of never being reborn.

"But for the mythologic mentality problems and solutions condense into a single, exemplary act which takes on a general value. The protagonist in a myth is all men combined into one: if he succeeds in his undertaking then everybody succeeds in it by following or imitating him. And when the hour of the New Testament struck, Man was Jesus. All the aspirations, expectations, anxieties, conscious and unconscious hopes of a collectivity were materialized in his person: it were enough that he undertake the great adventure which would conclude in triumph, it were enough that he alone travel the painful and perilous road of life, death and resurrection, and all could be reborn. If he succeeded, all would succeed: the Lord would become a friend again, perhaps more a friend than before, Satan would be beaten and reduced to impotence, order would be re-established, a new order within the framework of the old: the order of the New Testament. The great enterprise of the human spirit was summed up in that of Jesus Christ.

"Thus, while Man, the truly interested party, looked on, the Father, the Son and the Devil settled the business of the Redemption between them. As you see, the Mediterranean pattern for the ascent of new gods, Hebrew mythology, our modest results in the *terra incognita* of satanology, all would oblige us to posit the Devil's presence in Jesus' destinies, even in the case where he had not explicitly declared this to be so. And Satan behaved exactly as befitted Satan, both in the primordial sense and in the metaphysical sense of his essential self. On the one hand, brute and immeasurable force, without will, without thought and without initiative, but—almost in obedience to a chemical or physical law—forever ready to penetrate into the cracks of Creation and to receive it anew, if it gives way, into his indifferent and amorphous and infinite belly. Apparently always on the alert and waiting to swallow whatever exists, directly it looks to be unsteady or coming apart. But in reality it is the void alone that gather him in who loses his equilibrium. Satan does not act, he does but passively react to the provocation represented by the collapse of an existing order. Such is his role even in the human world: he comes on stage, or, to be more exact, man becomes aware of his presence when in his own despair he seeks a way out of conditions which have become intolerable to him. But man also discovers the other side of Satan: it is he who possesses the ways out! Satan stands there, passive, ready to devour him if he makes a mistake, but at the same time, in his passivity, he also offers himself: he offers the immense sterile wealth of all possibilities, for he is the one who is not, but could be—the raw material of omniscience, the All condemned to be Nothing. He remains standing there, he wants nothing for himself: indifferent, he lets you draw from his treasure whatever serves your desperation or your dreams: out of it you can create a new world, but if you have chosen badly, he takes you back into nothingness, with like indifference.

"That's Satan, *cher ami,* according to my satanological intuition, and you will now understand perfectly why the evangelists attributed no precise motive to Judas' treacherous act: whether because they were unable to identify it, and prudently preferred to pass on the matter; or because they understood indeed that there was no motive. Satan doesn't have motives, he doesn't hurt you, he doesn't help you: docile, or indifferent, he lets himself be exploited for your good or for your ill. Every one of your existential choices is articulated in the three acts of death, descent into limbo, and resurrection: you exclude yourself irreversibly from the old order, you attempt to install yourself in the new, at the risk sometimes of failing in the attempt, and when finally you manage to reintegrate the new within the old, you have re-arisen. But to travel this path of mystery common to the sons of gods, to humankind, and to the individual human being, you must first *understand* that the order, system, form of life you have lived in up until now is on the verge of crushing you, and you must *discover the possibility* of creating a new one for yourself: that is why Satan is present at the birth of every choice.

"In the earthly destinies of Jesus Christ, Judas fulfilled Satan's twofold function: he docilely let himself be exploited by him and passively conveyed him to his death, making resurrection possible for him. And then, hanging himself, he betook himself from the scene in good devil style. For this too is a characteristic of Satan: when man has managed to settle one way or another into his new order, Satan withdraws. And he makes no further appearance until the new conditions in their turn become very bad and intolerable: with an encouraging nudge from him, we then take it all apart and remake the whole thing. In simple language, that's life. And for mankind, that's History. We shall have further need of him for some time. But when at last we attain the perfect and unperfectable order, when man no longer has cause for, or the possibilities of, dreaming up something better, that is, when he has no further need for Satan, History will shut up shop. I sometimes think that must be the aim of the mysterious divine scheme."

*   *   *

During this last phase of my friend Dupin's long soliloquy, my astonishment grew to the point where I was unable to refrain from interrupting him:

"*Parbleu, cher ami!*" I exclaimed. "Don't you think you've strayed a bit outside the bounds of our investigation? Do you realize you have wound up making prophecies? Being the intelligent man you are, I can't imagine you believing in such absurdities."

Dupin's appearance was that of someone who from a state of semi-consciousness wakes again to reality. He smoothed his thinning hair, and smiled sheepishly. Then he composed himself and his face now wore a curiously bellicose air:

"I don't like being taken for an idiot by the one friend I have. All right, I admit that the fault is partly mine, for I'm up to the ears in this biblical atmosphere, and when I talk Biblical I sometimes get so enmeshed in it all that you can no longer tell whether I'm speaking on my own behalf or whether I am interpreting the thinking contained in the Good Book. You would have every right to laugh in my face if towards the close of my life I took up questions of the *Where do we come from, why do we exist, where are we going?* variety. You know me not as a person who gets bogged down in insoluble problems, but as someone who in the course of an investigation is keenly interested in what others have to say—in the present case, in what the Bible has to say. We have not strayed from the subject and, even if the ideas touched upon above do not fall exactly within the frame of our investigation, I can guarantee you that they are not prophecies on my part but indeed conclusions drawn from the severest analysis of the sacred text. These are interesting things about which we do not have to talk—but, on the other hand, with whom am I to talk about them if not with you?—who, I may add, are to blame for having interrupted me in my story and forced me into a long theoretical excursus. I find an almost sadistic pleasure in keeping you from eating. Nevertheless, go ahead, you have my permission to step into the kitchen and fix yourself a sandwich."

I took advantage of this authorization, while he made use of the interval to give himself over to the sacred rite of choosing, cleaning, filling with tobacco and finally lighting another pipe.

"In the course of my biblical readings," Dupin resumed as soon as I got back, "I was struck by two things. The first is that God had intended that man should live in Eden. The second is is that man, from his expulsion down to this day, has done nothing but try to recreate the conditions of the earthly Paradise. Our famous human intelligence, which I see as a simple physiological organ of service to survival, like the nose or liver, apparently has no objectives beyond reconstituting Edenic conditions. And what, in substance, are these so pined after Edenic conditions? Nothing other than security of existence, living for the sake of living, in an animal-like happiness, without cares and without sufferings, assured of one's daily bread and of what one eats along with bread, be it understood.

"Then I was struck by something else. I discovered to my great surprise that upon this point human aspirations and divine promises coincided. If you review the famous covenants, you cannot fail to notice that the Almighty always soothes consternated or desperate mankind by showering material blessings upon it. He allows Noah to feed on all the animals that populate the earth, and even to discover wine. He entices Abraham with the prospect of the Promised Land, Canaan overflowing milk and honey. The Lord seems to know them through and through, these favorite creatures of His, for whom nothing counts more than a well-filled stomach. That is why, among other upsetting feelings, He must have experienced some surprise, even some embarrassment, when in the New Testament covenant no one asked Him to better living conditions on earth. He must have thought mankind had gone clean out of its mind! Oh no, it's not without cause that it occurred to me to compare this historical moment to the crisis of adolescence. It is a phenomenon typical of puberty to feed upon dreams, upon illusions if you wish, and to scorn material things, don't you agree? Or was it destitution that affected his brain, forcing man to make a virtue out of necessity? But let's not worry about it, *cher ami*. What matters to us is that humanity lived for many centuries in accordance with the covenant of Good Tidings, and that meanwhile, and ever more insistently, it got back a taste for eating well and living agreeably. As usual, it was man who did not abide by the clauses of his covenant with God, and I do not think I am mistaken if I affirm that, at the present time, we are already living outside the framework of the New Testament. Not for a long time has the salvation of our soul constituted a primordial problem for us, and we proceed along the path of well-being without thinking that this can be pleasing neither to the Son nor to the Father. That it cannot please Jesus, guarantor of the latest covenant, seems to me beyond discussion. But it must not please the Lord either: He promises, and from time to time grants, the chunk of bread, sometimes the milk and the honey too, but according to the Bible's testimony (substantiated in this case by History), He does not appreciate man's taking too many liberties, infringing His laws, and beginning to become forgetful of Him . . .

"I was saying, dear friend—and, I remind you, it was still biblically speaking—, that the time is drawing near for a new covenant in which God and man shall have to re-examine their respective positions. The moment seems to be dangerous for both parties. As usual, alas, it is man who is incurring the greater peril. You'll recall the stages of the process: man becomes arrogant, God becomes angry, unleashes a cataclysm, and afterwards concludes a pact with man who is reduced to bare bones and frightened to death. I do not wish to frighten you in my turn, but I have the distinct impression that we are on a collision course with the divine order. We no longer pay any attention to the New Testament and day in, day out violate even the handful of divine laws that up until the other day were still considered to be eternally valid. We allow our possibilities to go to our head, we go about realizing them like madmen, but whatever the initiative we take in favor of our comfort, it boomerangs against us, against our interests, putting our survival squarely into jeopardy. I have no trouble imagining the opening lines of the next covenant:

" 'And the Lord saw that men were wicked, and He said: It is time to exterminate them. But whilst in the past I had always had to intervene Myself, I may now leave the task to them. Then, with the few who will be capable of reasoning, I shall conclude My covenant. Thus spake the Lord and upon the earth men began to die. By the steak they did eat and the wine they did drink were they poisoned. Then they fed on sea-weed and water, but were poisoned by them. Then, when of sea-weed there came to be no more, they ate each other, but it poisoned them. Unto men naught was left but the air to breathe, but the air was poisonous also, and they died from it. Then did the Lord say to His chosen: I shall make a covenant with you and with your offspring . . .' "

I had abandoned myself with lazy pleasure to my friend's pyro-technical performances; but now, he having interrupted himself, I realized that he was awaiting from me some sign of my interest.

"And what would the terms be of this new covenant?" I asked.

"I'm not a fortune-teller, you know," replied Dupin, pensive. "We must also allow for what the Son has to say—and perhaps, who knows, for what the Holy Ghost has to say as well. If we wish to hold coherently with the biblical line, this newest Testament, I'd imagine, would have to be concluded between men and the Trinity's mysterious third person. The truth however is that we know still less about it than about the two others. Nor have we any way of knowing how far humanity will have got with its self-destruction. I personally hope that History doesn't start all over again with bread earned by the sweat of the brow and children brought forth in sorrow. Instead I hope that History ends, but that man retains all his conquests, from the refrigerator to atomic fission. In my opinion, God will say to His chosen: 'You and those you elect with the help of the Holy Ghost must procure unto others the happiness of the Earthly Paradise, in order that they may return to the animal state, enlightened by that modicum of reason which suffices for worshipping Me.' Wouldn't you say that this solution would be satisfactory to both God and mankind?"

"But no worse end can be foreseen for the human species!" I exclaimed, almost indignant. "How would you have man give up his consciousness, his intelligence?"

"He won't have to give them up," Dupin promptly rejoined, a touch of melancholy in his voice. "Your expressing yourself this way shows that you too are under the spell of biblical language. Our hypothetical Third Testament will of course not begin with the aforesaid verses. Have you forgotten Satan? It will begin with the appearing of Satan, who will set his trap and offer his present. Listen to this: 'And the Devil said unto man: But why do you go on living with the forbidden fruit's taste in your mouth? Get rid of that unsightly swelling your neck ends in, spit it forth, and tell your woman to spit with all her might too: and you shall be like the beasts, happy and immortal, ignorant of Good and Evil, and you shall be restored to Paradise. Then they freed themselves of the remembrance of the forbidden fruit, and discovering their loins mysteriously covered over by a fig-leaf, they snatched it away.' Ah yes, my friend, you had forgotten about the Devil who, we've agreed, cannot absent himself at humankind's critical moments. As always, he appears and offers man the possibilities for extricating himself from the order which is about to undermine his existence. Those possibilities, as a rule, are always few, but at the beginning of the Third Testament there really will be no choice at all. Man will chose the one possibility available: the renunciation of his human consciousness, intelligence, mind, spirit, or whatever else it happens to be called. But, in speaking this way, we are still employing a mythologic language; reality is not so colorful. Naked reality is far more frightening. There it is . . . Human intelligence will die a natural death, dying of itself.

"Now don't make that dreadful face! Simply get the notion out of your head that Intelligence, the superb Human Mind is some independent entity, end in itself, autonomous value, uppermost objective of the sublimest aspirations, and reduce it instead to its original and simpler function of an organ, albeit typically human, serving existence and survival, and you will at once understand that it too must undergo the fate of organs which are no longer necessary to the functioning of the organism: it will wither away, atrophy like the appendix, and if it does not entirely die, it will be condemned to a seeming life. I would go almost so far as to say that it deserves this end, for under its influence we are due to see our very bodies gradually deteriorate: our legs, our teeth, woman's breasts and uterus, even our brain as it becomes ever more dispensed from the necessity of thinking, all these will end up as memories of bygone functions. And, when you come down to it, shall we really miss this famous Human Mind so much? In my view, the common run of mankind doesn't make inordinate use of it and I fail to see, from this point of view, any difference at all between the present and the hypothetical state of affairs: men do not live at the level for which they are qualified. Making slender use of reason, the human consciousness feels itself torn between the solicitations of unquiet instincts and the demands of abstract superstructures. Man would like to live in the somnolent torpor of animals satisfied by the pleasures of food and of sex. This rare use of his mental faculties in the course of his everyday routine tends only to worsen his situation, for on the one hand it does not allow his repressed instincts a free rein, and on the other it limits the intensity of his enjoyment of life. Getting rid of this damnable human consciousness will, in my opinion, make for a happy end to its career."

"Yours is a dark pessimism indeed," I remarked, ever more astonished by Dupin's divagations. "I never would have thought that you foresaw such a miserable end for our kind!"

"I may be even more pessimistic than you are able to imagine, *cher ami!*" he burst out heatedly. "The fact is I am convinced that the Third Testament is in operation already and that Satan delivered that little speech of his some time ago: I can't tell you exactly when it was, somewhere around the beginning of the last century. His ambiguous gift to humanity was the Machine, in both its concrete sense and in its symbolic and generalized sense, which includes the dizzying advance of the sciences, the incessant progress of technology, and their determinant contribution to the harmonious future well-being of mankind. You are already about to tell me that for the moment all that is visible of the ambiguity is the darker sides that will lead us to self-destruction. But the game's not over! Biblically speaking, we are in the descent into hell phase, the stage of settling in, the period of desperate attempts to arrange the absolutely new inside the framework of the old, from which we cannot and do not want to detach ourselves completely. More unexpected than the gift were its consequences: an avalanche of goods submerged us too swiftly, and we find ourselves a little disoriented amidst all that. But we'll be all right. A short visit to limbo always precedes resurrection. There is no cause for alarm. Do you perhaps believe that coming hale and hearty through the various glacial eras and floods was an easier business?

"And, furthermore, I am a supporter of the concrete sciences and technology (and you mustn't be misled by the fact that I still use candles for lighting, it's purely a matter of laziness), for their progress is the only constant in History and only in their sphere can one speak of any real progress: philosophy, the arts, the humane sciences, ethics do not advance, all they do is change as a result of progress alone, judging and evaluating it in its various phases. But I value progress above all because it is a gift from Satan. You know by now that it is not possible to turn these gifts down, for our survival depends on them. You cannot order progress to a halt! But over and above the material well-being it holds in store for us, there is a luminous, metaphysical side to this last gift from Satan. Has it ever occurred to you that with the forbidden fruit Satan made us the gift of a morsel of omniscience, and with the Redemption (or the work of betrayal, if you prefer) a morsel of immortality? He is in the act now of bestowing a handful of omnipotence upon us. Thanks to progress we are going to have at our command all the essential divine properties, in miniature . . .

"You now understand that one cannot renounce Satan's gifts; in our modern idiom we would say that the great essential and existential chapters of humanity's careers were more the fruit of an ineluctable necessity than of wishes and dreams, and that the great choice among the different possibilities for making our way out of dangerous situations always came down to the sole vital one, the very choice that was made. We are still here, alive and kicking, and this means that Satan's gifts are always good. Except, however, for one thing: we have always, in exchange, had to relinquish something, the something he wants in return. For consciousness, we had to give up the happiness of unconsciousness; for the salvation of our soul, the cherishing of worldly goods. But this sentence too is translatable into our modern idiom. Never has man given up anything: fleeing a situation that has become unbearable, he irremediably loses certain advantages he enjoyed hitherto; but it would be difficult to speak of renouncings when, with his acceptance of the gift of immortality in a hereafter, man sought to flee the stifling emptiness, the absurdity of a life of hardship and woe. Truly it seems that he did not make any renunciation and lost nothing in this exchange: the hunk of bread and the rags he was clad in remained his, even in the era of the New Testament. But wait a moment! Wordly goods extend beyond material goods, they also include the relationships we have with them. And the slaves, the poor, the forsaken, the humiliated, who took Christ's Word seriously and resigned themselves to the society that came to be built upon it, lost not only the possibility of obtaining goods they had never been able to possess, but also the capacity to dream of them and the capacity to struggle for them. In their terror of mortal sin and the prospects of hell, they lost all desire to enjoy the little the world offers even to the common herd. By shifting existence's center of gravity into the Kingdom of Heaven, they lost their love for the values of this life. As you can see, they who possess nothing also have a great deal to lose. Satan asks too high a price for his gifts!

"This is why I dare to affirm that for the gift of the artificial

Eden of the future Satan has demanded intelligence in exchange. Not that we'll renounce it: we'll lose it little by little, like an asset from another time become not only superfluous in this new stage of our journey, but impossible to use. Yes, and which would actually be dangerous, and would backfire! I'll explain. Just think a little! In possession of this morsel of divine omnipotence, Satan's latest gift, sooner or later, inevitably or perforce—in several decades or several centuries, and in spite of human stupidity and selfishness, conflagrations or cataclysms, halts and relapses of all sorts —we shall reach a high level of prosperity and security. This will be, since it will have to be, a well-constructed edifice, a complex and complicated organism, created, consolidated, controlled and protected by a few rare 'chosen of God,' off limits to those having no hand in the work, who will have to be content with enjoying the prosperity and security which that miracle of perfection guarantees. The Artificial Paradise will be a perfect and very complex, almost a high-precision machine, that profane hands will not have the right to touch; profane thoughts either. Any idea emanating from an incompetent person would wreck it. Furthermore, what sort of idea could be born in a profane brain regarding a high-precision machine? And, finally, why should it be born, when this machine distributes without respite, generously and impeccably, all the good things the human imagination is capable of dreaming up? Do you understand now why intelligence will end up by becoming dangerous, impossible and superfluous?

"They are probably very few who realize that this atrophying process of the human intelligence has been under way for some time now. Even today the greater part of the tasks which a few decades ago, or just a few years ago, depended on everyone's individual brain, have already been entrusted to specialized persons or machines. And we're still only getting started. Little by little we shall delegate all the functions of our intelligence to those, the men or the machines, able to make better use of it in our interest. That's how it will be because that's how it has to be: it is the condition imposed by Satan's gift. Some naïvely hope that the human intelligence, freed from preoccupation with "technical' problems, will open up more to the *humaniora*, will more eagerly devote itself to cultivating ideals of beauty, morality, and social organization. But any such hope seems to me an illusion sprung from the fact that whoever holds this belief is projecting today's situation upon the future. Today, and this today can mean decades or hundreds of years, a part of our intelligence, as we said, is used to overcome the difficulties that obstruct the road to the Artificial Paradise. But even that part of our intelligence, which has enough to keep it busy for yet a while, will also rapidly atrophy directly the goal and ideal are achieved. The intelligence lives upon goals and ideals, but goals and ideals are born of necessity, like History itself. When the Artificial Paradise has reared itself in History's former place, there will no longer be any goals, there will no longer be any ideals, the splendid Human Intelligence will expire through inaction and man will have to be content with unlimited well-being and constant security inside his gilded cage. Of course he will still have some leftover of brain to tell him what use to put his mouth and genitals to. And in spite of everything this vestige of reason will be superior to that of the beast, in as much as it will aid him to orient himself among the many buttons he will have to press his whole life long . . ."

I stared at my friend and gaped, not knowing whether he was in earnest or pulling my leg.

"And this splendid prospect, you believe in it?" I ventured, giving the adjective a slightly ironic emphasis to show that I hadn't been completely taken in. But Dupin did not seem to notice that irony.

"You have definitively made up your mind to confuse me with the Bible," said he with a fugitive smile. "All that is simply what I have deduced from my reading of the Bible. And if worse comes to worst, it will be one of my interpretations of the Bible. But, to conclude, I give you a glimmer of hope, which also comes from the Bible. If indeed the aim of the divine plan is to get man, rendered inoffensive again, back into the Earthly Paradise, rebuilt and with improvements by him, I believe that the Lord will leave His prodigal son in possession of a smidget more of reason than is required to pick the right button out of the lot. He will allow man pretty much the same amount of reason that He endowed him with at the time He created him: a reason scarcely superior to that of the beasts, but capable of conceiving of God, of worshipping Him and praising Him for all the magnificence of His Creation which, at long last, he shall thus, but only thus, be able to enjoy and contemplate at his ease. How do you feel about that? In my opinion, if you look at man's chances, that may be the best one he's got. It may also be the only one . . ."

"And you . . ." I began, dazed. But Dupin, waggling his finger at me, interrupted:

"Don't ask me again whether I believe in this or not. It is a fact that the Bible believes in God. The problem is now of knowing whether God really exists or doesn't. In the affirmative case, it will not be impossible to rediscover Him in a more or less faraway future. If on the other hand He does not exist, then I don't know . . . maybe it would be worth going to the trouble of reinventing Him . . ."

Dupin stretched his thin legs and with three sharp taps knocked the ashes out of his pipe.

"Sorry, I got swept away—but, you know, I'm a born chatterer who, in the absence of an agreeable partner, is apt not to open his mouth for years on end. At any rate, you've had all the answers I was able to give to your questions about the Devil. I think it's time we get back to our flesh-and-blood Devil, to Judas Iscariot, who couldn't have done a better job as Devil than he did. Through his betrayal he dealt a ferocious blow to the divine superpower, gave the Son a hand in his attempt at overthrowing the Father, and, finally, offered us his ambiguous gift: salvation of the soul and and the delights of the hereafter in exchange for contempt for the body and for the pleasures of this world. That's why he came within a hair's breadth of being raised to the honors of the altar . . ."

"It looks like you're really bent on amusing yourself at my expense tonight," I broke in, almost vexed.

But he let out a hearty laugh.

"All right, I'm joking, it's true, but it isn't a gratuitous joke. Perhaps you don't know that in the early years of the Middle Ages a Gnostic heresy, that of the so-called Cainites, held Judas in great esteem, for by betraying Christ and causing his death Judas had overthrown the tyranny of the Father, considered by those heretics to be a mere demiurge. And for my part I think very highly of a religious faction which had the wits to recognize that behind the bare, semi-historic account given in the Gospels lay a struggle between transcendent forces. That Judas was the object of veneration may seem distasteful and odd, but remember the honor enjoyed by the governor of Palestine, closely linked to the betrayer in the condemnation of later generations: in the calendar of the Coptic Church Pontius Pilate figures among the saints and his title to this glory is his ignominious yet precious collaboration in the work of Redemption. This means that for the great gift of Redemption a share of humanity, generally accused of ingratitude, owns itself grateful even to those who *indirectly* caused the Redeemer's death. From this it can be seen that for the primitive mentality the same person may be judged simultaneously a criminal and a saint, and that someone who has benefitted humanity (even involuntarily and to the detriment of the gods) may count upon some token of recognition. A Saint Judas would not be utterly impossible, thanks to his misdeed and to the grateful heart of the mankind redeemed by Christ.

"That Judas was not canonized seems stranger to me next to the recognition of Pilate's saintliness, if one considers that whereas the latter actually had nothing to do with Jesus' cause, the twelfth apostle contributed, unwillingly indeed, but directly, to its success; and even though the work of Redemption may not have had greater import for him than for the Roman governor, he did all he could to help the Master accomplish it. If his dedication and sacrifice did not earn him the glory of the Empyrean it is owing

solely to the fact that he was the Devil. Saint Satan would also be
the most absurd *contradictio in adiecto*.

"But now, *très cher*," said Dupin, raising his voice as well as his
forefinger in friendly warning, "I must beg you from here on to
hold off from expressing your indignation or your approval,
though I treasure them both. I should like, indeed, to move along
rapidly with the identification of the last milestones marking the
wordless dialogue that unfolded between a man destined to become
God, anxious to die under certain well-defined circumstances and
at a precise moment, and another man, who—though being the
Devil—had no reason at all to bring on his death. We know that
from this point on these destinies were under the unswerving rule
of a mythologic fate, and that the very fact of being the Devil for
Judas implied a congenital involvement which his wretched
human incarnation had no way of eluding. Thus you can understand why, despite his spontaneous horror and his energetic mental
protests, he came to serve, even to his own detriment, the desires
of his Master.

"This twofold enslavement, to Jesus and to Satan, made of the
twelfth apostle the unhappiest of mortal beings; and the road
which led from Ephraim to Bethany was certainly Judas Iscariot's
via crucis: proceeding down that road, he thought about dying. We
venture this hypothesis with the added confidence that comes from
the fact that, a few days later, Judas did indeed kill himself . . .
But we ask ourselves this question: once tempted by the idea of
death, why did he not kill himself right away, instead of
committing the most dreadful deed in the history of mankind?
However, had he done so, Judas would have put the Gospels'
exegetes before a ticklish problem. Had he taken refuge in death to
avoid the enacting of a vile intention he could have hoped for some
small amount of indulgence, if not of compassion: all things
considered, it is the worthier course to die honestly than to
preserve oneself for the doing of evil. But, in that case, another
question arises: would the Gospels exist? Would Christianity

exist? And last but not least, the exegetes themselves—would they exist?

"Judas had ceased to have any doubt that the absurd deed he was heading toward was the will of Jesus, and he did not ask himself whether submitting to that will was, on his part, indicative of moral superiority or of inferiority and the betrayal an act of generosity or of cowardice. It was later generations who beheld these problems in a simpler or more complicated manner. At this point, I would like to advise the right-minded, as they are called, who condemn him unhesitatingly and beyond appeal, to reconsider their rigid moralism. These gentlemen do not realize what a short step it is from the judge's bench to the defendant's! It would suffice, actually, if I put one simple question to them: 'Answer me, good sirs, with your hand upon your heart: had it been in your power, would you have halted Judas on the road to betrayal?' What an idea! Jesus himself did not try to do so; the theologians may say what they like, they wouldn't have done it either, just as, for that matter, no good Christian of today would do it: nobody, knowing the tremendous benefits accruing from the aforesaid fatal step, would have advised Judas against the betrayal. We are all accomplices to the Crime of crimes, and the one person in the world and in History who had nothing to gain from committing it, or to put it more exactly, the only one who had everything to gain from not committing it, was, precisely, Judas Iscariot himself! And if he committed it even so, that proves his supreme fidelity to the Master and his immense confidence in him. And that was enough for the twelfth apostle . . .

"In order to please Jesus, he hanged himself only after the crime and not before. But after having with superhuman strength performed his absurd task, wherefore he had not the courage to assume responsibility even though it was objectively indispensable, universally important, and desired above all else by the victim, he killed himself. His suicide thus belongs to the classical type, whose frequent examples in History call forth profound compassion from everyone, no matter who he is.

"As something to at least keep alive on there could have been that hope which never deserts even him who knows with certainty the end that must be inevitably his; in the present case, though, it is hard to speak of certainty as this is usually understood. He came to the deed which made him the most wretched of men by way of thinking, by way of signs and allusions, by way of a dialogue in which not one single explicit and unequivocal word was ever once uttered: room always remained for a minimum of uncertainty, and it was on this modest basis that doubt, with the hope it bred, enabled Judas Iscariot to continue to drag his life on ere he reached indubitable certainty.

"But how was this to be acquired? As more like an assistant than a shadow he followed the Lord's white-clad figure down the tragic road from Ephraim to Bethany, Judas once again was tempted to take hold of those straight and so indifferent and self-confident shoulders, and to shake them, and to force the Master to turn his face about, and to look with all his uneasiness into the the latter's dreamy, absent eyes, and finally to ask him: 'Say, O Lord, am I mad and the victim of morbid ideas, or do you truly wish me to hand you over to the law?' But by itself the act of imagining those dreamy and absent eyes, which would have turned a cold and unpitying stare upon him, broke in him the courage to rebel.

"That his soul thirsted cruelly for but one spoken word is shown by the famous episode of the anointing in Bethany which we might call, borrowing the standpoint of the twelfth apostle, 'the certitude of Bethany.' You doubtless recall the episode.

"After Mary, the sister of Lazarus, anointed the Master's head and feet with perfumed nard, and the house was filled with its heavenly fragrance, an indignant murmur arose among the apostles and all or some (according to the respective versions of Matthew and Mark) began asking why all that ointment had been wasted, and declaring that instead it could have been sold for more than three hundred pieces of silver and the money given to the poor. And they felt anger against her, Lazarus' humble and impassioned sister, as Mark recalls—but he might have added also: 'and against him.'

"The episode of the anointing in Bethany contains so many poetic, dramatic and symbolic elements that, curiously, it has occurred to no one to emphasize that this episode was also the most regrettable of all those reported in the Gospels. Indeed, we have to remind ourselves that they were but a few days away from Jesus' death, and therefore—in the estimation of pious believers—with a sense of the tragic end's nearness, Master and disciples ought to have been united in a profound and indissoluble spiritual onenness. Instead, we see the apostles for the first time daring to criticize the Master, in public and without reserve, mutually inciting and exciting one another. The fanatically enamored woman simply serves them as a pretext. Poor thing, what part has she had in this uprising? Had they all been as enamored of the Lord as she, or at least as enthusiastic and impassioned, they would have mainly praised her. Oddly, instead of that they are all horrified by the waste of ointment and money and, as though to excuse their indignation, they talk about the poor. Why all of a sudden did they become so niggardly? Or, the other way around, so charitable? And if it is too much to expect good manners and refinement from one-time fishermen and tax-gatherers, would not the mute pleasure of the Master lost in his dreams, or just his complaisance, have sufficed to daunt them?

"Jesus sits staring before him. Emerging suddenly from a sweet dream, he wakes to reality and it stupefies him. All during the woman's loving ministrations he dreamt that he was already dead, that he was receiving the unction that was due his corpse; he dreamt that he was already *beyond* the dreadful end, already in the tomb; absorbed in his tender sepulchral dream he perhaps imagined that those present, guests, apostles, disciples, were kneeling around his mortal remains, that they were tearing the clothing they wore and covering their heads with ashes, weeping. Instead, he is awakened by indignant grumblings and excited whisperings. At first he perceives only a mounting of unconcealed discontent.

But, suddenly, from within this swelling murmur a shrill voice stands out, piercing, almost lunatic, unexpected. Jesus looks up, astonished. And there now, in front of all the others, looms the one who would customarily keep back of the others. He is gesticulating, speaking at the top of his strident voice, this one who up until now has never made bold to address him at all. Thereupon Jesus realizes what is happening; thereupon also he understands the twelfth apostle, but only him. The eleven others do not interest him: a whole world sepates him from them at that moment. He bluntly puts them in their place, calls them to order, reprimands them: 'Let that woman be . . . The poor, you will always find plenty of them . . .' All that matters to him is to communicate the image that just before had laid hold of him: the image of his entombment. And to make it understood that in what she has done this woman has but anticipated the anointing of his corpse and that everything, therefore, is as of now over with, defined, henceforth immutable. Who is to understand him among all the apostles, full of unacknowledged hostility toward him because of the adventure into which he is about to drag them? Who if not the very one, the twelfth, who is waiting for this answer? . . .

"Never were relations between the Master and his disciples so strained as on that evening in Bethany. For anyone endowed with a minimum of psychology, it is obvious that the words spoken on either side are irrelevant and excessive, having regard to the motives that should have dictated them. Repeated here is a situation often exploited by dramaturgy, a climax in which two parties who had joined together in order to attain the same objective and had been in accord for a long time, finally come to the first tragic crossing of swords after numerous little dissensions that were never admitted to, after numerous divergences of opinion that were never discussed, after numerous affronts swallowed without a word, after numerous little disappointments poisoning the seemingly calm and peaceful atmosphere reigning between them. The repressed feelings erupt at the first opportunity. At issue is always something different from what the spoken words express: what is at issue is precisely what the words come to hide, to mask. At a time like this, depressed and made anxious by sinister omens, how could the disciples possibly worry about the money that went for the nard wasted on the Master's feet, or about the poor it might have been given to? There can be no doubt that for the eleven others as well the two days' walk from Ephraim to Bethany was full of unexpected agitations, unpleasant surprises, and bitter disappointments too. Off in the clouds, the Lord strode on at their head without deigning to say a single word to them. And when John, the favorite, urged on perhaps by Peter, made an attempt to find out where matters stood and whether they could count on the secondary thrones that ought to surround the Messiah's, the response was a short, sharp reprimand. None of them had a clue either to what the Master's projects were, or to what the true essence of his messianic mission was, and since in lieu of explanations he gave only evasive replies and did not hesitate to predict for himself an ignominious, absurd end, to occur before there would be time enough for conquering the throne of the King of the Jews, the souls of the apostles were filled with confusion and apprehensiveness. They began to realize that they had misunderstood, to perceive that nothing was the way they had imagined it.

"In the anointing they found something unspeakably scandalous, outrageously provocative, and on this they were all agreed, for all of them, for one reason or another, were angry with the Master. They themselves did not understand what in that humble act of homage so upset them. But they were all in a such a state of tension that one drop was enough to make the cup overflow: and behold, while their souls were being racked by a thousand anxieties and their confused minds tortured by a thousand worries, the Master sat down with that unearthly calm of his to abandon himself to a woman's amorous cajoleries! Jesus sat there, his eyes closed, a rapturous expression upon his face: never had their dedication, their fervor, their self-sacrifice procured him such thorough satisfaction as that abominable unguent of Mary's! This giving himself up totally to the enjoyment of the homage seemed a derision of their persevering faith, of their whole sacrificed lives.

"Not daring to do so with the Lord, they discharged all their ill-humor upon the rich and beautiful young woman, who from every particle of her supple body exuded the intoxicating magic of her sex. Indeed, swept into a kind of trance by her own overflowing adoration, she was all but groveling on the floor; and the while she lay there prone, drying the Master's feet with her golden hair and touching her avid lips to them, all around, as if by enchantment, the atmosphere built up of a world totally out of tune with the one where their feelings and thoughts were languishing. Oh, if it had been they who were in the Lord's place, wouldn't they have kicked that hussy straight out of doors! But instead, the Lord, his eyes closed and with a transfigured expression on his face, was plainly enjoying her adoring female attentions!

"At first they cast quick, meaningful glances at one another, then they began to fidget, though they themselves didn't know what was bothering them. Finally, someone hit upon the manner for liberating the nameless discontent that was stifling them, a not too offensive manner, one which might even prove pleasing to the Lord as well.

"When the others had begun to stir and indignant murmurings had begun to go back and forth, Judas, illuminated by a sudden intuition, had the feeling that here was the moment when he might succeed in extracting the long-awaited reply to his exasperating doubts. The emotions he had been repressing for days, for weeks, for months now erupted with irresistible force, a great wave of despair and bitterness burst the dikes of shame and modesty and fear, and he, who hitherto had always kept to the rear and uttered never a word, now elbowed his way forward, and to the chorus of the eleven others added his shrill, piercing voice, deformed by madness. Perhaps because of their excitement, those others did not notice it or did not attribute any significance to it. But John noticed, and was so struck by it that, with the passing of time, it was the betrayer's shrill and piercing voice that alone stood out in his memory

"And the Master too noticed his presence. More, he understood, at the same moment, that nobody was really concerned about the cost of the ointment and about alms for the poor—the twelfth apostle still less so than the others. Then he replied. Not directly to him, nor explicitly, but not in an ambiguous manner either. He spoke of himself as of a corpse: of the near future he spoke as though in the past tense. And when he saw his disciple turn white as a sheet, his soul was invaded by a hitherto unknown calm. Now he knew, with infallible certainty, both that Judas Iscariot had understood him and that he had never been mistaken about his twelfth apostle. Jesus was now persuaded that line by line, from deduction to deduction, the dialogue was proceeding with ironclad logic towards its conclusion.

"Jesus' words were followed by a mortal silence. The eleven, shamefaced, fell still: they realized they had committed an injustice toward the Lord, though they did not know in what it consisted. But the twelfth, like someone who has heard himself sentenced to death, felt the ground beneath him give way.

"All room for doubts was gone. The Lord's sepulchral dream would remain a dream forever if he, Judas, failed to act. The Lord would never have dared to dream had he not been confident that he would help him turn his dream into a reality.

"By now the die was cast . . .

"After having acted in accordance with the order he was given, his doubts took hold of him again, poisoning the last days he spent in the Lord's company. Was there yet a possibility that he might be mistaken? All is not lost, he told himself feverishly. Everything can still be straightened out! Indeed, with what results had he come away from his visit to the high priests after the grotesque entry into Jerusalem? They had treated him with great contempt, and for his part he had found nothing to tell them that they did not already know. Over the two thousand years that followed no martyr or confessor testified more solemnly, more vehemently in favor of Jesus Christ than did Judas Iscariot before the high priests! But nobody had believed him. The terms for him so familiar, so cherished, such as Son of God, Messiah, Redeemer, King of the Jews, from them fetched forth boundless hilarity. They made fun of him and reproached him for not presenting any proof. 'And so, just like that, we're supposed to believe he's the King of the Jews?' and they broke into hearty laughter. Did anybody believe it? Well, they certainly didn't, and they retorted that nobody would. And Judas realized with terror that not even the eleven had believed it. So then he began to swear and to implore their confidence: 'Believe me! For I *know*! I know that He is the Son of God! And is it so difficult for the Son of God to turn in a flash into the King of the Jews?' This reasoning gave the priests pause for a moment, but a moment later they fell to laughing again. 'And do you believe in him?' they asked. 'I believe, I swear it to you, I believe in Him as I believe in the Father, the One and Living God!'

"The high priests, who had gathered around him in ever growing numbers, observed his exalted behavior with astonishment. 'But what is it you're really after?' they asked him. 'If you believe in the man, why do you want us to lay hold of him?' What a sorry actor he made! He would have liked to have replied to them in accordance with the truth, saying, 'Just because of that! Because I believe in Him and because I believe that what He wants is right! And it's He who wants it, that you lay hold of Him and that you torture Him and then, without wasting any time, before Passover, that you crucify Him'—but was it possible to say the truth? Feverishly he cast about for other arguments, everyday ones, hence more credible. Oh, how at that moment he hated the Master who had forced him into this terrible and stupid role!

" 'And because I hate Him,' he whispered aloud, and it may have been said in the belief it was so. Then he added heatedly: 'I believe in Him, but I hate Him. You don't think it's possible to believe in someone and hate him at the same time?' The priests shrugged their shoulders. Exhausted, Judas looked at them beseechingly, and he turned to the commonplace arguments: 'Yes, I hate Him, for He is leading our people to disaster. He will redeem us, yes, He will open to us the gates of the Kingdom of Heaven, but He will bring the wrath of Rome down upon the Jewish nation! And upon you too! And I do not wish, by keeping silent, to become the undoing of my people!'

"Here the Judas of the legend would have recalled his mother's dream. He, who had committed all possible and impossible sins and was about to commit the most terrible of crimes, could he not at least avoid the one foretold even before he was born? Rather than lead his people to ruination, could he not save it instead? Might there not be one drop of good in the ocean of evil? But to History's Judas it did not occur to look about for self-justification. With revived hope he saw that the phrase 'the wrath of Rome' had made a certain impact upon the high priests. At any rate, a frown had appeared on their faces and there was a muttering going on between them. The wrath of Rome! Ah yes. Rome! The view that Rome took of matters was something they'd never neglected. Needless to say, in a case where a prophet or a candidate Messiah should threaten to provoke political conflict, he would be seized and handed over to the Roman authorities. Indeed, the case of this Jesus of Nazareth had already been examined from this so exceedingly important angle, but, to be honest about it, he had not been found to be very dangerous. What he had said and done so far was all within lawful bounds. Only once had he declared publicly that he was the Son of God, but, when cornered, he had very cleverly talked his way out. As for being the Messiah and the King of the Jews, he had said nothing to that effect up until now; so all in all, what did it amount to? To begin with, you'd have to prove that he truly considered himself to be these things, and then that he publicly passed himself off as such. But there was no proof, and there didn't seem to be anything urgent about the affair. Some intervention or other on the part of the religious authorities would have been reasonable and indispensable only should it appear that the crowd believed in him. But there was nothing to indicate that this sort of thing had occurred.

"The high priests then turned their attention back to Judas Iscariot, who looked at them wild-eyed, trying to make out their innermost thoughts. 'We'll think about it,' they told him. 'During Passover, we don't want to have anything that could arouse public opinion.' Then, on the verge of despair, Judas played his last card: 'Beware!' he cried. 'If that be the case, then Jesus, who is also called Christ—and who in very truth is Christ!—shall undertake to arouse the public. What hasn't happened so far is about to happen! What until now He has not said, now He will proclaim it. And what until now He has not done, now He will do it: before the vast crowd come to town upon the occasion of the holidays, He will declare Himself King of the Jews, and by virtue of His divine power He will ascend to the throne of the Kingdom. He is in a position to do so, for, understand this once and for all, He truly is the Son of God and the Messiah! I know whereof I speak.'

"The priests began whispering to one another again: it's not impossible that this young man does know something, and it's not at all out of the question that this Jesus of Nazareth, a sublime madman like all our prophets, and with a strong reputation as a worker of miracles besides, may be preparing a surprise; and one mustn't forget, either, that during the Passover holidays spirits tend to run very high and a mere nothing's enough to cause the crowd to go beserk. All in all, it might not be a bad idea to stay on the alert.

" 'So you think he's preparing a coup?' they asked him again. Thereupon Judas Iscariot understood that he had gained their attention and that he was on the right track. He gathered all his forces. 'I know that He is,' he said without hesitation. 'I live with Him, and I know whereof I speak. Capture Him before it is too late. You will find Him at any hour of the day on the steps of the Temple . . .'

"The priests improvised a little council. It was just possible that this man might be right. On the other hand, it could be a very risky business, during the Passover holidays especially, to arrest a prophet who was followed and revered though it were by only a few: all the others who, knowing him, would have laughed at him, would raise an outcry at the news of his arrest. One had to give it a lot of thought before doing something. And when they perceived Judas' anxious face, the trembling fixity with which he was staring at them, they advised him of their hesitations. The thing was not at all simple.

"Judas imagined he was looking again at the hypnotizing back of the white-clad figure, which had walked with such unconcern and with so much assurance from Ephraim to Bethany only because it felt that sustaining shadow behind it. No, he could not desert him, could not depart from the house of the high priest without having arranged anything! With a sigh he addressed a prayer to that straight, proud back: and in his imagination an almost imperceptible tremor ran down that spine. And at that instant, an idea lit in the disciple's brain. In a gesture betokening despair, he reached out his hands toward the priests and in an imploring, almost menacing voice cried out:

"'*I* am the one who shall deliver him to you!'

"The priests exchanged glances, then, bidding Judas to wait, they withdrew for a brief colloquy. All agreed that it would not be a bad thing to take the impostor from Nazareth quietly out of circulation; were he, in the end, to turn out to be the inoffensive fellow he seemed, they could always release him from jail and let him go about his business. If, however, he came out with some crazy declarations and persisted in maintaining them, here was an excellent opportunity to make a good impression before the Roman authorities and show their loyalty to the political power: it would in any case have been a courteous gesture to hand over a revolutionary, a political criminal. Actually, that idiot, that lunatic in the next room, apparently worthy of his master, was really a godsend: just let him set the hour and the place most suitable for the Galilean's arrest. Should he subsequently have second thoughts, he could go to the devil. Should Jesus have been brewing something, they would be able to nab him themselves, in the course of a night-time raid, while the public slept.

"After their brief colloquy, the high priests told Judas, who had been waiting in the next room and hoping alike for the success and the failure of his desperate enterprise, that his services were favorably viewed and were accepted. And to encourage his good disposition, they probably talked to him about the thirty pieces of silver. But who, in Judas' place, would have troubled himself about this insignificant detail? He longed to get out of that house, longed to rejoin his companions and, from the Lord's countenance, to measure the importance of what he had done.

"It is not possible to give even an approximate picture of his overall state of mind, since nothing comparable exists in the history of psychology; at most we may imagine a few predominating elements in his psychic spectrum. There must have been a certain little dose of mingled pride and gladness at having brought off the inhuman task with success. But this feeling of grim joy must have faded into nothingness, blotted out by atrocious doubts. What tormented him most was the sensation of having committed an absurdity, a deed both cruel and ignominious, without rhyme or reason, and that he would never be able to explain. He was carrying out the Master's will. And what if it hadn't been the Master's will but only an obsession of his own, the most enormous misunderstanding in the world? And with this, amidst all the unhappy man's sufferings, deadly doubt resumed its place in the forefront.

"This doubt had accompanied him to the house of the high priests, had remained with him throughout the exhausting discussion, and had faithfully accompanied him all the way back to where his companions abided. Jesus, with a single look, would be able to sweep every vestige of that unbearable doubt clean away. And when he entered, Judas sought avidly for that absolving look. He had the clear impression that the Master knew very well whence he came and what he had just arranged. But what conveyed this impression to him—and the realization caused Judas the utmost terror—was not a grateful or at least a sympathizing look from the Lord, but signs instead of sorrow and uneasiness, obscure allusions to the betrayer which made his blood run cold. His despair was at its height. Worn out in mind and spirit, he could not understand why the Master, the one who had suggested, imposed, ordered that desperate act of his, was now at every turn manifesting aversion, contempt and anger in his regard. Was it thus that he should treat him?

"Meanwhile other indications, being unable to put a complete end to his doubt, were the source of another doubt: doubt as to the rightness of his doubt. And in his desperate situation uncertainty itself was a remedy, for it left alive a glimmer of hope. From that moment on, indeed, the Lord had spoken more and more frequently and with perfect assurance about his imminent death, making masochistic use of prophecies from Scripture in order to corroborate it: and that seemed to prove that he was mindful of his services and that he was in hope of them.

"Only one true consolation remained to Judas: it was that despite his visit to the high priests, everything still depended upon him, upon what he was willing to do. Should he become convinced he had been mistaken, had misinterpreted the wordless dialogue and had not acted in accordance with the Master's will, well then, in that case he wouldn't go back to the high priests and wouldn't deliver the prey into their hands. And even if his initiative had set things in motion he would still be able to warn the Master in time and shelter him from danger.

"These considerations strengthened him in the absurd hope of not having to do anything further. If he had been mistaken, everything could come to a halt there and then. But he was not able to deceive himself for long. The Master's furious predicting, prophesying, alluding to baleful events at hand were incessant notification that his fate was inevitable. The wretch clung now to the last line of defense he was able to put up. He was going to remain insensitive, deaf, recalcitrant in the face of those allusions, those looks, those hints. He did not think of disobeying. But he made up his mind to obey only an order, an order expressed in unambiguous words. Yes, he would act, if the Master ordered him to. But without a precise order, no!

"The five days that went by between the arrival in Jerusalem and the Last Supper were the longest days in the life of Judas Iscariot. And they were as long as the last days of the man under sentence of death who does nothing else but wait for the end. For five days he waited every instant for the fatal order. But five days is a long time, above all five such days as those. And one wearies even of waiting for the worst of ills: and weariness in its negative sense is almost a kind of hope. Judas almost wound up believing that the order was not due to come.

"When at the supper the Master afterwards pronounced the order, which could not have been more precise and categorical, Judas was nearly unable to believe his ears. Though the atmosphere was dismal and laden with threatening clouds, the lightning bolt fell unexpectedly. And it made a definitive end of all doubt . . ."

Dupin fell silent and for a long time stared at his extinguished pipe. Then he looked up, and he said:

"I've finished, *cher ami* . . . I thank you for the patience with which you have taken part in the senile efforts of an amateur detective emeritus to dispose of the last case in the *evadenda* dossier. Without your providential presence I would never have remembered it, and had I remembered, it would have been to set it down in written form. Oh, what a lot of work you have spared me! Thanks, *cher ami,* thanks a thousand times over . . ."

"I'm the one who must thank you for the unimaginable surprise you had in store for me. It stands to reason that the remarkable conversation we've had is going to lead to something, and I can already foresee an enjoyable task for myself. You may have avoided for yourself the trouble of putting all this down in writing, but you very cleverly left me the duty, and the joy, of doing it in your stead. Others of your investigations have brought me money and glory in the past."

Dupin huffed affectionately, then with a small boy's blush, the sign of modest vanity, said:

"As always, I'll let you have the money and the glory; but this time you must do me a favor, and it is to satisfy my longstanding ambition of seeing in print a few modest pages that were born from my imagination and written by my own hand. You must solemnly promise me that for the opening and for the concluding of the book you are going to do you will use my fragmentary story . . ."

Now it was my turn to blush, for I had completely forgotten that I had not finished reading the pages contained in that slender folder.

"Ah yes, of course, your story. It isn't," I mumbled, " that I . . ."

"And to think," he laughed good-humoredly, "that if I detained you with my monologue it was mainly in order to establish a logical connection between the beginning of my story and its end!"

"I won't lose another minute," I reassured him, laughing, reassured in my turn by his laughter. "I am going to get back into it at once."

Dupin nodded his approval, and adopted his amiable smile. "Excellent. However, do please make sure that you finish it before the sun comes up. Even the most normal things can seem absurd in the light of day . . ."

Dupin's story (second part)

AND WHEN, WITH THE BITTER TASTE OF THE DIPPED BREAD IN HIS MOUTH, *Judas set out upon his fatal errand, doubt no longer accompanied him. However, he was tormented by an idea, an idea that had never entered his mind before: it had been brought on in all its terrifying reality by the malediction the Master had uttered: "Woe to the one who betrays the Son of man: better for him had he never been born!"*

Indeed, what was going to become of him?

What was going to become of him, not so much upon this earth, where we are free to end life even before its natural term, but in the beyond, where life is everlasting? "Better for him had he never been born!" And as he walked through the dark narrow streets of the outlying quarters toward the center of the city Judas understood, shivering, that his fate would be damnation.

The thought froze him in his tracks. With terror strangling him, he gave forth an inhuman cry:

"Have pity, O Lord!"

It seemed to him then that the Master was beside him. He was not walking ahead of him, as He usually did, and was not standing facing him either: He was truly at his side next to him and tenderly had slipped an arm under his. He gazed at Him with a wild expression at first, but so mild was Jesus' face, so kindly and smiling His gaze, that the apostle, in whose eyes He had never appeared so human, felt hope and confidence being born in him anew.

"Have pity on me, Lord," he stammered again, but now in a subdued voice, without even noticing that they had resumed their way.

"I cannot have pity on you," he suddenly heard the voice of Jesus say, a voice stamped by indescribable sadness. "You are engaged in doing the only thing that is left for you to do in this life, and all I could do would be to pity you were you not to do it. But I understand that your entire being rebels against the decision your reasoning self arrived at, with that poor reason of yours that surpassed itself in order to think accordingly with the divine mind . . . And you are free to act as you choose, you may withdraw your arm from mine and go the other way . . . But what then will become of you? And what then will become of me? . . .

The apostle was silent and his teeth chattered, such was his terror.

"I do not want to be damned, Lord," he managed to say at last.

Jesus gave a long sigh and, after a moment of silence, He answered, at first in a quiet tone, then with growing animation:

"If you turn back, damned you shall be! And everyone will be damned, for I alone, from the cross, can open the gates to heaven! Only once there can I gently wrest unto myself the power of benediction. Only then will it be possible to be saved, in my name. If you turn back, none of this will come to pass. And so no one will be saved. Even in future times humankind will remain under the yoke of the Father's law, and man will remain a toy, played with by the capricious hand that giveth and taketh away. Never shall the reign of free will come about! It is from the Father's arbitrariness I shall save man. Anyone who shall so will shall attain salvation in my name. When you shall have raised me up, I shall in my turn raise up the whole of mankind. But for that to be, I must die on the cross, tomorrow, in the afternoon. And that will not come to pass without you."

Judas, who had dimly followed what the Lord was saying, perked up with the concluding phrases and, impelled by an absurd hope, he raised his head.

"Then I too may be saved in your name, O Lord!" he cried.

But Jesus bowed his head, as though prey to remorse.

"You, Judas, cannot be saved," he said with difficulty, and at once fell silent.

"I do not understand you, O Lord," the apostle stammered, trembling in every limb. "Well do you know that what I am about to commit is not a sin . . ."

"Yes," Jesus replied, "I know. But I am the only one who knows, the only one on earth and in heaven. And even this can be to no effect. For you belong to the law of the Father and according to the law of the Father he is guilty who betrays his Master and a thousand times guiltier is he who betrays the Son of God. According to the law of the Father you are the greatest sinner in the world . . . and before that law I am powerless so long as I have not taken to myself the power of benediction; but without your sin this will not come to pass . . ."

They were arm in arm, and Judas' arm twitched. And the apostle exclaimed bitterly:

"And now you talk of sin, whilst a moment before you said that it wasn't one!"

"It is not one, no," Jesus flung back, "not according to me and not according to my law. But my law does not concern you, Judas; you are only its condition. In the eyes of my law you are not guilty, for your heart is innocent, it is not evil that you mean to do, you are yourself a virtual stranger to your deeds. What you shall commit, therefore, is not a sin, for in my law it is criminal intention that makes for the crime. But don't you see, Judas! My law does not provide for your case. My law absolves every sin if the guilty one is contrite. But how could you repent a deed for which you are not guilty and hence cannot feel guilt? My law makes provision for remorse, not for tragedies. Those singled out by fate will always remain within the Father's competence. I cannot do anything for you, Judas . . ."

"And the Father," cried Judas in a last effort, "O Master, do you think the Father may forgive me?"

Jesus did not answer right away, and in his silence there was something sinister.

"Yes," he said at last, "the Father might forgive. Until three o'clock tomorrow afternoon he might be able to forgive; after that, all the paths leading to the Father pass through me. But the Father is immeasurably great and unknowable. I do not even know whether He will want to forgive me. I, however, will bring him around . . . I will vanquish Him with your help. But this help that you are giving me will not avail you in the eyes of the Father. It will perhaps be your one unpardonable sin . . ."

Ever more stunned, Judas went on listening to those words spell out his irrevocable doom. And of a sudden in his soul there opened up an indistinct chaos, shapeless and without light, into which he felt himself sink, he together with the whole world, in a dizzying, benumbing fall that seemed unwilling to end before reaching Gehenna. At the same time tears came to his eyes and his weary steps drew to a halt. "So then I am lost, O Lord," he breathed in a faint voice, as though to conclude.

Jesus squeezed his arm compassionately, tenderly.

"I do very much fear, Judas, that you are in any case . . ." Then, softly and with a certain detachment, Jesus added: "You were born for the doing of evil, for the supreme evil . . ."

They looked at each other for a long time, both feeling just a little awkward, like two persons who, having successfully settled an important piece of business, suddenly discover, as they are about to exchange civilities, that beyond their material interests they do not have anything in common. But not even the thought of damnation was so unbearable for Judas as this stagnating of feeling. Just as after its eruption an appeased volcano will sometimes belch forth an unexpected last residue of lava, so from the apostle's spent soul sprang one last question, the most important:

"And you, Lord . . . do you at least forgive me?"

At this question there appeared on Jesus' lips that spontaneous, gentle and almost joyous smile produced among us simple mortals by the ingenuous questions of children we love. With an almost friendly impulse he again squeezed the apostle's tensed arm.

"Do I forgive you?" and in his voice resoundings of laughter gleamed like pearls. "Do I forgive you? It's I who must put that question to you!"

The apostle, who had never heard the Master laugh, stared at him wide-eyed. The figure standing before him seemed to him as if transfigured by the invisible rays of a youthful strength, which emanated from his triumphant aspect. This sudden revelation of the divine shook him to his depths and froze him at the same time. What could he reply to this question? Making an enormous effort, he withdrew his arm, moved back a step, gazed at Jesus for one more instant, and then bent his head before so much splendor:

"Thy will be done," he said.

His ears caught a triumphant sigh of relief:

"My will . . ." he heard, and these words too had the form of a sigh.

When Jesus looked up again the Master's figure was already moving away. And, overcome, the apostle murmured:

" 'Tis the Son of God . . ."

Everything was terrifying and terrifyingly beautiful. Still under the spell of the divine epiphany, Judas' hypnotized gaze followed that almost transparent figure, watching it vanish into the darkness of night. But suddenly it stopped and retraced its steps. The apostle felt his heart shrink, he was assailed by a premonition of something more terrifying still.

Come to within two steps of him, Jesus halted.

"Will you be receiving some recompense for your betrayal?" he inquired with ill-concealed excitement.

Judas went pale. But at the same time all his despair rose up within him, undoing the knot in his throat.

"How can you ask me such a question, O Lord?" he cried in a voice stifled by sobs. "What does it matter whether or not they give me something? Do you perhaps believe—"

"No, I do not believe anything," Jesus interrupted, "but it does matter, it matters more than you think. How much are they giving you?"

"Lord, why do you torment me?" Judas moaned, surrendering. "Thirty, I think—thirty pieces of silver. But . . ."

"Ah, thirty pieces of silver," Jesus repeated with satisfaction. And a light smile played over his lips. "Don't keep them, Judas. Throw the money in their faces."

Judas, at the end of his strength, pressed his two hands against his temples:

"Oh for pity, Lord!" *he cried with a voice that was no longer a man's.* "So then you believe . . ."

But with a mild and reassuring gesture the Lord interrupted him again:

"No, no, it's not you I'm concerned about, Judas Iscariot," *he said in a sober tone.* "It's about myself—about myself as always, and about my work. It was written by the prophet that the pieces of silver received in payment for the betrayal would be thirty, and that they would be cast to the potter . . ."

He saw boundless astonishment appear upon the apostle's tormented face, and he added:

"Don't fret over it, Judas. What you will do is return them to the high priests, and with your money they will buy the potter's field. At any rate, Scripture will be fulfilled. The work you do must be without a flaw, Judas."

Then, turning about, he set out into the night's darkness, where he vanished for good. Judas, the prey of confused emotions, a mixture of despair, of astonishment, of anger, of admiration, finally shook off his torpor. He was unable to tell whether or not he had been the victim of an hallucination. Everything, however, held logically together in the nightmare of their mysterious unspoken conversation. And at that instant the atrocious doubt arose in Judas' mind that the entire dialogue without words had been an hallucination, the monstrous fruit of his tortured imagination. But at the same instant he had the certainty also that he had interpreted it to perfection.

Finally, having decided to resume his dolorous way, he faced around. His feet felt rooted to the spot.

The house of the high priests stood right before him.